Luxe Is In The Air

Orchid Bloom

"In order to be irreplaceable, one must always be different."

- Coco Chanel

Chapter One

Phoebe did a final check on her appearance from the reflection of the perfectly polished elevator door. The tailor-made navy blue dress suit was impeccable and accentuated her slender figure. Her hair was pinned in place and rolled up in a neat French bun. The suede pumps in nude colour were elegant and chic, and the heels were of a height that was tall enough to be sexy but remained professional. She made sure she was not wearing any Maison H accessories.

Earlier in the week, she made a stop at a Vuitton boutique and spent a small fortune for today's interview. She was reluctant to spend the money. Now looking at the small handbag that could barely carry more than her smartphone and make-up pouch, she prayed that her interview was going to bring a return to her investment. Phoebe wanted to show her readiness to move from one luxury brand to another. She hoped that her interviewers would notice the little scarf tied on her handbag when she walked in, too. She'd to smuggle the handbag in a folded shopping canvas bag to work that morning.

The elevator doors opened. The Hong Kong office of Dion she was in was all about size and glamour. Black and white lacquered panels accented with light grey leather upholstery on walls, the cold and chicness ambience was a big contrast to the understated luxury of the Maison H office, where Phoebe was still employed, for now.

"My name is Phoebe Downlington . I am here for an interview," Phoebe told the receptionist, who she thought looked more like a model, about her appointment at 5 p.m.

"Phoebe! Good to see you again. Please come with me to the conference room. They will be ready for you in a minute." Rebecca, the head of the Human Resources Department, welcomed her warmly. She had a signature bob hairstyle and wore make-up that Phoebe suspected was the latest Dion collection. She could smell Rebecca's Miss Dion perfume a distance away. Rebecca was wearing an elegant cocktail dress today, versus the power woman suit from her previous interview.

"I am going to a vernissage after setting you up." As sensing Phoebe's eyes on her outfit, Rebecca explained about an exhibition of an up and coming artist she was going to that evening and urged Phoebe to hurry up into the conference room.

Phoebe's head-hunter, Adele, rang her nearly ten days ago and congratulated her on being one of the three shortlisted candidates to make it to the last round of interview. She and Adele had gone back and forth several times to set up a date for the appointment due to both her and her interviewers' frequent travel. Finally, a date was set. Adele briefed her that the interview would be with the top management of the division. She expected that the interview would be conducted the old fashion way, in person, probably during the management's business trip in the region, just like Maison H.

Hence, Phoebe was taken by surprise when she saw the equipment for a video conference had been set up in the conference room. But then Phoebe had not had a job interview in the past five years - things could have changed, even the way to have a job interview these days.

Sensing Phoebe's surprise again, Rebecca explained to Phoebe that since all four senior managements would like to meet with her, it would be more efficient to conduct a video conference; otherwise, it would never happen due to everyone's hectic traveling schedule.

Rebecca picked up the phone in the middle of a giant conference table and pressed one button after another.

"Bonjour, Phoebe is here and ready."

Within seconds, four men in designer suits appeared on the screen in front of them. Almost like a mirror image, they were also sitting at a grand conference table in a tastefully decorated conference room. The decoration of the room was nearly identical as the one Phoebe was sitting in.

"Phoebe, once you have finished, just leave everything as it is and you can be on your way. I am heading off to my event now, good luck." Rebecca waved goodbye to her colleagues in Paris, wished everyone a 'bon weekend,' and left the room.

The four men introduced themselves as Pierre, Bernard, Florian, and Nicholas. Pierre, Bernard, and Florian were the bosses of her superior prospect Sebastian, who she met in the last round of interviews, while Nicholas was the head of the global Human Resources Department.

For the first five minutes after Rebecca left the room, all four men talked amongst themselves like they had forgotten about Phoebe. She immediately felt uncomfortable and wasn't sure if she should initiate the conversation. As her interviewers could now only see her from the chest upwards, she regretted spending the money on the handbag and scarf. Yet, she tried to sit up tall to display composure and confidence. Phoebe was grateful that her complexion was still tanned and her usually brown hair appeared golden brown from a boat outing with friends over last weekend.

"Bon, Phoebe, tell me more about yourself." Thankfully Florian finally directed questions at her instead of the others.

"I am an American but have grown up pretty much in Asia as my father is a career diplomat. Thank you very much for the opportunity to have this intervieeeeew... hello, hello, caaaaan youuuuu heeeeeear me?"

Just as Phoebe started to talk about her job experience that would be related to the role she'd applied for, the signal was losing, and the image of her audience shook violently. Sitting by herself in the conference room, she prayed for the signal to come back. On a late Friday afternoon, she could see the office was pretty much deserted, so any help she could get was diminishing by the minute. After three rounds of interviews with different departments and her perspective immediate superior, Rebecca arranged Phoebe to have the last interview with the top management in Paris. She very much hoped to nail the job offer after today's meeting.

"Damn, the video conference screen just went blank on me!" cursed Phoebe under her breath when the last fraction of an image on the screen finally disappeared. "We'd be better off using FaceTime..."

"Allo, allo. Ok, the audio is still working, not very clear, but it will do for now."

"Are you still there? Can you come closer to the microphone please?"

Closer to the microphone? Phoebe wondered. The 'microphone' was sitting right in the middle of the massive conference table, and the cable was barely long enough to make it to the power outlet. The device was securely locked in a frame, and Phoebe remembered Rebecca asked her to leave everything as it was. She stood up and decided to get closer to the device. Staring at the giant table, Phoebe had no choice but to lean forward across the table to be closer to the receptor and speak louder, yet still not to her audience's satisfaction. Confident that no one could see her, she climbed up slowly onto the table, cautious not to tear her favourite dress, with her face closer and closer to the sound reception, to the point that she was almost kissing it. If anyone walked into the conference room now, they would see her on all fours, with her head close to the speaker and her head rotated regularly to either listen or to speak into it. It was almost like having a job interview while doing yoga, only Phoebe was in a suit dress instead of her Lululemon. It was as uncomfortable as it was awkward, so that Phoebe could not wait for the interview to be over.

"Phoebe, would you mind looking at the camera, si vous plait?"

Phoebe's heart nearly jumped out! She looked up, still kneeling on the table, with her bottom hanging in the air; all of a sudden she found her interviewers staring at her, first with a shocked expression, then with question marks on their faces. She quickly slid down the table, resumed her seat, and tried to explain the technical challenge. At the same time, Phoebe was not sure if she wanted the job anymore. She was sure these guys would forever remember her embarrassing interview moments for as long as she worked for them, and beyond.

Now her potential future bosses could see Phoebe clearly on the screen as they talked among themselves again as if she wasn't there. Then all of a sudden, it seemed like they had reached their conclusion. Without revealing anything to Phoebe, they thanked her for "trying her best" and making an "extraordinary effort" in the interview. They wished her a "bon weekend" and bid her "au revoir."

Chapter Two

Walking into the Armani Bar, the most popular hang-out among the sassy white collars in the city's financial district, Phoebe made her way through the Friday happy hour crowd to the outdoor terrace. The stunning weather of the day made this chic location more desirable than ever. Shades of orange gradually merged with the cloudless blue sky to create stripes of lavender colours that diffused effortlessly into the sunset canvas. The terrace of the Armani Bar was facing the harbour, which was glittering gold with a stunning backdrop of the tall and handsome skyscrapers. The bar was surrounded by a fashion boutique, make-up store, and even a florist of the same renowned Italian brand. Beautiful and stylish people favoured to frequent this place. Not only during happy hours it was popular with money hungry bankers, but during the day there was a constant flow of them hanging out nearby as there was a famous coffee stand-up bar just right outside the bar. This coffee shop served artisano coffee that costed over USD10 a shot. The kind that only the employees in the finance institutions upstairs in the office building could afford and could never get enough of.

At the corner of the terrace, Phoebe spotted her best friend, Ting-Ting, in her little black dress that had been tailor-made in a way that allowed her to turn the dress from a power dress during the day into a sexy cocktail dress in the evening, sipping her Cosmopolitan while flirting with a tall, handsome man who looked like in his early forties. Phoebe suspected the reason why the Armani Bar was Ting-Ting's favourite spot was because of a video of her modelling various hairstyles playing in a loop in the celebrity hair salon adjacent to the bar. Ting-Ting's family had an investment in the salon, and from time to time, Ting-Ting volunteered to be the model in their promotional videos. It was very effective in getting men in the bar to approach her, and most of the time, they found her look familiar but could not pinpoint where they had seen her. They often looked confused whenever Ting-Ting told her she was a model considering how petite she was, then Ting-Ting would explain that she modelled for a hair salon and reminded them to check out the videos on their way out of the bar.

"Fair bear! How did it go? Tell me you got it." Ting-Ting ditched her flirt right away and ran to Phoebe to give her a bear hug.

"Asshole, I could see the wedding ring mark on his finger," Ting-Ting whispered in Phoebe's ear and led her to a corner standing table, on which she had already marked her territory with her Maison H handbag and a cashmere shawl with an elaborated equestrian pattern.

"He could be divorced, Ting-Ting."

"Newly divorced, possibly with luggage, a.k.a. kids attached, is even worse." Ting-Ting always had a theory about everything and sometimes, in Phoebe's opinion, was too quick to make a judgement.

"So how did it go?"

Phoebe recounted the embarrassing event during the interview to Ting-Ting. Ting-Ting could not stop laughing at the expense of how Phoebe went on all four to catch the attention of her future bosses.

"I can't really tell if it went well or bad. Most of the time they just talked among themselves; there were four of them, by the way. I felt like I was in America's Got Talent and could be 'dinged out' at any moment."

"Which, I am sure you have shown them your 'talent' and 'flexibility.'"

Phoebe almost spilled her drink laughing at Ting-Ting's comment and her very fresh memory of the interview.

"Seriously, they will be lucky to have you, Fair Bear. You are from a bigger brand: you are from Maison H, for god's sake. A Caucasian from an aristocratic family. If anyone can sell luxury to different nationalities, that would be you. Besides, you speak fluent Mandarin - all the more cherry on top - and what the French would love for a Travel Retail Area Manager position. Wait until you see the Chinese's reaction when you open your mouth and speak to them in their language, a white girl speaking fluent Chinese!"

"Now the final interview's done, I'm not entirely sure if I want to leave the company. I love being there, it's almost like a family to me now after working there for five years. I heard it's very competitive and political at Vuitton. They said it's like swimming in open water with sharks circling around you."

"Be ambitious, Fair Bear! There was no harm to venture out to see the world and to swim with the sharks for a bit. You don't want to find yourself still in the same position five years more from today; worse, you may drop to *Cut & Paste* level if you don't find yourself something new and challenging to learn."

Phoebe shuddered at the thought of that. Many of their colleagues in the Maison H office came from the generations when paper, pen, and fax machines were still the main communication tools. As most of them were still staying in the same position and never felt the threat of losing their jobs, they had little motivation to pick up new skills or learn modern-day software. Few of them knew how to use basic Microsoft office software such as Excel and PowerPoint. One day, to Phoebe's horror, she found one of the senior managers took 'cut & paste' literally and helped herself with some glue and a pair of scissors in order to put a few reports together.

On the other hand, Ting-Ting had a theory of castes when it came to a French company. She divided the employees into a pyramid which resembled the one that represented the nutritional value of food, with only the food types replaced by nationalities. The bottom caste was the local employees, pretty abundant and easily replaceable. The second to bottom tier would be someone like Phoebe, a foreigner who had certain skills that the company wanted. After that would be Immigrant-French, of French nationality and of true francophone. The second top tier was the Caucasian French, and the top of this pyramid was a very tight, big boys club - a French employee, either from an aristocratic family and very often easily recognized by their remarkable last names, or from an alumni of the few elite business schools such as the HEC.

Ting-Ting believed that unless you managed to squeeze into the top two tiers, you would have to struggle to advance in a large name but small company like Maison H. The only way to advance upwards was to move sideways first.

Chapter Three

Ting-Ting was Phoebe's colleague, a Junior Manager in the Marketing department of Maison H. Working at a traditional luxury house where most of the employees worked their way to retirement, she and Phoebe bonded right away, being one of the few young ladies who often made fun of the out-dated mentality and resistance to the digital world of the oldies in the office. Ting-Ting gave Phoebe the nickname Fair Bear, as to how her name would sound like when spoken by their French colleagues. Phoebe didn't like it but loved Ting-Ting too much to resent her for that.

Everyone in the office thought Ting-Ting was born to do what she did. She had fair skin and a doll face that every Chinese girl would trade anything for. Ting-Ting was more on the petite size but with curves in all the right places. With silky dark hair and carrying so much confidence, she was even more popular with foreign men than the local Chinese who preferred a girl who did not always say what she wanted. She was born with what one would call 'having a golden spoon in her mouth.' She was raised by an army of Chinese amah's and went to a prestigious boarding school in the U.K. She went on to get her master's degree from a famous business school in London. Then, by her own choice and with much convincing to her parents, she studied art history in Paris. She wanted to live freely in the romantic city and probably romanticised the French men, before returning to the ever stressful city of Hong Kong; a city where there were eyes of her family or friends everywhere.

Born in the prominent family of the Lees in Hong Kong, she knew nearly all the old monies in the 'anyone-that-matters' circle, which made her the perfect marketing executive for the brand. Most of her uncles and aunts were the brand's VIPs. Instead of applying for a job, the brands lined up to invite her to join their Marketing and PR team.

Ting-Ting had actually spent a summer interning at the very same office that Phoebe had just had her job interview in. Ting-Ting later commented to Phoebe from her memory that the office reminded her of her family - complicated and competitive. In the end, she'd decided to accept the job from Maison H, who never knew they made the least attractive offer to Ting-Ting - but it was the brand she liked most and had the least complicated office environment to spend her carefree decade in before one day when she'd have to take over the textile empire from her father.

Because of her excellent performance, Ting-Ting was promoted to a managerial position literally right after her probation, and it was just a matter of time her immediate boss retired, got fired or moved to another company before she could be promoted again.

But, Ting-Ting was destined to return to her family business one day. For the time being, however, she wanted to enjoy being herself and work for Maison H. She was not ready to give up her freedom just yet.

Just as Ting-Ting came from a family of money in the far east, Phoebe came from a family of power in the west. Her great-grandfather, grandfather, and father were all career diplomats. All Downingtown's had to start learning a second language before they could walk. As the only child of her generation, for years Phoebe had been under tremendous pressure to carry on the family's torch. Phoebe loved living in different countries and experiencing different cultures; however, she was not a fan of politics and often found people she met through the 'family trade' shallow and full of agendas.

Not sure what her true calling was, Phoebe did a gap year of internship before college, at the U.S. embassies in a handful of places. Besides pleasing her parents, who wanted nothing more than her entering the Foreign Service, Phoebe had wished to find out whether she could enjoy the work when she was outside the shadow of her father. When the year was over, Phoebe was convinced that being a diplomat was not a career she aspired to. Her parents Claire and Johnathan Downlington finally gave up on pushing her when she failed the FSOT - the U.S. Department of State Foreign Service Officer Test. Phoebe suspected that her father would rather tell his peers that his only child had no interest in joining the foreign service than tell them that she had failed the FS entry exam.

Chapter Four

Phoebe tumbled into the Travel Retail industry totally by accident. After graduating from college, she had little to do before deciding on a job. She'd accompanied her parents to Buenos Aires for an inauguration ceremony of an important politician, hoping to get more inspiration in the more exotic part of the continent. While she spent most of her teenage years in Asia, her father had his posts concentrated in Europe and part of South America when she was little.

Not wanting to say she could not dance the tango whenever she told people she'd lived in Argentina, Phoebe decided to take some tango classes during her stay in Buenos Aires. It was during one of the evening milongas, a social Argentinian tango practice section in Palermo Soho, Phoebe met her future boss, Priscilla.

Priscilla was vacationing in Buenos Aires with her husband, Guillaume. Both Priscilla and Guillaume were Argentinian tango lovers. Unlike its ballroom counterpart where the dance was more theatrical, such as the male dancer biting a rose and spinning his female dance partner around, Argentinian tango was a lot more sensual. Its origin was in La Boca where prostitutes danced in a voluptuous style to flirt with the immigrants who were mainly from Italy and worked on the docks. Combined with the live music played by skilful and passionate musicians, Phoebe thought the Argentinian tango to be the most enticing music and the most sensual dance in the world.

Phoebe could tell there was an intense chemistry between Priscilla and Guillaume, although at that time she didn't know they were actually married. She was even more mesmerised by Priscilla's tango shoes. *Comme il faut*, that was the brand; the only brand Phoebe thought mattered when it came to tango shoes. They came in the style of nine-inch heels, in matching colours to the overall outlook of the shoes. Their spaghetti straps were covered in either silk, velvet, or textured materials like faux crocodile skin or snakeskin. They reminded Phoebe of Pucci dresses or Birkin, Kelly Bags on the feet.

Wearing a pair of those in bed can seduce any man you desire, Phoebe imagined a sex bomb spreading her body on a bed in only a pair of Comme il faut, while admiring the shoes on Priscilla. Staring at her clumsy salsa ballroom shoes she picked up back in the States, Phoebe was determined to ask Priscilla where she could find those beauties before the milongas ended that evening.

That was how the conversation started, and probably how most women bonded - over heels. She told Priscilla that she was a bored fresh graduate following her diplomat father to Buenos Aires and wanted to learn the tango. Priscilla asked Phoebe what she was going to do after going home. Phoebe told Priscilla honestly that she hadn't decided yet. Coming from generations of diplomats, Phoebe did not want to follow her father's footsteps. She wanted to find her own calling, although she did enjoy living in different countries and travelling around the world.

"Do you speak other languages?" Priscilla suddenly became very interested in Phoebe's profile.

"I spent the majority of my teenage years in Asia, Japan, Indonesia, and Thailand. I picked up Japanese, and I speak fluent Chinese. My father hired a Chinese nanny to look after me when I was three, as he believed China was going to be the future. In fact, my father's next posting will be in Beijing."

"Come work for me in Maison H - you are made for this job. The post will be based in Hong Kong, which is a cosmopolitan and fabulous city." Priscilla literally made Phoebe an offer on the spot, although Phoebe would have to be approved by Priscilla's boss before it became black and white. Phoebe nearly spilled a "yes," already picturing herself traveling around the world, but had nothing to do with any states or diplomats.

Chapter Five

Although disappointed that their daughter was not following a diplomatic career, both Claire and Johnathan were glad to hear that Phoebe had found a job at Maison H. It was a reputable company who made alluring products. Claire was particularly excited as she personally owned a handful of handbags from the brand and couldn't wait to learn more about the brand and upcoming collections through Phoebe. Johnathan was relieved that the posting would be in Hong Kong, which was one of the safest cities in the world. He had already known that his next posting was going to be in Beijing, which was only a short flight from Hong Kong. It was comforting to know that even Phoebe was now leaving the nest and going to lead her own life; their precious only child could still be close to them.

Claire helped Phoebe to prepare her relocation to the far east. She generously gifted her daughter a few accessories from Maison H that Johnathan bought her on some special occasions over the years, with her husband's blessings, so Phoebe would not feel pressured to spend her salary on getting something from the brand to display loyalty. In fact, Phoebe had never stepped into a Maison H boutique before being employed by the brand. She had seen many glamours brought into her world by her diplomat father, yet she had little interest in the name an item carried as long as it was of good quality and served its purpose. Phoebe's unfamiliarity to the luxury world ultimately took her a long while to get used to and comfortable with, in her role with the most luxurious brand in the world.

Claire flew to Hong Kong with Phoebe and accompanied her to look for an apartment, in areas that had been suggested by Priscilla, who said would be easy enough for her daily commute and at the same time within her budget. Hong Kong had the most expensive properties in the world, and Phoebe's humble budget only allowed her to rent a studio. Priscilla raised the idea of sharing a flat but growing up as an only child, Phoebe was not entirely warm to the thought of sharing a small living space with strangers. Fortunately, Johnathan gifted Phoebe a small fortune as a graduation present to set herself up in a place wherever she took her first job.

In the end, she settled in a one-bedroom apartment in Happy Valley on Hong Kong Island. Happy Valley was a little oasis within the busy commercial area of the city. It was an area favoured by the city's upper middle class who had made purchases of apartments in the area for generations. It was also preferred by some of the expatriates who were over the party scenes after living for some time in the city that never slept but still would like to enjoy the convenience of the location. The community was self-sufficient with supermarkets, wet markets, restaurants, bakeries, laundromat, etc. within blocks from each other. There was also a world-class horse racing course with sports facilities surrounding it as the heartbeat of the community. The horse races were run by a non-profit Jockey Club whose revenue was then invested into the city's numerous charity projects.

Phoebe's apartment was tiny but had a green view instead of buildings across the road. The apartment was also within walking distance to her office, which was a big bonus. Its vicinity to the horse racing course with a running track surrounding it meant Phoebe could maintain her habit of outdoor jogging. Within months, Phoebe had settled well in her new job as well as the new city.

Chapter Six

Coming from a diplomatic family, Phoebe was used to getting her clothes tailor-made. Among the to-do-list for her mother Claire Downlington in every country the family moved to, was to engage a capable tailor that came highly recommended and appoint him as their family tailor. There were numerous occasions that the family would need different costumes for, and this family tradition came in handy for Phoebe when she joined the luxury world. She was used to wearing clothes that fit like gloves and highlighted the merits of her figure. Not that she needed much of that. Inheriting the good genes from her mother, Phoebe was blessed with a long and slender figure. Her parents enrolled her into different local sports, and they themselves exercised regularly to stay fit. She grew up learning martial arts and was active in the school's sports team. It was essential for them to have a healthy body and mind to adapt to different environments, climates, and diets. Their roles involved many occasions that they were served with local delicacies. All of them had to stay active to burn off the calories.

Among the martial arts Phoebe had given a try over the years in different countries, Capoeira and Krav Maga were the ones she still practiced. She picked up Capoeira when Johnathan was posted in Brazil. It was a martial art combined with gymnastics, dance, and music that appealed to even a three years old. The sport was popular globally, and her mother Claire had always managed to find a maestro to train Phoebe - especially in Japan, where Brazilians were one of the biggest minority groups, and some of Phoebe's best friends were from her Capoeira class.

On the other hand, Johnathan had enrolled Phoebe into Krav Maga classes when she was old enough to do a kick and throw a punch. Krav Maga was a contact combat martial art from Israel that taught Phoebe to defend herself when she was attacked or kidnapped. Since then she was used to training once a week everywhere she moved to, and she was glad that there were several Krav Maga instructors in Hong Kong so she could continue the training.

Over the years in Hong Kong, Phoebe had tried a few tailors. She didn't have the sharp eyes and experience of her mother to decide a perfect tailor right away. In the end, she used the tailor who had been providing his service to Ting-Ting and her mother for many years. Her favourite was a one-piece slim fitting dress that fell just under the knees, with a wide collar that showed off her collar bone. She had the same style in various colours and materials that would suit different weather conditions and could mix and match with numerous coats as well as accessories such as the famous Maison H scarves. This way, she did not have to spend all her salary on branded clothes. She could also avoid the embarrassing situation of wearing clothes of other brands, knowing very well that she would never be able to afford Maison H clothes, and there was no clothing allowance offered to her as it was a privilege exclusive to store managers and very senior executives.

While Ting-Ting was in the local marketing department, Phoebe worked for the travel retail team. Travel retail was the glorified industrial term for Duty Free. Those branded perfume bottles husbands brought home every time to their wives from airports or airplanes when they went on a business trip. Travel Retail in the luxury sector was in a world of its own. While most of the luxury shops one saw in the city were owned directly by brands, those in travel retail, like in the airports or in downtown duty-free shops, were mainly concessionaires.

Luxury brands granted operators, who had the local expertise to bid at certain airports and to deal with customs, concessions to run their shops. Thanks to travel retail executives like Phoebe, it looked like any other luxury shops in towns. Yet, the brand might share the cost to start the shop. Some more popular brands even managed to negotiate zero contribution, the operators owned the stocks and paid for most of the operational costs. Therefore, the margin of travel retail was significantly higher compared to direct-owned stores, which was highly attractive to brands from a P&L, Profit and Loss, point of view. In addition, travel retail functioned as a window or communication to the world. Travellers of all nationalities and cultures who would otherwise never step into a luxury house would get to know the brand by just passing by in the airports.

In other words, travel retail was a sort of a paid marketing channel. At major busy airports, the pay was lucrative. That made Phoebe's job so important to keep the operational quality on par with the shop in town and to fight for the best location to have the brand exposed to the most number of customers.

Chapter Seven

Phoebe remembered the day she met Ting-Ting very well. The Maison H office in Hong Kong was in an inconspicuous building, just as low profile as the luxury brand was, and the Travel Retail office was on a different floor from the Domestic Market office. However, during the first couple of months when Phoebe started her first job, the Travel Retail Department was undergoing renovation, and the whole Travel Retail team and the Marketing Department of the domestic market were made to share the office space together.

In the beginning, Ting-Ting was on holiday, and she had no idea she was going to come back to a very unwelcoming arrangement of dividing her semi-open office into half. On the other hand, Phoebe was curious about her temporary neighbour, who came back from her Mediterranean holiday on her family yacht.

Priscilla had briefed Phoebe about who Ting-Ting was. Since then, Phoebe paid extra attention to the local Tatler page, and every now and then she spotted photos of Ting-Ting in some beautiful designer gowns, with her mother Edith Wong-Lee, at various fancy charity balls. She had yet to decide whether she would like her. Phoebe despised spoilt trust fund kids who thought they were entitled to everything they had in life. She had met enough of them growing up when her father often entertained the parents of these kids. She was trying to avoid them as best she could in the life she made for herself.

The day when Ting-Ting was back in her office, Priscilla's boss was visiting. Cecile spoke English with a heavy French accent and pronounced everyone's name in her own French way. Knowing very well who Ting-Ting was, Cecile always made an effort to stop by Ting-Ting's office every time she was in town. After making Ting-Ting give her a full account of her luxury yacht holiday in the Mediterranean Sea, Cecile introduced Phoebe to Ting-Ting.

"Ting-Ting, this is our new Travel Retail executive 'Fair Bear.' Fair Bear will be assisting Priscilla in her area. Since you are of similar ages, I expect a very close collaboration between you two…"

As Cecile turned away from Ting-Ting's office and moved on to say hello to everyone she thought that mattered, Ting-Ting gave Phoebe a head-to-toe scan.

"So, what is your real name? It's obvious that you are white, but you look nothing like a bear to me."

Silence fell between the two, as Phoebe returned with a similar scan. Suddenly they burst into laughter.

"P-h-o-e-b-e, Phoebe, my name is Phoebe. With the colour of your eyes, you look more like a bear than I do. I am more like a goat..." Phoebe referred to her Chinese Zodiac sign and extended her hand to Ting-Ting.

"Same here! No wonder we are both this white. Except your eyes are green as a cat's."

Since that day, Phoebe and Ting-Ting became as thick as thieves. 'Fair Bear' became Phoebe's nickname exclusively used by Ting-Ting. Whenever Phoebe did not have to travel, Ting-Ting would reserve her lunch hour to catch up with Phoebe. Ting-Ting often took the initiative to make reservations at nice restaurants that Phoebe otherwise would have no time to explore. Phoebe enjoyed hanging out Ting-Ting, who always caught her up with most of the gossip in the office as well as in the city, which most of the time involved her family or rival families.

Chapter Eight

Ting-Ting was very popular with men of all ages. Those who did not know her were attracted by her appearance and sassy attitude. Those who knew who she was, were attracted by both her appearance and the vast fortune she was destined to inherit one day from Simon Lee, being his only child. Growing up in a city safe as Hong Kong and with protective parents, Ting-Ting had been living in an innocent world and had never seen dangers.

On the contrary, Phoebe had spent most of her childhood years in South America and Europe, where kidnappings and attacks were more common. Phoebe was used to security details and training in combat, and even after moving to the much safer Asia, her father kept the security tight, especially after each terrorist attack on American soil or against Americans. It took Phoebe a long while to get used to living in a very safe city like Hong Kong and without bodyguards following her around. She kept her vigilance and never wandered on the streets late at night by herself without being on high alert.

From time to time, Phoebe would be concerned about Ting-Ting because of her frivolous manner. Six months into their blooming friendship, Phoebe invited Ting-Ting to go train with her at Krav Maga one evening a week. Ting-Ting found it incredibly sexy and fun to be able to kick ass in her Jimmy Choo's, and she committed to her weekly training as long as Phoebe agreed to party with her on the weekend. After all, if there was any chance to kick some badass in Hong Kong, Ting-Ting believed they would have to go out and meet some drunk perverts.

Her long years of training earned Phoebe the role of being the assistant instructor. She helped run a women's self-defence programme, and trained women in techniques to deter their attackers and run away to get help.

The moves that Phoebe taught Ting-Ting became handy on several occasions when she was in vulnerable situations; the most remarkable incident being a year after Ting-Ting started training with Phoebe when she was targeted to be kidnapped for a ransom. Ting-Ting reacted in defence by reflex from the training.

Ting-Ting went jogging every other evening after work around Bowen Road in the Mid-Levels. The kidnappers must have trailed her and studied her routine in advance, then planned an ambush. They waited for Ting-Ting at a spot where there was a big banyan tree, which provided them with cover, blind spots to on-comers, and soundproof in case Ting-Ting screamed. Luckily, they underestimated Ting-Ting's strength. They thought only one man would be enough to grab her as she was petite, while the other would bring the van over, ready for the exit. It was a two-man job. The moment the kidnapper had his arm around Ting-Ting's neck and his other arm around her waist, Ting-Ting reacted by reflex, holding on to one wrist and ramming her fingers straight into her attacker's eyes. Then she angled her elbow straight and unlocked the neck grip during the few seconds when her attackers screamed in agony for his eyes. Next, she wound her arm across her attacker's neck, held his head in place, and kneed hard at his groin. She released him, and her attacker immediately fell onto the ground, covering his private part with tears pouring down his face.

Not knowing if there were others following, Ting-Ting quickly snapped a picture of her attacker and ran for her life. As soon as she saw a group of runners, she asked for help and called the police.

Meanwhile, the attacker limped his way to his accomplice for help.

Thanks to Ting-Ting's photo, the police soon spotted them while searching in the area for the injured attacker. Both kidnappers were put on trial and in jail for attempted kidnapping. The news generated much noise in the city because of who Ting-Ting was. Despite the initial shock and scares, Ting-Ting enjoyed the limelight of her being a super-heroine and fending off villains.

Simon had since then assigned a driver and a bodyguard to follow Ting-Ting wherever she went. Phoebe had also become a superstar in the Lee's family. Both Simon and Edith appreciated Phoebe's positive influence on their rebellious daughter, and they treated Phoebe as family since she did not have anyone in Hong Kong. Edith and a couple of Ting-Ting's aunts also convinced Phoebe to show them a set of anti-kidnapping moves to apply in times of need. Being an only child, Phoebe saw Ting-Ting as the sister she never had, especially with much love from Ting-Ting's family, who never cared much about who her parents were.

Chapter Nine

Phoebe did not take her friendship with Ting-Ting for granted. Despite their fondness for each other, most colleagues of the domestic market did not see eye-to-eye with their travel retail counterparts. The domestic market staff thought travel retail people did not exert any influence in the brand, as the shops they managed were not owned by the house - they had to manage through their concessionaires.

Yet, Phoebe loved her job in Travel Retail for Maison H. She loved the energy at the airports. She had travelled to many different countries growing up but never spent much time at any single airport, thanks to the privilege of being with an American Ambassador and a dependent diplomatic passport. Her family was always whisked through secret channels and through the immigration checks in no time.

With her role at Maison H, she spent hours at any one airport at a time. Sometimes when her head was spinning from fatigue, and her feet were burning from hours of walking from one terminal to another, Phoebe would find a spot to sit down, close her eyes and take in all the sensations and vibes of the airport. The excitements of traveling to another country, the sorrow of couples separating from each other, the business travellers trying to make another work call or send out another work email before boarding, families calling home to say the last goodbyes, airport staff greeting each other and recounting their days, be them eventful or uneventful. Phoebe often felt energized afterwards.

Phoebe's role ensured her frequent travels within Asia as well as in Paris. She enjoyed the familiarity of the places and cultures in Asia. For the first time in her life, she was her own person, not the daughter of a diplomat. She enjoyed visiting all the landmarks and museums incognito, at her own pace.

When she travelled to Paris for work, she usually stayed for half a month. On weekends, she would take a long walk in her favourite arrondissements such as Marais, Monmarte, St. Germaine... and every time she would do some research in advance to check on the exhibitions in different museums to see if there were any she would like to go to. Her favourite museums were Le Grand Palais and Le Petit Palais on Champs-Elysees - not the Louvre where it was crowded with tourists at all times throughout the year. In the evenings, she would enjoy dinner with friends or colleagues she made during her years working for Maison H. She even found time to go to milongas, which never failed to amaze her as she often found gentlemen in their seventies or eighties dressing up elegantly to go to the social dancing. At first, she was unsure whether to accept the invitations from these gentlemen who dressed in their best suits and bowties, fearing they would not be able to bear her weight. They surprised her with every lift and swing they made. They were amazing Argentinian tango dancers and incredibly agile for their age.

Moreover, most of the people she met in travel retail were worldly, intelligent, modest, and at the same time, resilient. She believed it was due to the nature of the industry. Travel retail executives usually looked after a region or global interests instead of a single city or country. Their business counterparts and clientele were people from all walks of lives, different nationalities, and cultural backgrounds. Everyone was culturally sensitive and savvy, respectful, and had a sense of everything happening around them. Phoebe's upbringing was a big help for her to be attentive to the cultural differences, and know what and when to speak. The retail space at every airport was under tender every several years, which guaranteed things and power were never constant nor stayed with a single operator. This rule of the game kept everyone on his or her ground and to never be too arrogant, as what they had today could be gone the next day.

Every news and events around the world could have an impact on the traveling pattern; therefore, a good travel retail executive would keep herself or himself up-to-date with the news, both locally, regionally, and globally, such that their team could make adjustments accordingly and swiftly, either to capture a surge in sales or fine-tune the forecast to avoid overstock later on. Travel retail executives were also required to have fine financial acumen skills. There was probably no other industry besides a Forex trader involved in as many currencies as in travel retail. Travel retail executives were sometimes walking currency converters. Not only were they constantly traveling to different countries and keeping probably up to ten currencies themselves, they also had to be able to react to international currency fluctuations quickly in order to maximize business opportunities. A weakened Japanese yen meant there would be more tourists to Japan and more shoppers at luxury brands to enjoy the savings from the currency exchange. A capable travel retail executive would know to engage a conversation with the operator there to check on stock and replenishments to maximise sales, which at times meant covering the loss in another country.

On the other hand, since travel retail involved many more points of sale and operators compared to direct boutiques in the domestic market, travel retail executives had never ending expenses accounting and forecasts to do so they could meet their annual budget. Besides following up with shop managers on sales reports and displays to ensure duty-free shops were in line with the brand requirement, training new staff on the brand and regular staff on new products, Phoebe and Priscilla had to meet the operators several times a year to discuss future developments and open-to-buy for the next buying seasons, based on the inventory level, retail margin, and sales forecast for the coming season. It was a rare day to see the whole travel retail team in the office as everyone was a frequent traveller. Phoebe had her suitcase lying open 365 days a year since she was constantly in the middle of packing or unpacking.

Despite her hectic travel and challenging job, Phoebe loved living in Hong Kong. She had lived in half a dozen Asian countries growing up and found Hong Kong a truly cosmopolitan city. She made friends with the locals and people coming from all over the world. Nowhere else had the energy that vibrated throughout the city. Some might find the pace of the city stressful, while others found it invigorating and full of life.

From her first impression, Hong Kong seemed to be a concrete city where only skyscrapers existed. She was pleasantly surprised when she discovered that two third of the city was actually covered by country parks. There were numerous hiking trails and white sand beaches dotted around the city which she frequented whenever she could on weekends.

With the help of Priscilla, she rented a small place in a walk-up building. The building itself was back from the old colonial days when Hong Kong was still under British rule. It used to be a pawn house. It had very high ceilings, which was rare in Hong Kong. Phoebe adored the 1960s tile flooring, and a spacious balcony looking down to a temple and lots of greenery. Her apartment was in the area where buildings, both residential and commercial, spread up a hill. There was a little European import grocery store, a French Bakery, an Italian café… It reminded her of the quartier of Montmartre in Paris, which she visited a lot whenever she was there for work.

Working for Maison H was the cherry on top of the cake for Phoebe. She was convinced it was the only true luxury brand in the fashion industry, especially after learning about the brand history and how the products were made. She loved the fact that the brand invested most in the quality of the product instead of just some fancy products that could last for only a season. The company had a department that was responsible for sourcing materials and acquiring workshops that created the best leather available on earth- and Maison H would reserve this solely for its own craftsmen, while supplying the secondary quality leather to other luxury brands. Phoebe had never seen a single ugly product for as long as she worked for Maison H. Every item had a subtle elegance in it, and never failed to surprise and delight the owner through discovering its beauty and functionality bit by bit. Maison H never invested heavily in marketing either, like most other brands did. Besides investing in the quality and artisans who produced the items, they invested in hiring designers to produce the most stunning show windows.

Chapter Ten

Every year Maison H came up with a theme which all the new products and designs would be inspired from. The yearly theme would then determine the focus on the shops' show windows. Maison H was famous for their spectacular window displays. The brand spent very little on their marketing but reserved a mouth-watering budget to hire designers from all over the world to dress their shop windows. Every summer, window designers gathered in Paris to see the revelation of the theme for the following year. Although each designer was pretty much handed a carte blanche to use the display windows as their canvas of creativity, the designers from all over the world shared their works from the past year and brainstormed ideas for the next. These seminars and the liberty in creativity, empowered the designers to create theatrical and mesmerising displays in the windows of Maison H shops around the globe.

Angus was the appointed designer to dress all the show windows within the Asia-Pacific travel retail network. That accounted for over thirty boutiques, with four seasonal changes a year. Angus and his partner Zoe started an interior design company A to Z Designs several years prior to Phoebe joining Maison H. Priscilla's immediate boss Eric met Angus at an art exhibition. After chatting for a while about what they did, Eric hired Angus on the spot to give them a one season try, as Paris was not pleased with the window designer Eric was using back then. Angus nailed his first commission and received excellent feedbacks from Paris, while Eric got a pat on the back by the management, and Angus and Zoe had been dressing travel retail Asia-Pacific windows ever since. With more boutiques opening each year, Maison H travel retail became A to Z's only client, as the business was more than what Angus and Zoe could cope with.

Phoebe knew very well that Angus and Zoe could be well assured of their long-term appointment as long as they got the annual theme right. After all, it was a complicated operation. Not only did the designer have to understand the brand culture well, know what the headquarters wanted, the spirit and magic to enhance the products, and most importantly to Phoebe, to know the process to get the materials delivered and through the custom on time, without a fuss, and to arrange all the passes, he had to liaise with shop staff such that they could change the window display overnight after the shop closed, and reveal a brand new window to travellers the next day. Admiring the show windows of Maison H shops everywhere was definitely a highlight for Phoebe as part of her travel. Angus and Zoe never failed to wow their audience, while at the same time making Maison H products look like a million dollars.

Every now and then, being an art lover herself, Eric invited artists he met locally and overseas to have a special installation in the boutique at Hong Kong Airport. Once, the team had a collaboration with the local art academy and had their dance students do a modern dance in a historical colonial building while holding the brand's beautifully handcrafted tableware. The video was then played in a loop in the show window dressed up with bamboo and pieces from the latest tableware collection. The result was breath-taking. During the five years Phoebe had worked for the brand, she was blown away by many more similar installations.

Besides a stunning display window, another way to attract traffic into a shop was organising in-store animations. An animation could be a model demonstrating various ways to tie a Maison H scarf, or a skilled craftsman demonstrating the making of leather goods, such as a simple card case or a more complicated piece like a wallet. Phoebe liked the fact that the boutiques at the airports had no doors, except roll down gates at night for security, which looked a lot more welcoming to travellers. Whenever there were such animations in a downtown boutique, invitation cards would be sent out to VIPs and regular customers to visit the store and watch the in-store show. At airports, only a signage would be stood outside the store, and all were welcome. Some of the visitors had never even heard of the brand but enjoyed watching the magic of a skilled craftsman turning a piece of beautiful leather into a card case, while at the same time demonstrating the brand's signature stitches.

Chapter Eleven

Despite the limited opportunities available within Maison H, Phoebe loved the brand, its wonderful products, and the caring company culture. Part of the cons of being in a company who treated its employees well was limited internal mobility, as staff were reluctant to leave and willing to remain stagnant at their levels, for the comfort and shelter provided by the company. More than half of Phoebe's colleagues - whichever city they worked in - had been with Maison H for decades, contented, and planned to stay until their retirements, which was unheard of these days.

A year after Phoebe joined Maison H, the brand had created a campaign to encourage its employees to dream, and dream big. The luxury house invited all the employees to submit his or her wildest dream to the company's internal website, especially created for communication with employees. Among the thousands of ideas and fantasies one could only dream of, thirty dreams were then shortlisted for all employees to vote. In the end, only the ten dreams that received the most votes would be realised at the company's expenses. The 'dream owner' and a dozen other employees who voted for his or her dream, would go on an adventure to realise them. Phoebe thought it was a beautiful and incredibly generous initiative, especially when she was very lucky to be able to become one of the participants.

As a diplomat's daughter who had travelled and resided around the world, Phoebe was thrilled to join the 'Ainu Dream,' which she was delighted to read among the shortlisted dreams and voted for. The adventure was to live among the indigenous people in the far north of

Hokkaido in Japan for a week. Even after living for six years in Japan, as her father had managed to extend his term such that Phoebe could finish secondary school there, Phoebe could not imagine being able to share a meal with the forgotten native people in the country. The Ainu adventure turned out to be an unforgettable, a once-in-a-lifetime experience for her.

Phoebe was impressed by the colleague who organised the trip being able to find the indigenous Ainu people. She remembered she once visited a museum in Hokkaido on the Ainu people. There were many Japanese people who somehow had a bit of Ainu heritage, but few knew where they actually lived these days. The trip also allowed Phoebe to make friends and bond with colleagues from other countries. She acted as the group interpreter, which was much appreciated by everyone. There was one staff member from Japan who was supposed to join the adventure but cancelled at last minute as she came down with the flu. Phoebe's fluency in Japanese, however, ensured a smooth communication which was essential as they spent their days in the wilderness. At the end of the stay, everyone was exhilarated by just living the way the Ainu people lived. They grew their own food, hunted their own meat, weaved their own robes, played their own music with basic but adorable music instruments crafted by themselves, under roofs built by their own hands. By day three, everyone stopped checking their Blackberries; their minds and souls were liberated and refreshed by the absence of modern technologies, and instead, nourished by the spirit of nature and human survival.

Chapter Twelve

Five years later, since the milonga in Buenos Aires, Phoebe had learned everything there was to learn in her position, and beyond - when she covered her superior during her pregnancy and maternity leave. Phoebe was itching to move up but seemed to get stuck in the family-like company culture. The mobility seemed to be only available to those who held a key managerial role in the company, and Phoebe saw many of her older colleagues happily work their ways to retirement in the same position, as long as they were content and did not commit a crime. Most of her colleagues had been working comfortably in the same position for over a decade and had no intention to move up or elsewhere at all. They were very content to live and work in the cocoon of the brand. On the other hand, some of her French colleagues, especially those who came from an aristocratic family or the alumni of famous business schools, had been on a quick-ladder up through the organisation. Phoebe hated to admit Ting-Ting's theory on the caste system in a French company was proved right.

The only Maison H employee who did not belong to the top tiers of the hierarchy pyramid but managed to enjoy the enormous opportunity the House had to offer was a Chinese employee named Kannis.

At first, no one in Paris paid this young lady any attention. To anyone at the headquarters, Kannis was merely a trainee working several months here and there in different major Maison H boutiques across Europe. Then, all of a sudden, she moved from interning at shops to assisting the most senior executives and becoming the right-hand person to the big bosses of Maison H. No one would have believed Kannis was someone other than from money as well as lineage. Not only did she carry herself with an air of superiority, she did not seem to care about the obnoxious expenses even the Parisians detested about the city. Kannis was known to call a taxi and keep it waiting for her in front of the Atelier, which was located in a banlieue, while she smoked her cigarette. The meter started running as soon as the taxi driver took the order and started on the road, not from the pickup point. Maison H had the reputation of paying the least salaries among all luxury houses, and instead cared for their employees in other ways, like experiences and offering share options. Yet Kannis, as a management trainee, was able to afford an apartment in a privileged area of the Sixteenth Arrondissement. It was no secret that she would fly business or first class everywhere she travelled.

Chapter Thirteen

Phoebe did not have the pleasure to meet the legendary Kannis until the legend accompanied the head architect, who was also a member of the family that owned the brand, to come to Hong Kong for the renovation of the new Maison H flagship store in town. Phoebe was very surprised to find that Kannis was actually from Hong Kong, just like Ting-Ting.

"Fair Bear, I command you to leave your desk at six sharp, today. You will come to my place to get dressed. We are going to paaaaarty tonight!" Ting-Ting appeared at Phoebe's cubicle at 4pm and squealed with delight when Phoebe was deep in thoughts about Kannis, who'd just made a tour to meet everyone in the office.

"It's Wednesday today. It's a luxury that I'm not traveling in the middle of the week. I actually look forward to hitting my pillow by 10 pm."

"Wednesday is the new Friday! Come on Fair Bear. Kannis is in town, and she's leaving tomorrow afternoon. I won't miss the chance to party with my two besties," Ting-Ting shouted at Phoebe in excited whispers.

"Kannis? Your bestie?" Phoebe could not believe her ears. This Kannis sounded even more intriguing.

It turned out that Kannis Kwan, a.k.a. KK, was from a rival family of the Ting-Ting's Lee clan. While the Lee family was the royalty in the manufacturing world, the Kwan family was the leading developer in real estate, and not only in Hong Kong but across Asia. Kannis' father was more than just an acquaintance to the Maison H in charge – it was said her father helped Maison H to get the most prominent spot in various major Asian cities to establish its flagship stores. To Kannis' credits, although her family's ties opened the door wide into the company, she was an incredibly intelligent and accomplished young lady. She picked up the language wherever she went and quickly learned the trade. She treated both of her colleagues and superiors with respect and enthusiasm. She was well liked in general, and there was little resentment to what special treatments she enjoyed within the company.

Ting-Ting told Phoebe that Kannis was her childhood friend. They always ended up in the same school together. Kannis was a bit older, and Ting-Ting looked up to her. Since their respective families did not encourage their friendship, they often had to hang out in secret whenever there were the Lees and the Kwans.

"You have to come. I need you to be my chaperone, so it won't be too obvious that I am partying with Kannis."

"So you are just using me?" Phoebe raised her eyebrow and resumed her attitude of lacking enthusiasm to go out on a Wednesday night.

"I WILL help your dad to get that Birkin Bag for your mum's sixtieth birthday!"

"You are on, bestie!" Phoebe could not resist the chance to help her father to surprise her mother at her coming big sixty. The waiting list to purchase the renowned Birkin Bag was two to three years long, depending on the colour and leather one desired. Claire was not a shopaholic nor crazy about branded goods, yet she admired Maison H; the aesthetics of the products, and out of the world quality. She loved the structure and the elegance of Maison H's handbags. Johnathan gifted her an Kelly Bag ten years ago for her fiftieth birthday, which she adored. It was more challenging to get the Birkin Bag - the holy grail of women's handbag. Johnathan asked his daughter embarrassedly for her help a few months ago, after learning from walking into a shop that the wait would be two years or longer. He did not want to abuse his status, and never disclosed who he was to the sales lady. Instead, he hoped Phoebe could advise him which Maison H boutique on earth would have a shorter waiting list that would enable him to get one in time for his beloved wife's big birthday.

The evening turned out to be a great one for all three of them. First, they went to see horse racing in Happy Valley. Every Wednesday night, except during the hottest summer months, there would be eight races along the race course in Happy Valley near Phoebe's apartment as well as the Maison H office, where it enjoyed a panorama view of the race course. Besides gamblers who religiously went there every week to bet, more than half of the spectators were tourists or local residents who wanted to have a fun evening out and try their luck on the horses. The atmosphere was relaxed and at the same time, exciting. It was a happy place to be in the middle of the week. After enjoying the highs of the race, the trio moved to SoHo, where both Kannis and Ting-Ting were welcomed to the most exclusive clubs in town. At the end of the evening, before they called it a night, Phoebe admitted to Ting-Ting that Kannis was as cool and down to earth as she had claimed. Ting-Ting was glad that her two best girlfriends got along, and hoped there would be more occasions they could hang out together in future.

Chapter Fourteen

Phoebe spent her last day of her Japan tour in Osaka at the new store of the new terminal in Kansai Airport to ensure a smooth operation. She had spent a full week training staff at other airports, and last week training staff of the new shop as well as setting up the new store.

The day went by uneventfully. By noon, the shop had reached its opening target. Phoebe was right to line up certain products of new designs and colours to encourage impulsive buys of Maison H loyal customers. Feeling relaxed as 'mission accomplished', Phoebe started to loosen up and enjoyed engaging in conversations with customers, or travellers who just passed by.

Alex arrived at Kansai Airport with two hours to spare before departure time. The meeting was expectedly short. In fact, he did not understand why his company kept sending him to try to close a deal in Japan. Alex thought it was a total waste of time. How could they not come to a conclusion by now that the Japanese would only trust to work with a Japanese company? Yet, he enjoyed his every business trip to Japan, even knowing nothing fruitful would come out of it. He loved the culture, the food, and the seasonal change in this small but charming country. Even the food at a Japanese airport was excellent, and Alex found his mouth watered just thinking of which restaurant he should go to this time. He particularly loved the Kyoto style set that served the side dishes in such an aesthetic way that he nearly didn't want to consume, if everything was not so delicious.

Carrying a full tummy, Alex was reluctant to sit in the business class lounge and check his email just yet. He decided to go wandering the new terminal and check out the gadget store. He loved discovering new toys that the Japanese invented since the last time he was there. Alex often bought little things and put them aside at home in his 'gifts' cupboard, saving them for raining days when he needed a gift but did not have time to go shopping. Last time he bought several USB that resembled a puppy humping the laptop. Alex found it hilarious and put them aside for his teenage nephews, although he doubted their mother was going to find it amusing.

Alex walked pass the Maison H boutique and looked at its fascinating display window in which the focus was on men's accessories. The show window was staged like the platform of a metro station in Paris. There was no mannequin, but the products were displayed in a way resembled two men waiting at the platform dressed for different occasions. One in a tie that was twisted in a way as if it was flying, imitating the wind generated by a passing train. A pair of polished shoes and a briefcase were placed on the floor below where the tie was. Another one had a scarf wrapped around a hoop and was wearing a pair of suede moccasins. A sports watch was placed in a way one could imagine could be an arm resting across the lap.

Alex wondered if whoever set this window up splashed fresh piss around to make the staging more authentic, imitating the actual metro station in Paris which always smelled of fresh urine. He laughed at his own joke and reassured himself again that he did not need another tie. He was about to leave when someone caught his attention. A stunning brunette was talking to a couple of salespeople. Was she a difficult customer complaining? It didn't look like it as she was all smiles, and her gestures were more elegant than angry. Before knowing it, he walked into the store and in the direction to where the trio were standing.

Alex was even intrigued when he heard the same lady speaking Japanese to the two staff. Despite knowing only a few Japanese words himself, Alex could tell she was giving instructions to the two staff in uniform. The three ladies stopped and greeted Alex when they saw him walking towards them.

Phoebe was coaching the store manager and the staff who was in charge of the silk department to display a pattern of the current season, instead of the previous one. Every Maison H had a scarf mounting square above the silk scarf showcase. A scarf was displayed in such a way as if it was a valued artwork. For customers who already owned several

Maison H scarves, a pattern of the new season was very effective in drawing them to walk into the store again. Seeing a Caucasian gentleman in his thirties approach, the trio stopped their discussion and went on to greet him. Knowing the Japanese staff would be intimated to speak English in front of her, Phoebe took the initiative to serve this customer.

"Welcome to Maison H, would you like to take a look at our new silk collection?"

"Sure, I can make use of a new tie. The ones at home look a bit tired." Not wanting to give the wrong impression that he was married or had a girlfriend, Alex had no choice but to change his mind about needing another tie.

"Absolutely, it would be my pleasure to show you our new collection, this way please."

Phoebe led Alex to the tie section, found a white shirt on the men's ready-to-wear shelf, and placed it in a velvet lined tray above a standalone accessories showcase. Knowing all the ties by heart, Phoebe selected several navy blue ties of different patterns, and laid them next to the white shirt. Navy blue was always an easy start with a customer looking for ties. Judging from the customer age, Phoebe picked the geometrical pattern rather than the animal patterns, which were more popular among more mature male customers.

Alex, more interested in the presenter than the ties, tried his best to compare the patterns on how they looked against the shirts, so not to appear he was just there to chat up the stunning girl standing in front of him. She was wearing a perfume that was sweet like chocolate-orange but not repulsive - it was elegant at the same time, just like her. Unlike other staff who had a name badge on their uniforms, this lady did not have one.

"If I don't like the tie after I buy it, can I bring it back here to you to exchange?"

"Well, you won't have to bring it all the way to the airport here. Just go to any Maison H store in your home city and our colleagues there will be very happy to assist you. Besides, I am not based here usually; I'm just helping out as it is the opening day for the shop. I am normally based in our office in Hong Kong." Phoebe tried to engage a friendly yet professional conversation with the gentleman who had a strong English accent and was dangerously handsome.

"I am based in Hong Kong, too." Alex could not suppress his big smile. He quickly produced his business card and handed it to Phoebe, in the way the Japanese did, holding his card with both hands and with his head slightly bowed down, knowing very well that Phoebe had no choice but to exchange with hers in the presence of her Japanese colleagues.

Happy to have secured Phoebe's contact, even just her work one, Alex paid for all three ties that Phoebe picked for him.

"So much for not needing a tie…" Alex couldn't help but tease himself after stepping out of Maison H.

Chapter Fifteen

Phoebe went for a break at Starbucks after her encounter with Alex Brent, who worked for an investment bank in Hong Kong, which Phoebe would have never guessed. She'd encountered and flirted with many bankers in the city when she was out with Ting-Ting, and most, if not all of them, were arrogant. Alex looked more like the IT guy, albeit a handsome and sexy one. With his backpack and dark, thick-rimmed glasses, he looked so geeky that Phoebe thought he could, at the most, be working in the IT department for the famous investment bank listed on his business card. She doubted very much he wore any ties to work. Alex was actually wearing a T-shirt, although it fit and hung so nicely on his body that he turned Phoebe's knees soft just looking at it, and a pair of good quality chinos.

Checking her email on her Blackberry to take her mind off Alex, Phoebe wasn't paying attention to the traffic in the café and ran into a wall of muscle.

"Oh, I am so sorry. Gosh, it hurts." The muscle wall was rock hard, and she bet it hurt her nose more than the guy she ran into.

"Phoebe, are you alright?"

Looking up, Alex was giving her his geeky, but sexy smile, making Phoebe's knees weak again.

"I am very sorry, Mr Brent. I wasn't looking. I am so sorry. Are you hurt?"

"Alex… call me, Alex, please. No worries, I'm fine. You?"

Phoebe wanted to say she believed her nose hurt more but kept her mouth shut.

"When are you flying back to Hong Kong?" Alex tried to have a conversation with Phoebe and get more information about her before it was his turn to get a coffee. For the first time, he cursed the efficiency of the Japanese, as he saw the queue was moving forward quickly.

"I was supposed to fly back this evening for the weekend, but I just got an email from my boss to ask me to stay over for one more day to prepare the shop for the coming typhoon. So, I guess that will be tomorrow, and hopefully before flights get delayed by the weather."

Phoebe explained about the hurricane that hit Kansai Airport two years ago, which caused serious flooding at the terminal and all the shops inside. The damages were so vast that everyone who worked at the airport still shuddered at the thought of it.

The Kansai Airport Authority built a new terminal that was better designed to withstand extreme weathers such as a hurricane. The old terminal would gradually be closed down for refurbishment and reinforcement. Alex recalled the event, as he'd felt lucky his bank did not win the bid to invest in the airport - their loss came as a blessing in disguise. He made a decision before his coffee was ready.

Alex waved goodbye to Phoebe and made a quick call to his secretary.

Chapter Sixteen

After taking her luggage back to the airport hotel which she always stayed at, she asked the reception for another night of stay. She quickly changed into something more comfortable, went through the security checkpoints again and back to the shop to organise the typhoon preparation. Much to her surprise, by the time she got back to the store, she saw Alex there. Remembering from his boarding pass that his flight would have departed by now, she wondered if the typhoon had made a quick turn, and his flight was cancelled.

"The typhoon is here already? Is your flight cancelled?"

"Oh, my flight wasn't cancelled, it had departed already. I asked my colleague to change my flight to the evening one, so I'm now stuck in the terminal. So, if you could use a pair of hands, I would like to help you and your shop to get ready for the typhoon."

Unable to believe what she heard, and what a sweet gesture Alex was offering, Phoebe also felt uncomfortable that a customer would be carrying sandbags for them. She wanted to turn down Alex's offer, but before she could open her mouth, Alex pointed to some Japanese travellers who were not ready to board their planes yet, who'd also got themselves involved in helping – in typical Japanese behaviour to offer a hand in times of need.

This super typhoon would be the first test for the new terminal. Although it was believed the airport could withstand an even stronger hurricane, no shop was willing to take the risk. Hence, Cecile from Paris asked Priscilla to send someone, or fly to Kansai herself, to make sure the sandbags would be stacked sky high to stop rainwater from flooding the store and damaging the very stately and expensive stone tiles. Phoebe desperately needed some muscles to help her and her team, which was composed of mostly female staff, to do the heavy lifting. Alex was indeed a God-send in their time of need. Although mildly embarrassed, as the staff could sense that Alex had a serious crush on Phoebe, she was very touched by the fact that he'd postponed his flight in order to stay to help her.

Alex, Phoebe, and her team worked non-stop the following few hours to prepare the shop for the worst if the typhoon brought bigger damages than the new and stronger terminal could fend off. Not only was Maison H hard at work, but every single outlet in the terminal were all busy working towards the same goal, as the typhoon had now picked up its speed towards the airport. The brand's competition, which was located in the neighbouring shops, came and discussed how they could work together to build a stronger defence. It was exhilarating to work as one.

They were only halfway there when Alex's flight was called for boarding. Looking at Phoebe, sweating and carrying sandbags back and forth from the distribution counter, Alex quietly messaged his secretary and asked her to postpone his flight for another day, and book him a night of accommodation at the airport hotel.

"Alex, you missed your flight!" Glancing at her watch, Phoebe realised they had been working without a break for six hours and had built a wall of sandbags that they now required a ladder to get into the shop. Alex must have forgotten his flight in the heat of all the moving and stacking.

"Don't worry, I changed my flight to tomorrow. I booked myself into the Nikko Airport Hotel. I could use a nice shower after this. I'm not sure they would have allowed me to board the plane sweating and smelling like this."

"That would make the two of us." Phoebe could not suppress her laugh. "I think we can finish up here. We've done everything we can. All merchandises are now packed and stored away on high shelves or cupboards, and we've built a wall of sandbags as tall as us. If that does not stop the flood, I don't know what will."

After learning that Alex was going to stay at the same hotel, she invited him to dinner to thanks him for his labour and generous help. Phoebe took Alex to a restaurant that served Kyoto cuisine. The restaurant was a hidden gem, and normal travellers would not usually be able to find it. Those who worked at the airport took their important clients there for business meetings.

Chapter Seventeen

"I've been here on business a few times, but I didn't know such a restaurant existed. To be honest, the food here in Japan is so good that you can eat well even at a convenient store."

"The owner and the chef here used to work at the top restaurant at Park Hyatt in Tokyo. He retired and moved back to his hometown, somewhere nearby, and opened his own place. As we are at the airport, he's got the freshest ingredients flown in from all over Japan. The food here is top notch. He's trying to hide away from the Michelin guide to keep this within the knows and his loyal customers."

"The food is amazing! This could be a Michelin-starred restaurant."

"That you are wrong. Most Japanese do not like the Michelin stars. There was even one restaurant in Tokyo suing the Michelin guide because they gave it a star. The star had given the owner unwanted fame, and an unwanted queue outside his place every single evening."

"That... is unheard of." Alex enjoyed his meal and talking with Phoebe enormously. He thanked this typhoon for passing by when he was in Japan and fate had brought him and Phoebe together.

Phoebe and Alex carried on their conversations at the hotel bar when the typhoon moved closer and closer to where they were. With the music playing and wind blowing, banging on the window, Phoebe and Alex enjoyed the cosy environment in the hotel and each other's company; learning about each other, and feeling the tension built between them as the hours went by. They reluctantly left the bar when the bar staff informed them it was closing time. Alex, being the gentleman, did not make any advances, although all he could think of the whole evening was to kiss and undress the amazing woman that fate had brought him to meet. He walked Phoebe back to her room, said goodnight, and wished her a sweet dream.

"Would you like to grab a bite together tomorrow morning before our flight? I believe we are going to be on the same flight back to Hong Kong." Alex was hoping they would have breakfast the next morning then leave the hotel and check into their flight together, so that they could be sitting next to each other during the four-hour flight.

"That would be lovely, good night. Thank you so much for your help this afternoon."

The next morning Phoebe woke up and was greeted by sun shining into her window. She was so tired last night that she forgot to close the curtain. She turned on the news and was glad to learn that the typhoon had passed the Kansai area. The new terminal passed the test of the storm with flying colours. The relief team the government had sent, of stand-by workers, worked tirelessly in the early morning to clear all the sandbags in the terminal to get everything back into service before travellers began to check-in.

Phoebe and Alex had breakfast together in the hotel coffee lounge, both feeling relaxed as it was officially the weekend. They checked out of the hotel and in for their flight together. The ground staff at the airline counter thought they were a couple and arranged them to be seated together.

As the flight took off, both Phoebe and Alex enjoyed the bliss of a calm morning after the storm, with everyone around them wearing a grateful smile for the little damage the typhoon brought this time, and for them, it had brought the two of them together and marked the beginning of something romantic and beautiful.

Chapter Eighteen

After their fateful encounter in Japan, Alex asked Phoebe out when they were back in Hong Kong. Still not yet entirely over her last relationship, Phoebe approached Alex's pursuit with the utmost caution. With Phoebe's traveling schedule, she also found it hard to find time for a date during the week. On weekends, she was already committed to lots of outdoor activities with different friends. In the end, she asked Alex if he would like to join her to go hiking or out on a boat with her and her friends.

To Phoebe's surprise, Alex said yes, and for weeks Alex had been religiously picking Phoebe up from her home, joining her with her friends wherever they had planned going and doing, and then seeing her back in her apartment, without inviting himself in. Alex's relaxed attitude and his gentlemanly manners were a big hit with Phoebe's friends, both female, and male. Knowing Phoebe's history with her last boyfriend who hurt her deeply, her friends were being quite protective of her. They welcomed Alex into the group but did not encourage the relationship to progress. They adopted a wait and observe attitude towards this new man in Phoebe's life.

Early one Saturday evening, Alex saw Phoebe back home after a long day out on a boat at sea. As Phoebe and Alex walked into her building, the doorman apologised to Phoebe that the building was out of fresh water and power for the next few hours. Something went wrong, and the Water Department had sent technicians on their way to fix them, he explained. Phoebe was annoyed; she just wanted to have a long hot shower after spending a whole day at sea and on the beach.

"I guess I'm going to grab some clean clothes and go to my yoga studio to take a shower." As much as Phoebe was longing for that hot shower, she wasn't very excited about the idea of looking for a cab on a Saturday evening. It was going to be challenging, as many people would be heading out for dinner.

"Or you can come to my place, which is about five minutes' walk from here. You can take a shower, or a bath, while I cook something for dinner… how does that sound?" Alex did not want to pressure Phoebe into anything, but he was hoping to finally spend more alone time with Phoebe other than the return journey between her apartment and seeing her friends.

"How come I didn't think of that? Oh yes, you never told me you live in the area." Phoebe was touched by Alex's tireless gesture to pick her up from her apartment on every date with her and her friends, while all this time he lived conveniently nearby.

"Well, you never asked… now, may I have the honour to invite you to my bachelor pad?" Alex opened his palm and waited. Phoebe placed her palm into Alex's, and hand in hand, they walked to Alex's apartment, which turned out to be only two blocks away. Phoebe's heartbeat picked up as they had never been alone in a private space. She had never invited Alex into her apartment. Although they had held hands, they had not yet done anything more intimate than kissing each other on the cheeks the past few months since they started seeing one another. She wondered whether that might change tonight.

Alex's building is a recent establishment with a marble stone façade and a lovely courtyard in the middle after walking past the lobby. There were frangipani trees planted along a lawn where there were some older children playing before dinner time. The whole place was grand but not pretentious, just like Alex. His apartment was on the top floor of the building. There was only one unit on each floor to ensure the privacy of the residents. When the lift opened, Phoebe and Alex stepped into a small foyer where they could take their shoes off. As Alex lived on the top floor, the ceiling of the foyer was made of glass, which made the tiny space feel spacious. The area was warmed up from the sun during the day. Alex opened the door by entering a code into the digital lock and his fingerprint. Phoebe gasped at the view once the door was pushed open, and she stepped into a wide, open-plan space filled with lights from the sunset.

Alex's bachelor pad was a huge studio cleverly designed in a way that the sleeping area and bathroom were hidden to ensure privacy. The whole place was simple and tastefully set-up. The kitchen was modern, with a beautiful working station, equipped with high-end kitchen furniture and appliances. Phoebe wondered if Alex used his kitchen at all. The lounge looked welcoming and comfortable. Then Phoebe saw what the lounge led to. She could not believe something like this existed just five minutes away from her old and beat up apartment building. The wide, ceiling to floor glass windows opened up to a spacious terrace, which ended with an infinity pool looking out to the harbour. Phoebe was mesmerized by the view in front of her. Without thinking, she took her sundress off, and still in her bikini, she walked down the steps and into the pool. She swam towards the edge of the infinity pool and indulged into the last moments of the sunset.

Alex followed and swam towards her. He wrapped his arms around Phoebe's waist. Phoebe turned around and looked straight into his eyes. They started kissing each other, and within minutes they were completely naked in each other arms. Alex carried Phoebe to his bed. They made love quickly, with much passion to each other, as they could no longer stand the tensions building up between them ever since they met each other for the first time in Japan. Afterward, Alex took Phoebe to have the long hot shower he promised her. They made love again, slowly and gently this time, while cleaning and exploring each other's body.

After their shower, Alex prepared some fresh salad and made pasta for Phoebe. He put everything onto a tray with a wine bottle and two wine glasses, then he led Phoebe onto his rooftop. The sky was now filled with stars. There was a table in the corner looking out to the sea. Alex lighted up some candles, set the table, pulled one of the chairs out, and invited Phoebe to sit down. Phoebe saw one-third of the rooftop had been turned into a garden in which vegetables were grown. Looking at her plate, she realised where the salad came from.

"You are full of surprises, Mr. Brent."

Phoebe was surprised by how delicious both dishes were. They dined and chatted late into the evening. They made love again in bed and slept deeply in each other's arms. Both Phoebe and Alex quietly thanked whoever messed up the water supply in Phoebe's building.

Chapter Nineteen

Phoebe wished to give her company the benefit of the doubt, and not give into Ting-Ting's theory about French companies that soon yet. Therefore, she first went to Lorraine Pak, the Human Resources Director of Asia-Pacific, to talk about other opportunities internally.

However, since Lorraine was traveling back to back, Phoebe could hardly set up a meeting with her as she was barely in town herself. Luckily, she ran into Lorraine when they were both in Singapore for business. Lorraine was checking out while Phoebe was about to drop her luggage as it was still too early for her to check in.

"Phoebe, hey, what a coincidence! Look, it's very embarrassing for me to ask you, but can I use your credit card to settle the hotel bill? All my credit cards ran out of credit; the company hasn't yet reimbursed the travel expenses in time."

The staff at Maison H were responsible for settling all travel expenses, including credit card charges, until they were reimbursed. It had generated lots of pressure on the staff who travelled for work. While in the office, it took a long time for the expenses to be cleared and reimbursed as the senior management, whose signatures were required, were constantly on the road, too.

On the other hand, Lorraine was obsessed with handbags. During the stay of the latest seasonal buy in Paris, Lorraine had purchased several handbags as the brand had a couple of exciting designs come out. Phoebe helped her to carry one of the orange boxes back to Hong Kong. Lorraine paid the full retail price, but due to the tax exemption and price difference between continents, the handbags would still be less expensive compared to buying them in Hong Kong with staff discount.

Priscilla had warned Phoebe at the beginning, that if she was not cautious herself, she could end up like many young ladies in the industry, who looked sassy and glamourous on the surface but were all broke, or in deep in debt. Their average corporate salaries could hardly sustain their chase after the seasonal trends led by the luxury brands. Phoebe had been very sensible to her brand purchases and limited herself to a couple of items only at the annual staff sale. As her family moved location every three years because of her father's diplomatic career, her mother had taught her from young to declutter regularly, and trained her to have a core wardrobe and to have something for all occasions, instead of having many similar pieces.

Phoebe suspected that Lorraine could have reached the limit on her six credit cards after a shopping spree in Paris, plus knowing the turtle pace of the reimbursements, and worried herself if she would be in the same situation later, given the not very high credit limit on her card. Still, she did not hesitate to hand over her American Express to settle Lorraine's expenses at the same hotel she was going to check into.

Phoebe and Lorraine then had breakfast together at the coffee lounge before Lorraine left for the airport. Phoebe took the chance to ask Lorraine about internal mobility at Maison H.

Lorraine was a Canadian Asian; her father was Japanese while her mother a Korean. Although born and raised in Toronto, thanks to the limited English commanded by both of her parents, she grew up learning to speak English, Japanese, and Korean fluently. Lorraine had the look of a Japanese, temperament of a fierce Korean woman, and the mentality of a Canadian. For those who mistakenly took her at face value and thought she was a soft-spoken Japanese lady, they would be surprised by her direct, efficient, and no bull shit working style. Coming from a renowned headhunting firm, Lorraine had been hired into Maison H to modernise the organization, and enhance the function and influence of the Human Resources Department within the company. Phoebe was hoping Lorraine would be able to help her out of her static career in the company before she came to the last resort of quitting.

"As the HR Director of Asia-Pacific, I would like to ask you to be patient and assure you there will be opportunities within the company for you to advance. Keep on with the good work. But, speaking as a professional- talent personnel, I would advise you to venture outside and look for another good company to work for. That will be the only way for you to advance and enrich your own CV. I have been with the company for a bit more than two years. You can see I have restructured the organization, eliminated or merged duplicate roles. I also created an internal mobility bulletin board to make all internal availability visible and accessible for all employees to apply for. Despite all these tools I have offered them, this is still a very traditional company whose most senior management were born with entitlement. They have got to where they are by hanging onto what the family had left for them. It certainly worked very well to maintain the product quality as well as the brand value. However, in terms of opportunities open to common employees like you and me, I have my reservations. On the other hand, you are a bright young lady with lots of talents and skills. Do not limit yourself to just one company - go out and learn from another boss. If you cannot get a promotion from within, go and get yourself one… but probably at another luxury house."

That was why when head-hunter Adele came knocking on Phoebe's door as the fashion giant Vuitton finally branched into cosmetics, Phoebe, although being very fond of and loyal to Maison H, decided to meet with the head-hunter to see what kind of opportunities there were in the job market for her. Adele found Phoebe's profile on LinkedIn after Ting-Ting convinced her to sign up an account there to test the waters of the job market. Phoebe was hesitant to do that and felt it was like putting herself onto a dating site. After Ting-Ting's irresistible reasoning and persuading, she finally gave in and created a rather discreet profile of herself. She did not post any photo of herself nor list anything more than her professional experience at the travel retail team of a renowned luxury house. She believed that if another company were interested in meeting her, it would have to be solely based on her professional skills and experiences.

Vuitton was probably the most popular and successful luxury conglomerate in the world, and rivalled Maison H being the most luxurious. Vuitton fans had been waiting for the brand to branch out of its fashion and leather good lines, into cosmetics and fragrances. Earlier in the year, the brand held a high profile press conference to announce the news that everybody had been waiting for, for years. The products were already in the pipeline, and Vogue magazine even described the launch would be the most anticipated in the luxury world in decades. The fashion house had begun its aggressive process headhunting the best professionals in the industry to execute the launch. Other luxury brands started to get nervous, not only because of the competition but of the worry that their best people would be lured to work for the industry giant.

Yet, Vuitton Beauty passed on a stringent guideline about the team to recruit to its HR department. Cosmetics and fragrances were categorised as FMCG, 'fast-moving consumer goods.' Positions were usually offered to applicants who were from the same field, and were expected to have a solid knowledge of the high demanding sector. However, for Vuitton House, the launch was no ordinary FMCG brand - they wanted to sell their cosmetics and fragrances like their handbags. Hence, without Maison H even knowing, the brand approached several of its young executives, who were hungry for career advancement but had nowhere to go within the company, and tried to recruit them to be part of team zero.

Under this guideline, Rebecca, the Human Resources in charge, was particularly interested in Phoebe's profile. A solid five years in Travel Retail at Maison H, a daughter of generations of diplomats, raised and lived in all over the world, and with five languages in her pocket including Chinese and Japanese. Rebecca only learned the extra personal information of Phoebe from Adele, who'd managed to dig out more of Phoebe's background from other candidates she'd sought from Maison H. Rebecca was pleasantly surprised when she came across a photo of Phoebe with Ting-Ting who was under the limelight of the paparazzi every now and then, she thought Phoebe was perfect for launching Vuitton Beauty in Travel Retail Asia-Pacific.

Vuitton house was not the only one who had approached Phoebe. While Priscilla was on maternity leave, Phoebe took her place and went to the Cannes Travel Retail Conference to meet with their operative clients and prospects at the annual travel retail event. Once Phoebe met with other brands' Travel Retail Directors, there had not been a month that passed by that Phoebe did not get approached with a job offer.

Priscilla's boss, Cecile, the Global Director of Travel Retail at Maison H, was right to resist to let Phoebe go to Cannes. For years, Cecile had been trying to stop Priscilla taking Phoebe to the most important events in the industry. While Priscilla wanted to groom Phoebe and tried to include her in every single occasion where Phoebe could learn and shine, Cecile was worried once other brands met Phoebe, they would try to steal her away. She was right to be concerned, as Maison H was famous for paying staff with love rather than money. But to Priscilla, although knowing very well such a risk was high, she felt it was unfair to Phoebe to hide her from their competitors. With Priscilla on maternity leave and herself having some family emergency, Cecile was reluctant to let Phoebe go, as Asia-Pacific was an important region for the brand, and she simply could not leave the spot empty.

Phoebe was excited about going to the Cannes Festival - she had no idea about Cecile not wanting her to go. She used to ask Priscilla if she could go to Cannes with her as there was a surplus in their traveling budget and they were not too busy around that time of year. Priscilla would make up some excuse and encouraged her to take some time off and use up her annual leave. After a few times, Phoebe stopped asking to go. Therefore, she could not be happier when Priscilla broke the news to her that she would be her representative to Cannes this year while she stayed home to look after her new-born.

Priscilla had just had a baby girl, Emma, a couple of weeks before. Emma was a little darling, a Eurasian girl version of Guillaume. Her eyes were Mediterranean blue, and her cheeks were pink like a rose. Priscilla had worked very hard to push it as close to her due date as possible. She wanted to spend as much time with her baby as the short ten weeks' maternity leave the labour law allowed in the city. The government had recently proposed to extend the maternity leave to fourteen weeks, but it would take a year or two to pass the new law. Priscilla thought that her biological clock was ticking and she could not wait that long to have the extra four weeks off. So, she accumulated her annual leave for postpartum, too.

Emma came three weeks earlier than the actual due date, and Priscilla went into labour while she was having a meeting with an operator who was in town for buying another brand. It was a chaotic afternoon when Priscilla's waters broke. She thought embarrassingly that she had incontinence when she was in the final month of pregnancy. That was, until she first felt the stronger than usual contraction and she realised she was in labour. Lucky, her client from Taiwan was someone she had been dealing with for nearly a decade. Like any Chinese, the client was happy to be present and be involved in such a happy event.

Emma was born five hours later, and Priscilla was glad that she earned another three weeks with her baby girl after her birth - she would be off work for nearly six months. Priscilla thought that it would be a lot easier for her to breastfeed Emma until she started solid food.

Contrary to Cecile, Priscilla did not mind letting Phoebe meet with other brands' senior executives. She believed it was wrong to hold Phoebe back while she had so much talent to grow beyond even her capacity. Although she would feel sorry herself for loosing such a great help, Priscilla knew she would be proud of Phoebe the day when she left for a higher position elsewhere. Therefore, Priscilla extended her maternity leave and sent Phoebe to Cannes, amid opposition from her superior.

Chapter Twenty

The Cannes festival was the biggest annual event for the Travel Retail industry. Everyone who mattered in travel retail turned up in this stunning French Riviera city which was otherwise famous for its resort and film festival. It was usually held in the fall after everyone was back from their summer vacation. It was said that was to uplift the post-holiday depression. It was a showcase of the upcoming new products for the brand or to reveal the exclusive travel retail items, as well as for the brands to meet with operators to review business and discuss future projects. Not only was the event an important industry networking convention, it was also glamourous, with all the big brands competing to have the most luxurious décor, and senior executives dressing their best in their brand outfits, hopefully sponsored by the brands and not out of their own pockets. The best champagnes, wines, spirits, and cigars from the tobacco, wine, and liquor vendors were all out for everyone to enjoy. To top all this, every year, the organiser hired a famous band or DJ to entertain the executives, every single evening. This year the most anticipating performer was DJ David Guetta. He was currently the hottest DJ after launching his own album and did a few Billboard songs with big stars like Sia. Phoebe could not wait until lunch break to tell Ting-Ting that her trip to Cannes was confirmed and who she heard would perform at the event.

"If you are going, so am I, Fair Bear!"

"It's a travel retail event, dear. As much as I would like my best friend to tag along, I'm afraid you won't be able to find an excuse this time."

"C'est moi, Ting-Ting, you are talking to, I always find a way. Did I tell you my uncle Tony had acquired the exclusive distributing rights of Valentina's Secret in Asia two years ago? He goes to Cannes every year now, and has been trying to invite the whole family to go, just to show off his brand and models. I will give him a call this afternoon. Just don't let him know we are besties, or he will try to recruit you."

"Not a bad idea if I get VS's underwear for free."

"There's no free lunch, Fair Bear. My uncle is filthy rich but stingy as hell. My mum told me he makes three staff share a three-star hotel room when they are on a business trip. And to be reminded daily of how un-model-like your body is, imagine how depressing it will be." Ting-Ting was referring to the big screen at the reception area in his uncle's office which played a decade worth of Valentina's Secret annual big runway shows in loops.

In the next two weeks, Phoebe prepared for Cannes frantically, due to the last minute approval of her trip there. With Priscilla guiding her remotely and daily Skype calls with Cecile in Paris, Phoebe was ready for the show just in time. The premium travel retail event was more for the perfume team, which was independent from the fashion team as it was categorised as FMCG - a completely different operation. While on the fashion side, Maison H had standalone stores at the airports or in downtown duty-free malls, the fragrance side was more mobile. As a result, it was forever pitching with new products and promotions to the operators to get more prominent locations and exposure. The convention in Cannes was a fantastic platform for the perfume team to meet with operators worldwide and to get a glimpse of what the competitors had in the pipeline in the year to come. Therefore, Phoebe's mission was more to be present, and to review mid-season sales with all her clients, since they'd just done their seasonal buy in summer, less than two months ago. On the other hand, Priscilla reminded Phoebe to keep an eye on the Perfume team, in case they tried to persuade the operators to assign more space in their Maison H stores to display perfume. Although revenue was revenue, it did not fall into Priscilla's Profit and Loss!

Chapter Twenty-One

The flight from Paris to Cannes was only one and a half hour long. Phoebe's flight from Hong Kong landed in Paris before sunrise, and the layover was brief. She arrived at the 5-star hotel that Maison H had a contract with, before the check-in time. The concierge invited Phoebe to use their pool by the seaside before her room was ready.

Once Phoebe stepped into the pool area, she felt less annoyed that her room was not available earlier. The 9:30am sun shone gently on her skin, and the breeze kissed her cheeks. She was in Paris in July for the spring-summer buying season but was unlucky with the weather. It was cold and rainy during the two weeks she was there. She was pleasantly surprised by the warm weather towards the end of September in Cannes. She quickly changed into her bikini and spent the next two hours sunbathing by the pool. She dozed off a few times listening to the sound of waves in the Mediterranean Sea. Phoebe thought it was the perfect recharge before she had to go to the convention centre to meet Cecile that afternoon.

Phoebe expected the booth décor would be luxurious and the vendors would spare no budget to stand out among the competition. Still, she was in awe when she arrived at the venue, which reminded her of the World Expo on a smaller scale. The convention centre was literally turned into a luxurious shopping mall in a five-star hotel. The so-called booths looked more like proper standalone boutiques. It was extravagant to build something like this solely for a one-week event. You could find everything you needed there: clothes from all the fashion brands which focused on their travel-friendly items such as sports jackets, one item that

Maison H sold very well the traveller; the shoemaker giant Signore F. showcased their signature ballerinas in the newest candy colours and in kitty, low, and high heels. Watches ranged from USD20 for plastic pieces to USD6,000 stainless steels with a famous Swiss-made movement, that all told the same time, and skincare and make-up products, so that one could go to the conference hall from their bed, and get fixed with all the cosmetics products available at the convention centre. Chocolates, caviars, champagnes, wines, and even water – all would give you a headache just to decide which one to taste first. There was nowhere else one would want to be if there was ever an apocalypse.

Phoebe's mission was to review the business with the operators of the boutiques under her and Priscilla's management. She had to assure the business partners that all would still be in her capable hands while Priscilla was on maternity leave. Phoebe was also to gather information about the operators' agenda at the convention. Any business development of the operators would be of her interest, too, as it would impact their open-to-buy budget in their future seasonal buying.

By the third day, Phoebe had finished all the meetings with her clients, so that allowed her some free time to visit other booths. She first went to the big brands that were usually Maison H's neighbours at the airports or downtown duty-free malls she was in charge with. Phoebe wanted to see what their travel retail exclusive items were and noted down the features and estimated retail prices. These would provide important insight for her and her clients when they did their next buy. She introduced herself and met with most directors of the competition, who were surprised and delighted to learn about Phoebe from Maison H.

She walked past Vuitton beauty, who did not have much to display as they were keeping everything secret for their big launch. The team there just wanted to talk about business and negotiate with operators based on the anticipation by the public built up. Phoebe felt a bit embarrassed and guilty about the interview she had merely two weeks ago. Nonetheless, Sebastian, who would be her immediate superior if she got the job, spotted her visiting and talking to other brands. The next spare moment he had, he rang his colleague Rebecca from their Human Resources Department, to send the agent representing Phoebe the offer with a slightly increased salary, as soon as possible, before other brands could approach Phoebe.

After finishing her business obligations, Phoebe went on to see other vendors that probably had nothing to do with her. She went to visit Ting-Ting at her uncle's Valentina's Secret booth. She had to admit Ting-Ting was right again about her uncle showing off. The VS's booth had to be the most dramatic one in the whole go-big-or-go-home Cannes Travel Retail Premium Annual Conference. A runway was built in the middle, and around the booth were several miniature Asian iconic sceneries installed, representing the cities where he had the exclusive distribution rights for Valentina's Secret. After a couple of bellini served at the Chandon booths, Ting-Ting and Phoebe sang, 'It's a small world after all,' laughing at the Disneyland resembled set-up, giggling between themselves to no end. Not sure if it was the ridiculous booth set up or the super-hot runway models, no one could deny Ting-Ting's uncle had done a good job drawing probably the biggest crowd at the conference. Ting-Ting guessed rightly that all the models came from Eastern Europe, whose hourly rate was a fraction of those of their French counterparts. 'If you could pay less, why pay more?' was the forever motto of Ting-Ting's financially cautious uncle.

Ting-Ting and Phoebe were the first ones on the dance floors and the last to leave every night during the event. They knew it would be years if it would happen again before the two of them could be at the Cannes event again. The two best friends enjoyed dancing to the beat of David Guetta and sang their lungs out along to the DJ's top hits, such as 'Titanium' and 'Work Hard, Play Hard.'

If I ever get the offer from Vuitton Beauty, Phoebe thought to herself, *this would be the highlight of my time at Maison H - with my colleague and best friend Ting-Ting.*

Chapter Twenty-Two

A week after returning from Cannes, Phoebe received a call from Adele.

"Congratulations Phoebe! Vuitton has made you an offer! I'm going to email you the contract. Have a look and give me your answer in two days. Don't make them wait - many candidates would kill for this role if you turn it down." Adele was more anxious than Phoebe this time as HR from the brand made it very clear the bosses wanted Phoebe and Phoebe only. If only she'd known that when another week passed by, and when all Travel Retail executives would be back at their desks, more than five brands would ring her and asked about Phoebe. Then she would have waited and tried to find the best deal for Phoebe and herself in terms of commission.

Thirty minutes later, Phoebe received Adele's email with an attachment of the contract draft for her comments. Vuitton had offered her the position of the Area Manager for Vuitton Beauty; a title Phoebe had been waiting for years for at Maison H, and reporting directly to Sebastian who was the Travel Retail Director for Asia-Pacific. However, when she looked at her area of responsibility, she had to pause a couple of times in her head to read through all of them, namely, Hong Kong, Macau, China, Taiwan, Thailand, Singapore, Malaysia, Indonesia, Cambodia, Vietnam, Japan, Guam, Saipan. For any other brand, these areas would be concluded as Greater China for Hong Kong, Macau, China, and Taiwan, while South East Asia for the rest after Japan and Mid Pacific, (Guam and Saipan), that usually fell under three different area managers. So, shouldn't she be called the Regional Manager? She rang Adele to clarify that point.

"Well, apparently it was just for the initial launch as the product line was still slim. The 'area' would be divided later, once the brand found the right candidates. Look on the bright side Phoebe, Vuitton Beauty had the confidence in you being able to look after all their clients and would provide you the right tools and support." Adele had raised the same question earlier and was merely repeating what Sebastian told her, eager to close the deal with Phoebe.

"I applied to be the Area Manager for Greater China, Adele. I have been in Travel Retail long enough to know the areas you described to me easily cover over two hundred points of sales. Don't give me the rubbish that I should be flattered that they think that I'm a superwoman; I know the frogs well enough that they are just being tight and want me to do everything. Seriously, tell them no one can do a good job having to look after such a big area." Thinking of her parents who would move to Beijing soon, Phoebe wanted to focus on Greater China, where also all the exciting developments were going to be in the next years to come.

Adele had no choice but to go back to Sebastian and relayed a similar message but in a nicer tone. Sebastian pressured his boss in Paris to release more budget for hiring - gone were the days when the brand name alone could attract candidates to enslave themselves for the pure glamour offered by the group's name. They needed to offer something more robust these days to attract talents, apparently.

Sitting at the bar of his usual hang out as well as most French in the city, Pastis, Sebastian scratched his head. He tried to think of a solution after hanging up the phone with Adele, who'd just informed him that Phoebe turned the offer down unless her area of responsibility could be reduced by two-thirds of what had been proposed to her.

Sebastian thought he had hit the jackpot upon receiving Phoebe's profile from Adele's talent search firm. With a solid five years of all-round experience at Maison H travel retail, and several major Asian languages in her pocket besides being a native English speaker, on paper, Phoebe sounded perfect to him and ticked every box on what he was looking for in an area manager. He wondered why no other brand had recruited her already. However, as he had friends at Maison H, he knew very well everyone was as low profile as the brand itself, and most were contented where they were. He also guessed that probably Phoebe was not physically appealing, hence had not gained attention from elsewhere.

So, with such an expectation, he was stunned when Phoebe walked into his office for the second-round interview after meeting his colleague at the Human Resources Department. Phoebe had a royal presence about her. Sebastian suspected it was because of her aristocratic background. Her long brown hair was tied up into an elegant French bun. She wore a smart light grey work dress that looked like it had been tailor-made for her. When she talked, her green eyes sparkled. Sebastian loved the fact that she smiled a lot and appeared genuinely interested in what he had to say to her. He was sure both the operators and front line sale staff would love her. He rang his boss in Paris right after the interview and asked to expedite the hiring process.

Sebastian wanted to sneak in more areas into the contract as he wanted to have enough budget to bring someone from Paris to take up the marketing role instead of hiring a local or someone who was already based in Hong Kong. This meant he had to reserve part of the budget to offer a housing allowance to this candidate. In fact, he did not want any other candidate but Nadine; Nadine used to intern in his office in Paris when he was still based there. They flirted a lot with each other and Sebastian couldn't wait to bring her over after learning that she was now working full-time for Vuitton Beauty after leaving business school.

The property prices had risen a lot in Hong Kong, and the international school fees of his three children did not help, either. In France, having three children meant you could get allowances from the government, but in Hong Kong, expenses increased exponentially from the third child mostly due to the shocking school fees at international schools. The only way to work around these was to merge three area manager roles into one. He thought he would work harder and together with Phoebe at the beginning, and once Vuitton Beauty had developed, he could ask for more budget to add onto another headcount.

Nadine squealed with joy when Sebastian shared with her his plan to bring her over to Hong Kong. Nadine was an ambitious girl and knew that a position in Asia that covered China would give a powerful boost to her CV. She hinted to Sebastian that they could take their flirting to another level should his plan succeed. Sebastian regretted telling her about the plan too soon. He offered to increase Phoebe's base salary, which she rejected as well. Sebastian suspected no one who had experience in travel retail would take on such a big area to launch such a high profile brand.

Without surprise, Adele came back with a flat 'No.' By this time, Adele said a few brands had started to ask around for Phoebe, so she was going to give Sebastian just three days to close the deal with Phoebe; otherwise, she would walk away and hook her up with someone else.

It must have been Sebastian's lucky night because he met a young chap that evening who could be the answer to his prayer. Twenty-eight-year-old Benoit relocated to Hong Kong fewer than three months ago. Sebastian thought he was one of the hundreds of Frenchmen who left his country and moved to Hong Kong every week, hoping to find a job which was proving to be harder as the years went by. He felt lucky to be born a couple of decades earlier when there was still hope of employment in France. Sebastian wasn't interested in them as it meant tedious dealing with HR over visas and tonnes of paperwork, for someone who lacked in experience and possibly gratitude.

Benoit, however, was different. He'd moved to Hong Kong with his wife whose company transferred her to Hong Kong. He gave up his job at an export and import company as his wife's company offered an expatriate contract to her, which included a housing allowance and school support for their future children. They agreed it was an opportunity they should not pass on as they were both still young. It sparked interests in Sebastian as it meant Benoit had a dependent visa, which allowed him to work in Hong Kong without much administrative hassles to the company. After hearing Benoit talk about what he used to do in France, Sebastian thought he could dress it up and make his experience applicable to travel retail. Most importantly, Benoit was desperate to find something to have a fresh start in Hong Kong, so he was willing to take on anything with a pay cut on top.

Before the end of the week, Benoit was offered a job to be a junior travel retail manager for South East Asia and assisting him in managing Japan and Korea, two more important areas. He agreed to reduce Phoebe's area of responsibility to Greater China alone. Phoebe accepted the initial offer in the end before any other brand could approach her. She just had to go over the contract in detail and sign it. Sebastian shared the good news with Nadine. He couldn't wait to be able to have Nadine to himself in Hong Kong, finally.

Chapter Twenty-Three

Phoebe went to visit Priscilla at her apartment; she wanted to tell her about her job offer from Vuitton Beauty before handing in her notice. She wanted to get her boss's blessing before tendering her official resignation, and to tell her she was finally leaving her nest after Priscilla recruited her in Buenos Aires more than five years ago. She trusted Priscilla would give her honest and fair career advice. She also felt sad that this would mean giving up a boss such as Priscilla who was also her mentor.

Phoebe stepped into Priscilla's apartment when she gestured her to take her shoes off, worrying they would make a noise that would wake baby Emma up.

"It took me nearly an hour to rock her to sleep," Priscilla whispered and helped Phoebe with her bag, making sure she would put it on the chair as gently as possible. Phoebe glanced around Priscilla's three-bedroom apartment. She was only there a couple of weeks ago, and it seemed that the space had been filled up with more baby gears.

"Sorry, this place is a mess. The music rocker takes up the whole living room, but I can't live without it. It's the only thing that can save my arms. It helps Emma stay asleep for more than one hour." Priscilla apologized for not having time to freshen up herself, either.

Phoebe loved the change in Priscilla after Emma's arrival. Her face was glowing. Priscilla usually kept her appearance impeccable and would never allow a piece of her hair out of place. The first time Phoebe came to visit them, she was shocked to see Priscilla wearing a blouse that was full of stains. Priscilla said she gave up after changing for the fourth time before noon, the very next day after she and Emma came home from the hospital. Her daily target these days was to be able to take a shower or brush her teeth. She also owned t-shirts for the first time in her adult life, which were large enough to cover her engorged breasts and easy to be lifted up to breastfeed on demand. Yet, nothing made her prouder than the rose cheek, chubby baby asleep in the baby rocker with lullabies playing softly from the built-in speaker.

"To what do we owe the honour of your visit during your precious lunch break… with my favourite food?" Priscilla raised her eyebrow when she saw Phoebe showed up at her doorsteps with a bag of takeaways. She could smell the noodle soup with dumplings from her favourite lunch joint, and she was always starving from breastfeeding Emma.

"Did you piss off Cecile or an operator?" Priscilla interrogated Phoebe, although in her heart she suspected Phoebe might have some big news to break - after all, it was more than two months after Cannes. Priscilla expected someone might have made a move already.

Phoebe told Priscilla everything and handed her the contract from Vuitton she'd printed out secretly in the office. To her relief and surprise, Priscilla went through all the contract selflessly and cautiously. She reminded Phoebe to request a couple of important amendments to the contract. Then she gave Phoebe her full blessings and asked her not to hesitate to put her down as her reference.

"It's time for you to leave the nest, Phoebe. I am going to miss you by my side, but at the same time, it will not be fair to keep you at Maison H without laying out a clear career path for you, while you are still young and full of talents. I think Vuitton Beauty will be a good opportunity for you, and they are damn lucky to have you!"

With Priscilla's encouragements, Phoebe went back to Adele with an initial 'Yes,' provided that the changes were made to the contract as per Priscilla's advice, and to be given enough time for Cecile to find someone to cover Priscilla and to recruit her replacement. The timing wasn't great, but it was not the worst, either. They were in mid-season, so it was all about following up with the sales and training the staff. Priscilla could work remotely on that, and Cecile could chip in to help. Priscilla said it was time to call on Charlotte, the Global Travel Retail Training Manager, to have a tour in Asia. She was going to find the budget to cover the cost to hire a translator in each country.

Sebastian agreed with all minor changes on contract requested by Phoebe within a day. He did not want to procrastinate the recruitment further. Phoebe handed in her notice before the end of the week, which led to Cecile's long phone call to Priscilla, with many 'I told you so,' and once again regretted approving Phoebe's trip to Cannes, despite Priscilla reminding her repeatedly that Phoebe had already been approached prior to her trip to Cannes.

As soon as Phoebe had officially resigned, the truth that she would finally be leaving Maison H and start a new chapter in her career sank in. She was incredibly sad to be leaving the cocoon of the caring company she had been working for since she left college; a brand that she adored so much, and her colleagues who had since long ago become more like families. Yet, she knew it was time for her to go. Staying would mean becoming stagnant in her growth, professionally.

Phoebe was glad that there was still one more seasonal buy she had to go to Paris for, which would allow her the chance to bid farewell to everyone she knew there before starting her job at Vuitton. When she came back, there would be the opening of Maison H's new flagship shop in downtown Hong Kong, which was regarded as the biggest event of the year and for the brand in decades. Then she would take two weeks' holiday before starting the new job. She was hoping to go somewhere with Alex as she knew there would be lots of chances for her to see her parents in Beijing as she would be in charge of China in her new role. Claire and Johnathan had just started stationing in Beijing the year before. It was a big deal for Johnathan considering the importance of China to the U.S. these days.

Chapter Twenty-Four

Twice a year there would be a major collection preview and order in the banlieues of Paris where Maison's H atelier was situated. Each shop manager, as well as regional sales and marketing executives like Phoebe, had to be there to choose products for their own shop. It was a very different buying process compared to other luxury houses where it was most of the time centrally controlled and decided. It was a brilliant strategy as not all shops would be carrying uniformed collections. Besides, it was a good selling point to indecisive customers that if they did not buy the product she liked there, she might not be able to find it in another shop.

The atelier was built with a good intention to be present in a suburb to give a boost to the area as well as enjoying the low cost. However, with the increase in the number of unemployed immigrants as well as the crime rate, the atelier became increasingly surrounded by security to protect the brand's property and its employees. It was ironic to see very senior management drive a battered vehicle, and locked all their Birkin and Kelly Bags in the trunk before driving out of the building's basement carpark. During the buying season, the security was multiplied by three times, and one would expect a presidential visit if they didn't know better. Asian buyers were notorious when it came to flaunting their possessions.

Madame Queenie was Maison H's joint venture owner in Thailand. She came every time with her entourage of six assistants to serve her majesty. Besides her diamond buckled Birkin, crocodile-skinned Kelly Bags, she wore jewellery that could easily cost more than a pied-a-terre in Paris. The manager of Women's Ready to Wear never challenged their order on sizes as she knew very well Madame was merely picking clothes for herself and her friends instead of the general public. She had two bodyguards who would travel around the world with her and her entourage. Maison H's security team usually arranged Madame Q to be the last one to board the luxury coach to get back to Paris.

Phoebe drank in all the larger-than-life characters for the one last time she was there at the buying venue. She knew she was going to miss every single moment of it - how the global director unveiled the annual theme on the first day of the buying week, and the 'shop until you drop' closing line, before everyone was invited to the private collection preview at each department. The product managers and their teams spent months to create an enticing space that would make the new products look magical while at the same time welcoming to the buyers. Even in between the buying corners, thoughtful gestures and decoration were set up for the comfort of the visitors and discoveries of the Maison H universe. Phoebe even said goodbye to the giant machine that squeeze juice out of oranges that rotated in a wheel non-stop to supply a glass of vitamin C to the staff and buyers - another ironic reminder of the caring company she was about to leave.

On the last day of the seasonal buy, Phoebe packed all the documents and items to be sent back to Hong Kong, then dropped the box at the courier room for the one last time. The venue was deserted. Most of her colleagues had already left for the weekend. She sat at a corner in the lobby café and went down the memory lane of the very first time when she was there until the very friendly lady from the concierge came to remind her they were closing. Phoebe picked up her bag and shook hands with the security officers she had become friendly with over the years, who told her that they were sad to learn about her departure and wished her all the very best. As Phoebe was heading back to Paris, she found herself filled with emotions that knowing she would probably never be back to Maison H atelier in the Paris suburb again.

Chapter Twenty-Five

After the long week of exhaustive buying, negotiating between metiers and operators, Phoebe had enough and was ready for an evening of doing nothing. She just wanted to hide in her hotel room and ordered room service.

"Fair Bear, come on, it's TGIF Friday. We have to go out. KK is taking us to a club opening tonight."

"Ting-Ting, I am dead tired. The only place I am going to be tonight is my hotel bed. Wait, who's this KK? Why does that name sound familiar?"

"Kannis Kwan, KK. We went out together when she was last in Hong Kong, ring any bells? She's been living in Paris for more than a year. She is on the VIP list of all the hottest clubs in Paris."

"Of course, I remember Kannis Kwan; everyone was talking about her in Pantin. And I know that she's been living in Paris for some time. Since she was your childhood friend, I guessed that she must come from money. Although, you never mentioned that her influence has stretched all the way here to Paris."

"Just between you and me, Kannis is the daughter of Charlie Kwan. As you may recall from what I have told you, our families are not exactly friends."

"You mean Charlie Kwan, the biggest real estate developer and the richest guy in Hong Kong, that Charlie Kwan?"

"Yes, but don't tell anyone. Kannis does not really want anyone here to know about that. The history of our families is more complicated than a spider web. Our families are enemies, but we are friends. We went to school together. We only hang out openly together overseas. Otherwise, we will hear no end from our families back home. Our aunties always compare us two and intentionally put us into competition. But who cares? Life is too short to be bitchy. She is cool and great fun to hang out with. Both Kannis and I just want to enjoy life, and what we do, that's why we are both out of the family businesses. Kannis may seem very career hungry, but it's just a front - she dreams of getting married and having three kids. Three kids! What is she thinking? Charlie convinced his golf mate, who was someone very senior within the family in the company, to take on Kannis as his protégé and let her be a management trainee, as soon as he heard I joined the marketing team in Hong Kong. So much for competition. Kannis is only too happy to comply, in order to be with her French boyfriend who she met in London when we were in business school there."

"Hmm, very interesting and naughty of you to keep this from me for so long, even after we last partied together in Hong Kong."

"Well, it's really the first time Kannis and I are in Paris together since she joined the Maison. Last season she was still interning in shops around Europe. So have I convinced you to come party with us tonight?"

The club that was having a grand opening that night was situated by the Canal Saint-Martin. Kannis, who came with her boyfriend Jereme, first picked up Ting-Ting and Phoebe from their hotel in the eighth arrondissement, then a couple of Jereme's friends along the way. When the limousine that Kannis hired stopped near the club, Phoebe could see a line that stretched along the canal.

"Ting-Ting, I don't think I have the energy tonight to queue in this pair of heels for hours before getting in," Phoebe whispered to Ting-Ting, hoping Kannis their host could not hear her.

"Kannis' father is one of the investors of the club, we won't have to queue."

"Then why are we stopping here, at the end of the queue?"

Before Phoebe finished the sentence, one of Jereme's friends exclaimed, "Ooo lala. Chaud, chaud, chaud."

The group turned their heads towards the direction where clapping and whistles came from. A line of beautiful women, naked except only a pair of Christine Louboutin and underwear, each holding a tray with a champagne bottle and sparklers on top, skilfully covering their breasts, marched along the canal between the waterway and the queue leading to the newest night club in Paris, *Gondola*. One by one, the models that the club hired to build up excitement among the crowds entered the club. Before the last model went in, she turned around towards the canal. A luxurious boat approached, and when it came into view, the crowd in the queue went crazy. Steve Aoki, one of the hottest DJs in the world, appeared spinning a record with his iconic music, surrounded by dozens of stunning dancers who were on board. The last model served Steve a glass of champagne, then Steve waved at the crowd while running into Gondola with his entourage.

"Oh my god, what an opening! It is going to be all over social media within the next thirty minutes. Congratulations Kannis, your father, did great!"

"Daddy's PR team did great, I bet he didn't lift a finger to make all this happen. Come on, let's get in before the crowd gets impatient and start pushing."

Despite waking up the next morning with a splitting headache and her feet aching from all night dancing in her nine-inch heels, Phoebe did not regret going clubbing with Ting-Ting and Kannis. It was such a fun night, and Club Gondola was all chic and luxurious. And Ting-Ting was right again - Kannis was a nice, down-to-earth girl, wherever they were hanging out together. It was such a shame that their families were not fond of each other that they had to be friends in secret.

Chapter Twenty-Six

While Phoebe was done with her seasonal collection buy, there would be two more small collection previews in between seasons for Ting-Ting that she would have to fly back to Paris for, besides the major Spring-Summer and Autumn-Winter collections. Only the ready-to-wear and haute couture would be presented at these small collection previews. These were also the occasions that Maison H would invite its VIP customers of each shop to Paris, and were offered the opportunity to be the very first ones to order the pieces. Maison H would fly every single guest in business class and pay for all the hotel accommodations, hoping the house would recover the expenses from the order – and that would not be a problem, as the VIP guest usually competed unofficially to be the top spender at each collection. These VIPs would also be invited to the Maison's 'defile' as the visit was organised during the fashion week. Before the guests left Paris, they would be entertained with a spectacular dinner, usually at a prominent venue, and the room would be decorated with the brand's chandeliers, transported to the venue just for the occasion, while the tables were dressed with the Maison's luxurious table and crystal wares.

While it all sounded glamorous and extravagant to its extreme and not an entirely tough job for anyone, it had been proved, season after season, that Ting-Ting was the only one who could sail through the event with ease. It was because she knew the chemistry among these old monies from Hong Kong; who was friendly with whom at the moment, who was not talking to whom, who was rumoured to be having affairs with whose husband, and so forth. The house needed someone like Ting-Ting who was in the know to keep the right guests close, or far apart, so the whole event would go smoothly without an incident or worse, a scandal. The focus would be on shopping rather than fighting, which the house learned the lesson well before Ting-Ting joined the team, when the orders were a record low because the brand screwed up the seating arrangement and wrongly put several rivals in close proximity to each other. Another equally, if not more important task for Ting-Ting, was to communicate between her colleagues in Paris and guests from Hong Kong to make sure no one would be ordering the same piece of clothing and to have a major fashion clash when the guests appeared on the high society magazines back in their home city.

In recent years, there had been an increasing number of the nouveau riches, especially those who relocated to Hong Kong from Mainland China. There were more and more of them becoming the top thirty spenders of the brand as the years went by. Whenever there were new guests who flew to Paris for the collection previews, Ting-Ting would arrange special visits to the 5/F of the brand's flagship shop on Rue Faubourg Saint Honore. It was a museum as well as an archive that showcased every important item that meant something to the brand or marked some historic milestone in the brand's journey to stardom. The idea was to tell the new guests the brand's story all the way from its beginning, to let them totally immerse in the house's rich universe, while at the same time appreciate the brand's value as the brand appreciated them as clients.

On the other hand, the buying seasons for the shops that Phoebe usually went to were a lot less dramatic and extravagant. Yet, the house still invested in creating the environment for the buyers to experience beyond imagination the fantasy of the yearly theme. Exclusive caterers were brought to the atelier every season to serve amazing food and drinks to buyers during the break. Music was carefully selected to create the right ambience. The idea was to keep everyone fed and in a delightful shopping mood during a long week of exhausting buying.

Maison H was probably the only luxury house that had such an extensive product mix. From its desperately sought after leather goods and silk products, to lesser-known products but still enormously popular among shoppers, namely, jewellery, watches, ready-to-wear, accessories, tableware, perfume, to the bigger pieces of furniture that the house pushed to develop in the last decade. Despite having the widest range of products, every single one was beautifully designed and made with both aesthetic and functionality, carefully thoughtful and brilliantly executed. The brand's motto was, 'Don't make an ugly product as there would always be someone who buys it.' Very true, indeed. Maison H had a department called Industrial, which was in charge of sourcing all the materials for making the brand's products. Over the years, the brand had acquired top leather suppliers and workshops, which allowed the house to pick all the top pieces of leather before selling the less than perfect ones to other brands. How very smart was that? Like McDonald, the brand believed in properties. Most of the real estate where the brand's shops were open all around the world were actually owned by the brand. As a result, the brand had a very sounded financial base and a healthy cash flow.

Therefore, it was not hard to imagine how taxing it would be to prepare the buying for such a wide offer of products just for a single shop. Each shop must have a thorough inventory and sales analysis to study the stock levels and performance of each product. Then a better-be-accurate business plan for the season would be drawn to decide the open-to-buy for product category.

Phoebe and her colleagues in the travel retail team also needed to rub a non-existing crystal ball, hopefully, to predict what would tick in the coming seasons to impress the customers enough to take the products home. The usual challenge between shop and product teams in Paris would be the balance of the orders. The shop, expectedly, would like to carry only popular products in order to meet the sales targets. The product team, on the other hand, would like the shop to carry a wide range of products, that would represent the core of the seasonal collection, as well as meeting the material distribution they wished to achieve. It was easier to pressure the directly-owned store manager to comply. However, for Phoebe, it was an enormous challenge, season after season, to convince their operators to order in accordance to their guidelines – especially since the style Asian customers preferred was usually vastly different from their European counterparts, which her Paris colleagues believed would rather sell. After all, the operators would have to own the stock if they did not sell it on. And as the stock arrived, it was Phoebe's responsibility to help the shop to sell them, too, as the operator would often say, 'you asked us to order this, now help us to sell it.'

Models were hired not only for the ready-to-wear department but also for the silk products, too. Maison H was famous for its scarves. Indeed, each season it produced so many scarf products in a range of sizes, shapes, and colours, that it was essential to help the shop managers to decide what and how many to order. One easy way to do it was to have a model to demonstrate. A pattern that when laid flat open could look entirely different when being worn. Maison H always hired the same model, Valerie, as the model, must know the brand products well and practice in advance how to showcase the best of every single scarf.

Valerie was an expert in tying the brand's scarf, and there were at least fifty ways to tie a scarf. Because of her skill of making every single Maison H scarf wearable and desirable, Valerie was often booked by Maison H stores around the world to have in-store animation to promote the seasonal scarves. It was a guaranteed sell-out the scarf cabinet, both new stock and old, during the several days of the campaign. So, whenever shops that fell under Phoebe's responsibility needed a boost in their scarf sale, she brought Valerie to the shops. Over time, they developed a solid friendship that they were still in touch many years after Valerie had left Maison H.

For decades Maison H had had its flagship store in the same space that the brand owned in Central. It was prime real estate, but the store was no longer big enough - ever since the house decided to expand its Home Department. To showcase the brand's craftsmanship on the beddings, a bedroom had to be set up to create the luxurious ambiance that the brand deserved. A 'study' also had to exist to showcase the beautifully handcrafted writing desk. On the other hand, other prestige brands had built spectacular flagships stores in the same area over the years. Maison H's discreet shop windows and entrance became too understated, and an overall update was long overdue. With the climbing commercial rent in the city, a second tier brand was exiting the area. It was a perfect spot and space for the brand, and without much hesitation, the management in Paris gave the green light to take over the lease.

Kannis, having worked as the personal assistant of the in-house architect who oversaw all shop renovations for the brand and due to Kannis' family influence in Hong Kong especially in the real estate sector, was appointed the Project Manager for the relocation of the flagship store in one of the most important cities for the brand. Everything had gone smoothly so far, and the grand opening was less than a month away. Just when Kannis was ready to hand over the project to the Hong Kong team, the CEO of the company asked Kannis to stay in charge until after the opening party. She would work from the Hong Kong office in the last two weeks leading to the opening and reported directly to him.

Being the Marketing and PR Manager and personally knowing all VIPs on the guest list, Ting-Ting naturally became the person-in-charge on the Hong Kong side. That meant Ting-Ting and Kannis would be working very closely together in the coming days, on a very high profile event of the most prestigious brand in the world. It would have been fun for both Kannis and Ting-Ting, as the two were close friends and knew the operation and everyone by heart, if the two families were not enemies. They had been taught from a young age not to get involved with anyone nor have anything to do with each other, and now it looked like they would have to keep the collaboration a secret, as it would be the secret to the success of the event.

Chapter Twenty-Seven

Kannis' father Charlie Kwan, at six feet four inches, was unusually tall for a Chinese man. Kannis inherited his height and could work as a model if she wanted to. He was also handsome in a dandy way. At sixty-two, Charlie felt and looked better than ever, and his girlfriends were getting younger in each relationship. When he smiled, a deep dimple appeared on the left of his face; people said it was this dimple that kept him looking young and charmed so many ladies. He was particularly fond of mingling with actresses, and was said to have fathered several children with different movie stars. But among these children, only two he admitted in public as his own. Kannis as the older daughter, and a younger son, Liam Kwan, with another woman. However, no one knew who their mothers were - it was like the two kids appeared from nowhere. Yet, Charlie loved both Kannis and Liam to bits. He nurtured them well and gave them the best opportunity to see the world and succeed. Kannis looked like the female version of Charlie and inherited his height. No wonder no one could guess who the mother was. Being brought up in an untraditional household, Charlie did not see his son as his only heir. He groomed and nurtured Kannis the same way he did Liam. He believed responsibilities and rewards to be allocated according to capabilities and credits, instead of one's gender or identity. He often said to journalists who interviewed them, if both Kannis and Liam turned out to be useless freeloaders, he would not hesitate to pass on his real estate empire to a capable employee instead. Luckily for Charlie, both Kannis and Liam graduated from top business schools, and their internships at the company since they were sixteen showed great promises. Even Charlie's most competitive employees came to respect and love the duo and were willing to teach them all they knew for them to take over their father's empire one day.

Ting-Ting's father Simon Lee was a soft-spoken gentleman. He was an ordinary looking man in his mid-sixties. His family was from the working class. His grandfather worked his way up from being a clerk at a textile company to the CEO then took over the business from his boss, who had no children and saw him as his protégé and successor. Ting-Ting inherited her good looks, and petite but sexy figure entirely from her mother, Edith. Edith was in the film industry in the late sixties, and at one point the biggest female movie star. She was in many classics that the older generation still enjoyed watching today. At the peak of her career, Edith suddenly quit the entertainment industry and went overseas to study for two years. When she came back, she announced she was done with acting and married Simon. After marrying him, they had Ting-Ting, and Edith helped Simon manage the PR of his company. Thanks to her fame, she helped his company to achieve great success and established the Lee family as one of the richest and successful textile companies in Hong Kong. Simon's siblings, hence, Ting-Ting's aunts and uncles, benefited from Simon's success and engaged in related businesses such as import, export, and retail.

Charlie was a smart and successful businessman. It was rumoured that his mother was a mistress - a 'kept woman' of an English tycoon during Hong Kong's early colonial days – and that Charlie was their bastard child. Charlie looked Eurasian, and he went to a prestigious private school then to Hong Kong University. In those days, it was impossible for a single mother to afford that. So, one believed the rumours were true, and that although it could not be admitted publicly, Charlie had received support from his secret wealthy and powerful father. After his mother passed, he inherited a small fortune and with that money he bought acres of land. He soon made his first million, which he invested in more lands and properties; millions then turned to billions.

While the Kwan family was small and their real estate business brought them enormous wealth and gave Charlie equal power to have influence over the government, their reach was also global; the Lee family was big, and their network was wide and more focus on local. Coincidentally, the roles of Kannis and Ting-Ting at Maison H reflected this dynamic. Both Kannis and

Ting-Ting were well-known among the high society circle in Hong Kong as they were both heiress of two powerful empires in the city. Before long, the news of the collaboration between Kannis and Ting-Ting could be read on the city Tatler's page. The anticipation of the reopening of the brand Maison H was pushed to sky high. It was the event to go to for everyone who knew anyone in the city.

Chapter Twenty-Eight

Ting-Ting and Kannis thought of a way to maintain the peace for as long as possible for the biggest event they were ever put charge of. They decided to hire a pair of models, one male, and one female, to hand deliver the invitation to every single VIP around town over the span of a week. The invitation card was expectedly luxurious to the extreme, and the brand spared no expense for the event of the year in one of the most important cities for luxury brands in the world. The 'envelope' was, in fact, a leather clutch with the guest's initials embossed on the cover. The 'invitation card' itself was another piece of the brand's sought-after leather in another colour with the event details printed on top in gold paint. A mini scarf was enclosed with the pattern of an illustration of the new flagship store façade. The guests were invited to bring the mini scarves with them in lieu of the invitation, and in the fashion of their imaginations.

Ting-Ting and Kannis worked with the Communication Team in Paris zealously in the coming month to prepare for the big day. The theme of the event went without saying - it would be the same as the brand's annual theme, 'Dream Big and Wild.' Both Kannis and Ting-Ting pulled their strings and played all the cards they held among their vast networks in Hong Kong. Once they confirmed their ideas were feasible and got approval from Paris, they had their designers and contractors work day and night to meet their deadline. With her current position as the Global Merchandising Manager, Kannis also worked closely with the merchandising and logistics teams to arrange a shipment of exclusive and exquisite products to showcase during the opening day - for the purpose of wowing the guests and be cleared off the shelves before the end of the event. The revenue on the opening day would set the tone and pace for the rest of the opening month. A big earning on this day would also give a strong boost of confidence for the sales team for many months to come. Therefore, Kannis pinned the pictures of these products up with a photo of the potential customer next to it, as if she was solving a serial murder. She consulted with Ting-Ting from time to time, who laughed at her board every time they Skyped. Kannis made changes according to Ting-Ting's instructions as no one knew what the VIPs liked better than her.

Phoebe wanted to get involved in the final and biggest event during her last days with Maison H, so she proposed to Cecile that she would like to invite the heads of several operators in nearby cities to the grand opening. Cecile welcomed the idea and initiative, thought it would be a good gesture to counter Phoebe's departure and Priscilla's absence. Thanks to her friendship with Ting-Ting, she managed to get a dozen travel retail guests on the VIP list. Phoebe knew Cecile would be pleased, and she was glad to be able to do something nice for the team before her farewell.

It turned out that Cecile was very pleased, because it usually never occurred that the domestic market would invite any travel retail clients to their events unless she strongly requested or asked as a kind of favour. Ting-Ting made Phoebe promise her parents would come and support. So, Phoebe invite Claire and Johnathan, who'd already planned to go as a private mission to their daughter's work event. The senior officials within the Hong Kong administration caught wind of that, and also accepted the invitation from Ting-Ting to appear at the grand opening. The rumour was that everyone who mattered in Hong Kong, and the General Consulate of the American Embassies in Beijing, would be at the reopening of the flagship shop. This was when the management in Paris finally realised who Phoebe was, and questioned Cecile why on earth she was letting her go, and to Vuitton, of all competitors. Cecile woke Priscilla again when she was napping with Emma and shouted at her to no end, only this time Priscilla turned her into mute such that Cecile was not going to wake her precious baby girl up.

Chapter Twenty-Nine

D-Day finally arrived. All the paparazzi in town gathered outside the Maison H new flagship store in Central overnight to get the best spots to snap as many photos as possible of everyone who was anyone in the city. The new flagship store occupied four floors of the corner space in one of the most expensive buildings in the city where two major avenues met. Perfume, Men's Ready-to-Wear, and Women's Fashion Jewellery occupied the ground floor, so the shop always smells luxurious and heavenly for the first moment's someone pushed the door into the shop. Men could not be bothered to go up, so their section was strategically located for the easiest access, while the usually colourful fashion jewelleries, with new arrivals every month, would be attractive enough for female customers to come to check out regularly.

The opening was scheduled at 3pm. With Charlie pulling strings, Kannis managed to convince the authority to block the avenue where the shop was located for the parade they'd prepared. Kannis and Ting-Ting came up with the idea to hire the retired racehorses which the city was famous for from the horse riding school to do a parade, to showcase the brand lineage with its handcrafted saddles and riding accessories. For the riding school, it would help them to promote the sport to the public. On the other hand, numerous celebrities, high ranking officials, and movie stars had been invited. The authority finally gave the green light to block the busy avenue for several non-busy hours in the afternoon for the grand entrance and opening of the Maison H flagship store.

The government welcomed the festive and prosperous atmosphere the shop opening created. It was a much-needed contrast to the last occasion where the avenues were blocked a few years ago during the Occupy Central social movement. Thousands of people, most of them young working class or students, took over main avenues, flyovers, and roads stretching across the major financial and commercial centres in the city to protest against the government. The occupation was eventually named the 'Umbrella Revolution,' for no violence or weapons had been involved except umbrellas. It lasted for several months. Businesses were seriously affected, the operation of the city badly disrupted, and morale in the society was at its lowest.

So, the Chief Executive Officer of the Administration welcomed the festive display of the grand opening and liked the idea of getting the public involved. To dissolve the worries of the government that the brand would further highlight the gap between the rich and the poor, Ting-Ting came up with the idea of working with the charity Dreams Come True, which helped child cancer patients to realise their dreams in their last days. Some of their dreams were to ride in a carriage as Cinderella or watching magic shows. Over thirty children and their families had been invited to the opening, and the children were the first to enter the parade. Professional child entertainers had been hired to help the children dress and create their fantasy for them.

Guests were advised to have their vehicles stop at the beginning of the Queen's Road Central, as a carriage would bring them to the store. That was where the magic began! Ting-Ting, through the connections she had with the production team of the most popular shows in Macau, a city adjacent to Hong Kong and the Las Vegas in the Far East, hired several horse carriages. The carriages were decorated with the brand items from the Home Department for the comfort of the guests.

The weather was thankfully perfect on the day, and the open carriages allowed the paparazzi to take photos and the guests to show off their Maison H looks and sought after handbags! The scarf that was gifted to the guests, along with the invitation, proved to be a brilliant idea. The guests were very creative in wearing their 'tickets' to the event. While most gentlemen used them as pocket squares, the ladies tried different playful ways to stand out. There were ladies who wore them as bracelets, belts, headscarves, or on their handbags in different manners. A few daredevils wore them as a top with different degree of exposure, bareback, as a bandeau, etc.

After the parade in the carriages led by the most handsome horses and jockeys dressed in the brand equestrian outfits, the guests were invited to sit in the row of chairs that had been set up on both sides of the avenue. As the last carriage left the avenue, Gotan Project was played, and from afar male and female models dressed in the coming season Maison H Ready-to-Wear, and accessorised with the house's jewellery and bags, walked down the avenue as if it was a long runway. The crowd went wild, and clapped and whistled, as the models got from one end to the other one by one.

Ting-Ting hired a few magicians to go around the shop and delighted the guests with the classic magic tricks, only using objects of the brand. The guests nearly fainted when the magicians turned the USD500 per piece Maison H scarves into a flower or a pigeon! Models continued to showcase and try on clothes and accessories for female and male guests in the respective Ready-to-Wear areas.

The Home Department on the third floor was temporarily turned into a dining room where the brand chandeliers were hung. Maison H tableware, crystal champagne flutes, and napkins dressed the tables where the guests would be seated to have a dinner catered by a Michelin starred restaurant in the city. The merchandising team selected a collection that had gold and silver plated onto the rims of the tableware. Along with the crystal chandeliers and glasses, the whole dining room was mesmerised with sparkles and elegance.

The dinner was an intimate fair, with only one hundred guests invited. The guest list was generated purely based on spending. Speeches to thanks the guests for their loyal support throughout the years were delivered. The pinnacle of the dinner was an auction of several antique items, generously donated by the brand, to the highest bidders, while the income would be donated to the guest charity of the opening. As Ting-Ting and Kannis expected, several of their aunts and uncles went into battles to bid over the unique leather goods. The auction successfully raised over one million dollars for the charity. Everyone was pleased with the outcome. After desserts were served and more champagne poured, guests were invited to browse freely in the shop as the shop staff would bring out all the exclusive items for the guests to view and order.

Before the end of the evening, the reports and photos of the event spread across the front pages of all local newspaper and magazines and was covered by major network and social media worldwide. At closing, the team of the store was proud to announce that nearly 70% of stock on display were claimed, and the opening achieved a record high one-day revenue in the brand's history.

The CEO of the brand came to congratulate Kannis and Ting-Ting for the unprecedented success of the grand opening. To put on such a great show in the busiest part of the city in such an elegant way, it was indeed a big and wild dream, come true!

Chapter Thirty

After the last of the guests had left the shop, Kannis and Ting-Ting helped the team to wrap up. With more than thirty staff, it was done quickly and efficiently. Everybody could not wait to get to the after party to celebrate the success of the opening; the opening that had been planned and prepared for, for more than eight months. Ting-Ting and Kannis had booked a table at the hottest club in town. Charlie Kwan was one of the silent partners of the club and offered to pick up the tab, so no expenses had to be signed for by the brand management.

Kannis opened three bottles of Dom Perignon she brought from her father's house and served a glass to everyone who was either changing into party clothes, refreshing makeup, or styling their hair. The shop designer had generously assigned a spacious room for the staff and designed in a way that they could relax during breaks or sit comfortably while attending training.

To be discreet, Ting-Ting and Kannis split and jumped into different cars to leave the shop and to reunite at the restaurant to avoid media attention. They first went to Sevva, which was located on the top floor of the building across the road of the new flagship store. Sevva was a high-end restaurant bar and decorated luxuriously from the entrance to the washroom. It opened out to a vast terrace which one usually called it as the hanging garden in Hong Kong. The three-sided terrace offered the view of the famous Victoria Harbour as well as the neighbouring prestigious and historical buildings of the city. On a clear night like the night of the grand opening, the view was breath-taking, and the height of the building gave one a feeling of suspension in the air. As Charlie owned the building per se, Kannis had the biggest table reserved for her at any time she was in town and would like to bring friends over for drinks.

Kannis, Ting-Ting, and the team of the flagship store had a wonderful time at Sevva. They swapped stories of the day and evening; such as the competition between two of Ting-Ting's aunties to become the highest spender of the day, which helped to push the opening day revenue to a record high for the brand. The party enjoyed the bliss after the success of the event they all worked very hard to prepare for over the last few months.

Ting-Ting then suggested to go dancing at the current hottest club in town, Boujis. The party then divided into two in which the younger, single ones went dancing with Ting-Ting and Kannis, while those who had kids waiting at home kissed each other goodbye and wished them a fabulous time clubbing. A long queue was seen waiting outside Boujis, waiting for access into the club. Kannis and Ting-Ting marched into the club with their entourage in their usual elegant and charming manners, cheeking kissing the bouncers at the door while slipping a big tip into their palms. The VIP semi-open room was waiting for them, with several bottles of Dom Perignon sitting in ice buckets, and champagne flutes lining up on the tables ready to get the party started.

Kannis and Ting-Ting each had their own friends joining the party gradually while their colleagues left one by one to head home. Phoebe also finally joined the party with Alex, who was visiting her for the weekend, after having a very nice dinner with her parents at the renowned Mandarin Grill & Bar.

Ting-Ting was exhilarated. She knew she did a fantastic job with the grand opening of the new flagship store. It was going to be talked about by the media for days and a major achievement on her CV. Looking at her best friends Phoebe and Kannis dancing with her at the club, in her tipsy head she was thinking, '*Life is Beautiful.*'

Chapter Thirty-One

Wendy took the key of a Yamasaki motorbike off her colleague, and started her evening shift. She worked for a tabloid magazine. On days when there were big events in the city, the reporting team took shifts to follow the targets 24/7. Her colleague briefed her about the day's events of the grand opening, and reminded her to look for something juicier. Wendy doubted there would be any, as most of Maison H VIP were not the likes who would go club hopping in LKF, the notorious area for a fun night out in Hong Kong. Yet, she needed something to stay employed; with the print media shrinking by the day, she had to find something writable, something even unrelated to the day's event, in order to survive. Wendy had several bouncers of the hottest clubs on her payroll, to inform her at once whenever there were fights, troubles, or dishonest relationships of anyone who was anyone that she could report. She just received a message from the bouncer of one of the clubs telling her he saw Kannis and Ting-Ting, arm in arm with each other, stepping out of Club Boujis. Everyone knew the two families' rivalries, so it caught Wendy's interests. Checking her watch, it was 3:30am. She spun the Yamasaki around, and within a few minutes, she was on the tail of the limousine that picked the duo up.

The vehicle that picked up Kannis and Ting-Ting drove in the direction to the Peak, which could either be Kannis' or Ting-Ting's family house as they were both located in the most exclusive residential area in the city. Wendy kept a reasonable distance between her bike and their car so as not to arouse suspicions. She was not sure what the storyline could be, but since she had nothing so far, she had nothing to lose by following, either. All of a sudden, she felt a wind at her back created by speeding cars. She spotted a white Porsche pursuing a yellow Lamborghini, which was followed by a red Ferrari. Wendy could tell all the sports cars were going at a minimum of 120km/h.

"Those idiot-rich second generations," Wendy cursed under her breathe. She hated those youngsters who were born with a trust fund and apparently, an open garage to expensive sports cars that they would speed around town in, to impress girls or race against each other.

Then she heard a squealing noise followed by a loud bang. Wendy rode to the source of the noise and saw the car that was carrying both Kannis and Ting-Ting had crashed into a tree. There was a long skid mark left on the road; a wild guess by Wendy was probably the car made a quick turn to avoid something coming very quickly from the opposite direction. Wendy took a quick snap of the scene in front of her before she dialled 999 for help. While waiting for the ambulance to arrive, she went to look for the injured passengers to see if she could give first aid. However, the airbags were all released, and she didn't want to risk moving the injured who had all passed out but seemed to be alive and breathing. Wendy heard the sirens in the distance, and she quickly took her smartphone out and snapped as many shots as possible of both Kannis and Ting-Ting, unconscious and lying in the seats waiting for being rescued.

After giving her statement to the police on the spot, Wendy rode to the Queen Mary Hospital, which was the nearest to the scene. She wanted to find out how seriously injured the passengers were, and to be the first one to report that. On the other hand, she was glad that she'd held her speed and not pursued the car at a close distance. She did not want to get involved with the police for her job. In any case, she was pleased with what she got tonight, although she felt terribly sorry for the injured.

Chapter Thirty-Two

"Phoebe, where is Ting-Ting? Is she OK?" Simon and Edith ran towards Phoebe and asked after Ting-Ting as soon as Edith received a call from the hospital informing them she'd been injured in a car accident.

"Hi Edith, Simon, sorry, I can't really tell you much, I've just arrived here myself, and the nurses said the doctors are operating on her."

Phoebe only found out about the accident less than an hour before. She was trying to call Ting-Ting to help her pick up the Maison H scarf she'd carelessly left at Boujis, after rushing to go home with Alex earlier. Only it was the hospital staff who answered the call and asked her how they could contact Ting-Ting's family.

After looking frantically for a doctor to ask about Ting-Ting's condition, they learned that Ting-Ting was in a stable condition. The surgery went well, but the doctor told her Ting-Ting's kidney had taken a rather bad hit and would need a transplant as soon as possible. Both Edith and Simon volunteered to give one of their kidneys right away, but after running a few tests, they were told that neither of them were a compatible donor.

"We are very sorry about that Mr and Mrs Lee. Our current waiting list is over eighteen months long. Since Ting-Ting is your only child, your best chance is to ask your extended family members who are also willing to take the test."

Down the other end of the room, Phoebe spotted Kannis walking towards the nurse's station to ask about Ting-Ting's condition; she herself had just been bandaged up for minor injuries.

"What happened Kannis? Didn't you leave with Ting-Ting in your family car? Are you alright?"

With tears in her eyes, Kannis told Phoebe that their car steered away from a speeding car which was trying to overtake them on a rather narrow road over the hill. Being Kannis' driver, he instantly steered towards the direction such that the impact on Kannis would be kept minimal. That meant Ting-Ting's side took a relatively worse hit.

Kannis was full of guilt and wished she was the one who was in the operation theatre.

"You are the one who got Ting-Ting into this situation; none of you Kwan's are good for us!" Simon nearly charged at Kannis if not for Edith stopping him.

"Ting-Ting is not my only child, doctor…" Speaking apparently with much difficulty, Edith turned to Kannis and was about to tell the world the most shocking news.

"Kannis, I am your mother, Ting-Ting is your baby sister, please help her…" Edith then broke into an inconsolable sob.

While sitting in a corner in the waiting area, Wendy could not believe her luck. What she had just heard was the breaking news of the decade. She knew she had hit the jackpot that night. She quickly snapped another shot of the bereaved Edith and the shocked face of Simon, then along with the crash scene plus a recap of the night's event, she emailed it all to her editor-in-chief. She was no longer worried about getting laid off. Instead, she could taste a promotion in the air.

Without thinking much of the consequences to her own well-being, Kannis asked to speak with the doctor in private. She volunteered to be Ting-Ting's kidney donor and urged the operation to be done as soon as possible – not only for Ting-Ting's sake, but also before her father caught wind of that, and who could come and stop her.

Thanks to Wendy, the news quickly travelled to Charlie's ears. But what Wendy did not know was that Charlie had a small stake in nearly all print media in Hong Kong, and he wanted to be on top of the news before they reached the public - and on a day like this, he felt all his years of investment had been paid back.

Charlie rushed to the hospital to check that Kannis was alright and to be with her after the news broke. What he did not expect, was by the time he reached the hospital, the operation of Kannis donating a kidney to Ting-Ting had already begun.

"She what?! Kannis is giving your daughter a kidney?!"

"Charlie, Kannis is my daughter, too… we have no choice. If Ting-Ting could not have the transplant as soon as possible, she is not going to make it."

"A daughter who you did not raise. If anything happens to Kannis I will never forgive you."

"Shut up, Charlie! You and Mimi ripped the right to raise my child off me. They are both my flesh and blood. You have no idea the pain and guilt I've been carrying all these years. Kannis is old enough to make her own decisions, and she decided to save her only sister. Now please, put our daughter's well-being before all our personal sentiments."

Charlie knew he was in the wrong and was too much a coward when it came to his mother. Edith was right; he only had himself to blame for not having stood up to Mimi. He put his emotions aside, and went to find Wendy, the reporter who was going to expose the story that Kannis and Ting-Ting were both Edith's daughters. This was going to dig up lots of ugly stories and would be talked about for years to come.

The waiting area had been blocked off by Charlie's bodyguards as soon as he'd arrived, so he was sure that except for Wendy and the medical staff, no one had heard the arguments. Charlie offered Wendy a cheque under the condition that she was never going to write anything about the evening incident. Charlie was going to talk to the doctor and the nurses and plead for their discretion. He knew it was just about buying time before the story leaked, but he hoped he could buy enough time for both Kannis and Ting-Ting to recover from the surgeries.

Chapter Thirty-Three

Edith and Charlie met each other at the premier of a movie that starred Edith more than thirty-five years ago. Charlie had made a small fortune by then and was attracting actresses like nectar to bees. Edith was rather unmoved by his wealth, which made her even more appealing to Charlie. Her refined features and creamy skin were rare for a Chinese girl from the south. Even before becoming a movie star, she was pursued by men who came across her life. She was studying to become a secretary when she was discovered by an agent who took a long time persuading her to join the movie industry. Actresses did not have a good reputation back in those days. Except those who were super movie stars, most of the actresses were regarded lowly, just above prostitutes, as they usually had to expose more skin and acted in the kissing and sexual scenes which were not decent to be seen in public in their generation. Unfortunately, Edith's father was ill at that time and needed the money to pay for the medical treatment that was not available in the public health system. Edith was a rare beauty and a natural when it came to acting, so she was selected to play major roles in one movie after another. Within a few years, she'd become the most desirable actress in the film industry.

Charlie was infamous for being a playboy. He loved chasing after actresses and breaking their hearts. The only exception was Edith, and he fell head to toe in love with her. Despite being rejected by his pursuits time and time again; Charlie did not give up but only became more determined. He even severed all his relationships with all his girlfriends, to prove his intention to Edith. Charlie also discreetly helped Edith's father by hiring a specialist from the US to fly to Hong Kong to treat him until he was on his way to recovery. Edith did not find out until one day when she went and visited father at the hospital between her hectic shooting schedules, and saw the doctor fussing over her father in his ward. Edith finally granted Charlie a date and was pleasantly surprised to discover the real Charlie. The playboy was more of a cover to drive away all the gold diggers while deterring his mother's push to have him marrying the lady she deemed matching to his status. Charlie's mother, Mimi, although being a mistress herself all her life, regarded herself highly as she came from an aristocratic Chinese family. Her 'taipan' was the most powerful expat in Hong Kong, who was only married to his wife on paper; she lived in the United Kingdom until the day she died without stepping a foot in the city to visit her husband all the years he lived here. Everyone regarded Mimi as the real 'taitai.' Yet, her taipan was a lot older than her and passed away when she was only forty years old, and Charlie, sixteen.

'Kept women' in those days were often rewarded with properties by their 'masters.' Hence by the time of Charlie's father's death, Mimi had already wealth in real estate. Revelling also certain fortunes left to her from her taipan, Mimi became more arrogant than ever. With Charlie building their wealth further, Mimi led an extravagant lifestyle and would only hang out with the high society. She had been trying to arrange dates or even marriages for Charlie with the daughters of friends from her tight social circle. Charlie, being a rebel at heart, never laid an eye on any of the ladies his beloved mother raved about.

So, Mimi thought it was another fling between Charlie and Edith, until the day Charlie told her that he would like to marry her! There was no way Mimi would give Charlie her blessing. Mimi tried many classic tricks one saw in movies on Edith as she did not want to upset Charlie. She believed Edith was just like all the other actresses; whoring herself out and trying to score a taipan for herself. She even tried to buy her out with quite a fortune which to her surprise, Edith was not interested at all.

After dating and being completely in love with each other for nearly eight months, one day, Edith found herself pregnant. With much shame, she shared the news with Charlie and asked if he wanted her to abort the child. Delighted and angry at the same time, Charlie got down on one knee and asked Edith to marry him. Edith did not expect such a reaction from Charlie, and she nodded her head while tears ran down her cheeks. The playboy was tamed, finally.

Charlie brought Edith home to officially introduce her to Mimi and was sure the news of the baby would please his mother to no end. Charlie could not anticipate Mimi's reaction in a thousand years. Instead of being overwhelmed with joy for being a grandmother soon, she was outraged. The mother and son had a big row, which ended with Mimi faking a faint or a heart attack that Edith could hardly remember. She could only remember Mimi shouting, 'gold digger' and 'whore' more than a dozen times at her, and at one point, that 'bastard child' she carried in her womb was not Charlie's.

In the end, Mimi's illness to the news and her threat to severe the mother and son tie with Charlie prevailed. Charlie gave in with the only condition to keep the child himself and set Edith free. Charlie arranged Edith to wait for the birth of her first child in the US before she showed, so she told the world that she was burnt out and wanted to pursue her studies in the United States. She picked Communications, and with the credits she did before entering the entertainment industry, she managed to finish her degree in two years even with taking a semester off towards the end of her pregnancy.

She could hardly bear the separation from her child, but back in those days, single mothers were looked down upon badly. She would not be able to support both herself and the baby if she could not work. To upkeep her image and get roles in movies, she had to keep her front as the innocent girl who every man fantasized about. Charlie promised to love their baby girl with his life, and no one would ever know this secret except themselves and his mother. They named their baby girl Kannis, after the name of the character Edith played in the movie during the premier in which they met.

Unfortunately for the two lovers, by the little time after when Mimi passed away, Edith was already married to Simon Lee and had given birth to a little girl who was three years younger than Kannis - this little girl was Ting-Ting.

Chapter Thirty-Four

The light above the operating theatre indicated the transplant surgery was still going. It had been ten long hours. Everyone had started to show fatigue. Except for Edith, the mother of both patients lying on the operation tables, who never stopped pacing back and forth, praying the operation would go smoothly, that both her girls would get through the surgery, and would recover to their healthy selves again. Edith prayed to God and the Almighty of the Universe that not only she would forgive Charlie and Mimi, she would also try her best to make everyone friendly to each other so that Kannis and Ting-Ting could be sisters without any interference for the rest of their lives.

To everyone's relief, the surgery went smoothly, and everyone in the waiting room heard the good news from the leading surgeon with tears in their eyes. They agreed that everyone should go home, rest and freshen up before Ting-Ting and Kannis woke up from the anaesthesia.

Ting-Ting woke up with a cracking headache and her body hurt like she had been hit by a bus. The first thought that came to her was she had the worst hangover she'd ever had after the big party celebrating the success of the new Maison H flagship boutique. Then she remembered the car crashing into a banyan tree before everything went black. Her whole body was in pain, and she did an overall inventory that she still had all her limbs, and touched her face to check everything was still in the right place. She sighed with relief and looked around her. She was in a hospital ward by herself. All of a sudden, a horrible thought came to her, and she pressed on the button to call for help.

A nurse rushed into her room and checked everything was fine. She asked Ting-Ting if she felt any pain now that the anaesthesia was supposed to be wearing off.

"Where is Kannis? Is she alright?" She demanded an answer from the nurse right away.

"You mean the woman who was admitted to the hospital with you? Sorry, we can only reveal a patient's situation to their families."

"Get me off this bed, NOW!" Ting-Ting could not suppress her worries after hearing Kannis had also been admitted to the hospital and struggled to get out of bed, only to find herself connected to different machines to monitor her vital signs.

"Ting-Ting, please stay in bed, you just had surgery."

"Mum, I need to go find Kannis, she was in the car with me!"

"Ting-Ting, Kannis is fine. She's just next door. We can go see her when you feel better. I have something to tell you first."

Edith told Ting-Ting everything.

At first, Ting-Ting was elated to hear that Kannis was actually her biological sister. Then the truth sank in, and Ting-Ting was outraged by Edith hiding the fact from her, and the families on both sides had been trying to discourage them from seeing each other.

"We have wasted so much time, all these years when we could have been sisters. I felt so lonely growing up being the only child, how much I wished to have a sister, just like Kannis."

Ting-Ting asked Edith to leave her room - she did not want to talk to her, nor see her. Ting-Ting was not sure if she could ever forgive her mother for denying her the right to grow up with her only sister, and how it was only when they were near death, and Kannis giving up one of her kidneys for her, they were told the truth.

On the other hand, she was grateful for Kannis sacrificing herself to save her life. She was overjoyed to have Kannis as her sister… and she couldn't wait to spend more time with her before she had to return to Paris, to make up all those years they had missed each other.

Chapter Thirty-Five

Kannis and Ting-Ting gradually recovered from both the kidney transplant operation as well as the car accident. They spent their days hanging out in the garden, and evenings in each other's room to catch up with all the stories growing up, secrets about boys they had dated - things that sisters who were very close would do. They both felt like being children again, only they were free grownups now without the supervision of adults. They could do whatever they liked. They made plans to go traveling together once they had fully recovered.

Ting-Ting had been refusing to see Edith, who was heartbroken but at the same time could not blame Ting-Ting for being mad at her. Edith could only hope with time Ting-Ting would forgive her. Edith went to see her brother Tony a few times and cried the tears she had stored up all these years. Tony was the only one who knew all the secrets between Edith and Charles, as he was the one who helped to liaise all the details between the two past lovers. Contrary to the public's speculation that Tony had got rich after Edith married into the powerful Lee family, Tony actually built his own wealth with a little help from Edith, who loaned Tony the money she'd made from movies to start his first business. Growing up with nothing, Tony had the habit of being cautious with money. He never agreed with the extravagant lifestyle led by some of Simon's families. Despite being one of the super riches, he still took public transportation and packed a lunch box for work, hence the mean reputation for being tight. Tony felt sorry for his baby sister, but back then he knew that one day the two sisters would learn the truth and understandably be mad at their parents. He decided to go visit Ting-Ting in the hospital and see how she was.

"Uncle Tony, did mummy send you? Tell her I still don't want to see her."

Tony walked into Ting-Ting's room in the hospital with a massive bouquet. Ting-Ting could not help but smile at it. She was sure 'tight Tony' must have spent a fortune on it. Knowing her uncle well, and that he never spent money for nothing, she suspected he came for Edith.

"How is my favourite niece doing?" Tony gave Ting-Ting a kiss on her forehead, a kiss on each of her cheeks then a final peck on her nose, just like each and every time he saw her ever since she was a little girl.

"First of all, I am doing as well as one can after a car accident and a kidney transplant. And as of two days ago, I was your only niece. Because of the terrible fact your sister had hidden from us, you have another pretty damn cool niece who I can't wait for you to meet."

"You will always be Uncle Tony's favourite niece. And I had known about Kannis ever since your mum was pregnant with her. At your age, it is very hard for you to imagine what it was like back in those days, how much pressure your mum was under, how helpless she was in her situation and opposition such as Mimi's, your paternal grandmother."

"Are you saying that I should kick you out, too? Think of all those years Kannis and I had lost to be with each other!"

"Ting-Ting… Do you think you and Kannis ended up in the same boarding school, university and business schools by coincidence? We arranged it. After Mimi passed away, Edith begged Charles to let you two to be at the same schools so that even though you could not be sisters, you could still be friends for life. Of course, you both did brilliantly at school, so it was never a problem to put both of you in the top schools. Your mum was very proud of both you and Kannis."

Ting-Ting recalled all those years at school, and how Kannis always ended up being her 'big sister' at school; the senior student to help with a junior. Kannis also took gap years traveling and interning at Charles's company before starting universities, to then end up being in the same year in graduate school as she was, despite being older.

"And Kannis working for Maison H? But she was all in Europe instead of being here…"

"Charles thought Edith was going too far to want you two working for the same company, plus Charles had his own plan for Kannis. She had been trained from young to take over his empire from him. Plus, Kannis wanted to be in Paris to be with her French boyfriend. In the end, they settled for Kannis being a Management Trainee that allowed her the flexibility to be where she wanted to be."

Before the end of Ting-Ting's stay at the hospital, Ting-Ting and Edith were talking again. Edith had opened up to Ting-Ting and told her the love tragedy between her and Charles, and the endless drama once Mimi, Kannis' grannie, was involved. Ting-Ting understood now the hatred her mother had for Charles was as much as the love she used to have for him. Edith thought Charles was a coward not to be able to stand up for her nor grant her the right to be Kannis' mother. Charles begged for her forgiveness after Mimi's passing. Yet, Edith thought it was too little too late, and she was already pregnant with Ting-Ting. Because of the fame of both families, Edith did not want the story to become exposed and cause an unnecessary scandal that would eventually affect the baby she was carrying, Ting-Ting. No one else knew the background story and that Kannis was Edith's daughter, except Uncle Tony.

Uncle Tony remained friendly with Charles and throughout the years acted as the indispensable ties between Edith and Charles on the affairs of Kannis, with the goal of arranging 'coincident encounters' for the two sisters to get to know each other. Ting-Ting would not have been able to comprehend the challenges her mother faced if it was not for the numerous drama series' playing on television all the time on the love tragedy and drama revolving around rich and powerful families. The fact that Edith was a famous actress, and both men involved came from the most powerful and wealthiest families in Hong Kong, that would ensure the scandals that Edith believed would generate. She was protective of the baby that had been born and the one to be born.

Meanwhile, Kannis had already left the hospital and moved back to Charles's house where he hired nurses to look after Kannis until she fully recovered from the operation. Ting-Ting wanted to do the same but was forbidden by the doctor as she had her car accident wounds to be taken care of. Edith brought Chinese soup that she cooked herself to help boost Ting-Ting's strength. Edith told Ting-Ting she had been visiting Kannis as well, and working on rebuilding the relationship with her other daughter. Ting-Ting felt sorry for Edith and could imagine the tough journey Edith had ahead for her. Given it was not an easy task for her to forgive Edith, who had raised and loved her all these years and was one of her closest friends. She told Edith she had her full support to bond with Kannis again.

Kannis adored Ting-Ting. Growing up, they always ended up in the same boarding schools. They had always been the underground besties. They kept their friendship a secret to keep the peace between the two rival families. Charles, as a single father, raised and nurtured Kannis more as a boy than a girl. Hoping Kannis would take over his business empire one day, Charles trained Kannis to be tough. With the masculine environment at home and a brother, Kannis had always regarded Ting-Ting as her little sister she never had; the person she grew up doing all the girlie things and gossiping about boys with. Now she was not that sure if she wanted to have that 'dream come true,' as the indications it came with was too much to take in. Kannis wanted to have a mother so much growing up, but now she was a grown up and independent woman, she knew she no longer needed a mother figure and had no clue how to build up the bond between mother and daughter from scratch. She didn't hesitate to donate a kidney to Ting-Ting, even without finding out they were sisters. The revelation had merely brought them even closer than before.

On the other hand, would she be jealous at Ting-Ting that she got to be loved and spoilt by their mother growing up, while she found herself time and time again, shedding tears at night hoping that she had a mummy to love her?

Chapter Thirty-Six

Edith and Kannis went to grab some lunch together after visiting Ting-Ting. Bored of the food served in the hospital's cafeteria, they went to a nice restaurant in Central to treat themselves to some great food, now that Ting-Ting had made some good progress on her recovery. It would be very soon when Ting-Ting could go home. After lunch, Edith asked Kannis if she could spare another hour because she would like to take her somewhere. Extending her stay in Hong Kong only because of Ting-Ting, Kannis actually did not have much to do. Although she didn't know how to be a daughter to Edith, who was literally a stranger to her, she reminded herself to keep an open mind and give herself and Edith a chance to be part of each other's life again.

Edith instructed her driver to take her to an address that was familiar to him; the address that he had been taking Edith to at least once a month throughout the years he had been working as Edith's family driver. He had learned to be discreet being the driver of a rich and famous family. During all these years he guessed it could be a young boyfriend she kept in a common apartment, and he created fantasies in his head whenever he was instructed to wait for her nearby, each time for an hour or so but not longer than three. Only now she was taking a family member there he was no longer sure whether Edith was having an extramarital fair anymore.

Edith opened the door to an apartment that looked like it had been decorated and set up for a young family. Kannis stepped inside and found photo frames standing across tables, cupboards, shelves, or hung all over the walls. The colours of the furniture were of baby pink and white. When she looked closer at the photographs, she was shocked to find they were all photos of her childhood and that of another little girl. It was not a mistake that the other girl was Ting-Ting. Kannis and Ting-Ting were in the same outfits in most of them, just at a different times and different places.

"This place is…" Kannis had a guess, but she could not stop herself from asking.

"I have been keeping this apartment for thirty years. This is the place where I could be by myself and shed my tears from the pain of having to give you up. A place where I can display your photos, and look at you sisters in the same outfits I bought you."

"YOU were the secret Santa who sent me a package every year?" Kannis looked closely at the dresses she wore in those photos again and came to the realisation - every Christmas she received a big box from a Secret Santa which she was most excited about. There were always beautiful things inside that she loved. She always thought it was a trick by Charles, who sent a female staff to get all the girlie goodies for her. She kept teasing Charles to stop the trick as she was not five anymore, Charles would laugh it off, and Kannis found daddy's gesture funny but sweet. Last year she found an autographed first edition of the first hardcover book of her favourite author, which she thought was incredibly sweet and thoughtful of her father. Only now she realised her mother was the one who had been lavishing her with all those thoughtful gifts she loved all these years.

"I was putting these aside and hoping you would be able to read them one day. This apartment will also belong to you; I have instructed my lawyer to pass everything here over to you when I am no longer around." Edith handed over a box full of bundles of cards and letters to Kannis while hoping God would let her live longer to make up the lost time with her daughter.

Kannis opened the letters and cards as soon as she got back to her room in her daddy's house. There were more than a hundred of them, about a handful each year, dating back to when she was two years old. There were birthday cards for each of her birthdays and Christmas each year. There were also letters at random times of years handwritten by Edith to express how much she missed Kannis and how much she wished she were there with her and Ting-Ting, her baby sister.

"I showed you these not to ask for your forgiveness, but to let you know that you have been loved by your mother all these years. There was not a day passed that I did not think of you, miss you, and wish I could hold you in my arms." Edith's tears ran down her face when she begged Kannis not to forgive her but to give her a chance to be her mother and be in her life again.

Chapter Thirty-Seven

Phoebe had been to Bali over a dozen times during these years working for Maison H. The brand had a downtown duty free boutique. She regularly went for meetings, staff training, and new shop openings. Over time she became a VIP guest at the resort, and she usually received an upgrade to a fabulous room. Every time she wished she had someone to share all those luxuries with. For the first few times, she had dined at the restaurant, but later she ordered room service. She felt particularly lonely and sad when she sat next to families or a couple who'd come for a vacation.

Phoebe was heartbroken, embarrassed, and hurt from her last relationship with Rayan for a very long time. It was a big deal for her to try it again with Alex. For the first few months after they spent their first evening together, Phoebe still felt very insecure. Ting-Ting suggested and planned for her to invite Alex spontaneously to join her on business plus leisure trips on very short notice. Alex accepted them all with delight, and turned up on time at the spot as he was told by Phoebe. With the observations and blessings from her friends, before long, everyone could tell how smitten Alex was with Phoebe, and welcomed him into her world.

One of these test trips with Alex in Bali turned out to be a wonderful weekend getaway for Phoebe, and made up for all those lonely trips she had ever made here. She once swore she would never come back to this sad place. However, after spending time there with Alex, she thought it was one of the most romantic, yet spiritual places on earth.

On their last day there, Alex surprised Phoebe and took her to the Bulgari Resort for lunch. The resort was one of the most spectacular ones on the island. It was built on a cliff among the Uluwatu mountains. From every corner at the resort, visitors looked out to a view where the sky joined the ocean. Phoebe had never seen anything like that in her life. The resort was landscaped in a way that every room and dining facilities had nothing to obstruct its view. Therefore, the paths within the complex were all slopes. The only way to get around was by a golf cart. The architecture of the resort simply took Phoebe's breath away. She was impressed by Alex's effort to find a place to reignite Phoebe's fondness of the island. She wondered aloud how the room would look like in a resort like Bulgari.

After paying the bill, Alex asked to see the restaurant manager. Phoebe tensed up and worried there was something wrong although she could not think of anything - the lunch was perfect.

"My fiancée and I are thinking of having our wedding here, so we are hoping to get a tour. Do you think anyone here can arrange one for us?"

Phoebe's jaw dropped and she covered her face from embarrassment or to stop herself from laughing so as not to expose Alex's lie.

The restaurant manager explained Alex's request to the front desk who sent the concierge over within minutes and offered to show the engaged couple around. Although it was a lie to trick the resort to show them the guest rooms, ballrooms, and the spa, Phoebe enjoyed herself immensely when Alex squeezed her hand, or gave her a peck on the cheek or lip every now and then during the tour. She couldn't help herself, but imagined if they would get married one day at this resort.

Chapter Thirty-Eight

Phoebe planned to fly to Beijing over the coming long weekend, which was a public holiday and shared with her parents the news of her new job. She also wanted to introduce Alex to them. For a few weeks, Phoebe had been waiting for the right moment to ask Alex; still painfully remembering her last boyfriend always made up an excuse not to meet her parents. Phoebe was very close to her parents and did not want to keep the relationship from them as soon as she felt it was going to get serious. To her relief, Alex accepted the invitation with much enthusiasm.

Phoebe was the only child of Claire and Johnathan Downlington , who were high school sweethearts. They graduated from high school and went on to attend the same college. They got married upon graduation and had Phoebe soon afterwards. Johnathan got into the Foreign Service Department, as expected, with his brilliant academic record and a father as a career diplomat, who trained and groomed Johnathan to become one from the day he could walk. Claire Downlington was a professional diplomat's wife, who followed her diplomat husband around the world, looking after their daughter, managing the family to settle smoothly at each post Johnathan was sent to, and to entertain guests, big and small, from all over the world for her husband.

Being a diplomat did not pay well but enjoyed great benefits, especially when at a posting overseas - spacious accommodation in a prominent residential area or on a military site, with allowances on education, childcare, etc. On top of all this, was a prestigious status that would draw all the invitations to important social gatherings. As a representative of the most powerful in the world, everybody wanted to be friends with the Downlingtown's.

The house where Claire and Johnathan lived in Beijing was near the airport, yet it was an expansive and expensive area outside the city centre where many spectacular villas were built. Why these newly built houses were popular among the affluent group was mainly due to the cold weather in Beijing. In winter, the temperature could easily drop to sub-zero. These houses were all installed with floor heating and large double glazed windows which allowed the sunlight to fill up the house generously.

Phoebe spotted some new artworks her mother had acquired in the past few months since the relocation, among all the other artworks her parents had gathered over the years from each country they had been posted in. The style was contemporary, and Phoebe could guess they were from certain artists who were very popular at the moment - she had been to their exhibitions at some art galleries in Hong Kong.

Other than the artworks, the house's colour theme was red and grey. All decorations were spot on. The impression was elegant and welcoming, while remaining tasteful. Phoebe always admired how her mother managed to put together a beautiful home from scratch in such a short time wherever they moved to.

Phoebe stayed with her parents while Alex stayed at a hotel, arriving late on the Friday evening. Both Claire and Johnathan waited up for her arrival; they greeted her briefly then went to bed. The next morning, she asked Claire and Johnathan at breakfast if they minded her bringing a friend to join them for lunch. Claire was intrigued to hear that, and she raised an eyebrow and looked at her husband. Phoebe had never brought any 'friend' home, and for all they knew, her last relationship ended so badly that Phoebe had not dated anyone else in the past two years. Knowing their daughter, they did not push it - they told Phoebe that any of her friends would be welcomed to join them.

They went to a little restaurant by the lake in Hou Hai. It was a glorious day, the sky was blue, and the sun shining. They promenaded the charming lanes in the area after lunch, then explored the 798 Art Zone, where they spoke to the artists and galleries to understand the current trend and art scene in Beijing.

Claire and Johnathan were pleasantly surprised by Alex. He was relaxed while being respectful. He was a typical British gentleman while exceptionally knowledgeable about American politics. His view was worldly, which was much appreciated by Johnathan. The most important thing was that he seemed to be very kind and thoughtful towards their daughter. They both secretly hoped that the dating was going to get serious between the two.

The next day they went hiking on the Great Wall. The view was spectacular, and they all had a fantastic day out together. The last day of the long weekend, Claire and Johnathan excused themselves to let Phoebe explore the city with her new boyfriend.

Phoebe and Alex did the touristy thing, and visited Tiananmen Square and the Summer Palace. They had dinner at one of the courtyard restaurants in the famous Hutong district. Alex casually mentioned that his boss was thinking of exploring the China market, and that there would be a chance that he would be relocated to China, and if that would happen he was hoping it was going to be Beijing. He liked how cultural the city was and that Phoebe's parents lived there was a bonus. Since Phoebe travelled most of the time during the week, it did not really matter where he was during the week as long as they committed to be together on weekends.

Unfortunately, Phoebe's heart sank upon hearing this possibility. Her experience with a distant relationship was not a good one. After flying back to Hong Kong, she could think of nothing but Alex's possible relocation in the near future. She even contemplated the thought of cutting her losses and breaking up with Alex before things got more serious.

Chapter Thirty-Nine

By the last two weeks of her days at Maison H, Phoebe had already had over a dozen farewell lunches. Priscilla was back in the office every other afternoon to catch up with work, and also to interview candidates to replace Phoebe, although no one she had seen was to her liking so far.

"You have really spoilt me with your talents and help. I'm not sure if I will ever be able to find someone to replace you." Priscilla kept repeating this to Phoebe which made her feel worse. With a young baby, Priscilla needed Phoebe more than ever. Having a new hire would mean longer hours in the office and more traveling days to introduce her replacement to each operator. Phoebe felt as guilty as she was grateful towards Priscilla, for all she had cared about her like a sister as well as giving her the wonderful years in her career.

The last day was an emotional one for Phoebe. She went to each floor of the Maison H office to say goodbye and hug every colleague she knew or ever worked with for the past five years. Everyone wished her the best of luck. The Travel Retail team gifted her a Maison H cashmere shawl, which was of superb quality. Phoebe was touched by the gesture and very reluctantly, she handover her laptop, blackberry, work keys, etc. to the office manager and bid farewell to probably the most amazing chapter in her career.

After she had done the difficult farewell to her company, Phoebe mustered her courage and confided with Alex her intention to end things before their relationship got more serious. She told him roughly about her last relationship, which was long distant and ended with a broken heart. She had no heart to try the same thing again.

"Phoebe, first of all, I'm glad that your last distant relationship did not work out; otherwise, I would have never had a chance to be with you. The relocation has not been confirmed yet. Please give us a chance to see how things go. Maybe you will have got bored of me by the time they send me away? What has been confirmed so far is that I really like you, and I think I am falling in love with you. I give you my word that I will fly to wherever you are every weekend, every holiday to see you. If you still do not feel comfortable, I will change my job to stay in the same place with you. Does that give you the confidence to give us a try?"

Phoebe raised the issue with Alex a few times more as the day of Alex's relocation approached. She wanted to give Alex a way out to start fresh. Nevertheless, Alex told her with more certainty each time that he would never give the relationship up just because they would be living in two different cities. In the end, Alex convinced Phoebe to give their relationship a try and give him a probation period to prove to her that he would make every effort to go see her on weekends - he assured her that things were going to work out just fine.

Chapter Forty

Phoebe enjoyed working and living in Hong Kong, although most of the week her 'working' was all over the region. Still, she tried to make the best of her time when she was in Hong Kong. While most people who only ever visited Hong Kong had the impression that the city was overcrowded and only had skyscrapers, Phoebe soon discovered the very unique and amazing hiking experiences the city had to offer. Two-thirds of the city landscape was covered by country parks. Most of the hills in the city were close to the water which offered hikers a stunning sea view every stop they made along the trail, with the backdrop of the vibrant city filled with skyscrapers. Dragon Back trail was Phoebe's favourite where on a fine day, one could see not only the harbour but all the natural landscape around Hong Kong Island.

The city itself vibrated with an energy that Phoebe had never felt anywhere else in the world. When she went out with Ting Ting on a Friday night, they could easily meet people of at least a dozen different nationalities - Hong Kong was truly a cosmopolitan of Asia. While at home, when there was no one else but herself, Phoebe loved enjoying the snack she brought back from Japan while watching the local TV drama. With the streaming technology these days, she saved the series' while she was away and treated herself half a dozen episodes when she did not feel like going out. She particularly loved the drama and power struggle among the emperor's concubines in different periods of Chinese history. She knew very well that was something brewed over the years by her nanny Aimee whom she watched similar TV series together with on evenings when her parents were out or hosting dinner. The stories were often dramatic to the extreme with lots of tears from the actors and actresses. Phoebe and Aimee used to cry together, watching TV, and her parents would be shocked to see her eyes and face the following morning at breakfast.

With Alex still living in the same city and calendar, Phoebe enjoyed living in Hong Kong more than ever. Both Phoebe and Alex enjoyed being outdoors; they explored the national country parks and hiking trails that surprisingly, the concrete city was abundant of. They would spend hours chilling on a beach, where there were many spread across the city, or going out to sea with both their friends that took them to little islands that few would venture to. Whenever there was a long weekend, they would spontaneously book a flight for a destination weekend as the city was a travel hub in the region.

By the time Alex's company confirmed to relocate him to develop their market in Mainland China, both Phoebe and Alex felt more secure and confident with each other. The relationship had advanced, and Phoebe felt secure enough to live in two different cities. In the end, Alex was to be relocated to Shanghai. He made a commitment to Phoebe and booked his tickets to either Hong Kong or Beijing for the six months to come. He also planned getaways for the coming few public holidays with Phoebe, all to destinations she had ever mentioned she would like to see one day. The gesture was sweet, and gave Phoebe the confidence to give a distant relationship another try.

Both Phoebe and Alex embraced the coming changes and challenges that their relationship was going to put to the test, with Alex going to be relocated to Shanghai soon to set up an office there as well as to develop the Mainland China's market for his firm. After the transition period promised by Vuitton Beauty, Phoebe would be responsible solely for Greater China, which meant she was going to spend the majority of her time in China. She offered Sebastian to stay at her parents' house while in China, in return to be based in China half of her time in order to increase her time to spend with Alex.

Chapter Forty-One

Both Alex and Phoebe had three weeks off before Phoebe had to start her new job at Vuitton Beauty and Alex relocating to Shanghai to set up an office there for his company. They decided to go farther away for a rare, long holiday. They both agreed Brazil would be a perfect choice. They could hang out on the beach and sip caipirinhas, and visit touristic sights across the country.

Alex and Phoebe had a fantastic time. Besides caipirinhas, Phoebe enjoyed watching guys exercising on the beach in Rio de Janeiro. The scene made her feel bad for not joining them cycling, rollerblading, playing beach volleyball, or working out on the gym bars that were set up along the coast, instead of lying on her tummy to sunbathe all day long. The Brazilian men were both handsome and fit. They were such eye candies that Phoebe could not help but snap picture after picture and send to Ting Ting. Ting Ting swore she was born in the wrong city and made Rio her city of retirement. Phoebe and Alex visited the infamous slum which was an eye-opening experience for both, they took many photos under Christ the Redeemer statue, and watched a spontaneous Capoeira hoda fight on the beach… After enjoying a fun boat excursion along the Amazon River, they took a flight to the border to see the Iguazu Falls, which was breath-taking.

Their three weeks' adventure had completely unwinded both Alex and Phoebe; it had taken their mind off work, relocations, and their coming long distant relationship. They had their focus on having a great time and enjoying each other's company. At the end of their holiday, they were very sad to return to reality but had no doubt their love for each other, they were both positive about being able to handle the distance between them, and committed to making all the effort that it would take to see one another.

Phoebe started her first day at Vuitton Beauty. Despite having prepared herself that Vuitton Beauty would be very different from Maison H, she had to admit she missed the warm, friendly atmosphere, and all her colleagues who treated her like a family at Maison H. By comparison, it felt like she had been spoiled in the past five years, most of all by the office's tea lady, Ah Ling. Ah Ling was like a hen mother figure in the office, who would only serve everyone fresh coffee and water after each colleague's arrival in the office, not before, and let it cool to a lukewarm temperature by the time Phoebe sat down at her desk. If Ah Ling heard a colleague's voice sound like being under the weather, she would make a soothing tea made of mandarin peel and honey, which the mandarin peel was hand prepared by herself at the beginning of each year and fermented until end of the year for the flu season. The only perk so far was Phoebe's office; she finally had one of her own, with a door. The office had a sea view and even its own printer! No more standing in a queue to wait for her own printout nor dealing with paper jams for other people.

Sebastian made an effort to welcome her. He briefed her what had been done so far to prepare for the launch of Vuitton Beauty and what was expected from her. He introduced her to everyone, and arranged inductions and training for Phoebe with all the key colleagues such as the finance controller, marketing manager, etc. Although Phoebe wished Maison H could be more up to date in terms of software, she felt the Vuitton Group was taking the technology side to the extreme. By the end of her first week, she had accumulated more than fifty login IDs and passwords which required a little notebook to help her to keep up with all of them - to centralise and streamline the management and reporting for all the brands, the group had a system for everything. Indeed, Phoebe suspected that some of the systems were going to make her job more complicated than necessary. It also made her spend most of her early days trying to master the computer software instead of focusing on the work itself. Sebastian had asked his staff to help Phoebe with the system, but none of them seemed to have the time nor the will to help her.

Everyone was super busy and reassured Phoebe that in time she would be able to master all. Besides, the competitive culture in the company made everyone reluctant to spend time or make an effort to help one another. P&L was the running principle of the office, and whether there was any return to everything.

Phoebe looked forward to trying Vuitton's first-ever fragrance. She loved the Maison H perfume and expected something spectacular from Vuitton, too. When Sebastien handed her the Vuitton perfume bottle, it looked as luxurious and fashionable as it's leather bag was. The glass bottle resembled the shape of a travel trunk. The edges and corners were wrapped up with leather with the brand monogram embossed on them as if the bottle itself had worn a harness. It was probably the most gorgeous and expensive looking perfume bottle Phoebe had ever seen. Sebastien handed Phoebe a little jar of coffee beans to clear her sense of smell as his office was filled with a mixture of the cologne he wore and cigarette smell, and asked her to try the scent. He asked Phoebe to test it on her skin so she could see how the scent evolved on human skin over time.

Phoebe gave a little press to the pump of the stunning Vuitton perfume bottle, making sure she was not too rough after Sebastien told her that it was only a prototype. She was then overwhelmed by the fragrance's top notes. It was floral while at the same time musky, and no mistaking, an expensive scent. Yet, to Phoebe's disappointment, the scent was vaguely similar to some perfumes of other brands she'd tried at the duty-free beauty shops before. She made compliments to Sebastien to be polite and told herself that she would wait for the middle and base notes before she made her judgement. Throughout the day, Phoebe sniffed her own wrist to see how the notes of Vuitton's first perfume had become, and further to her disappointment, it was nothing mind-blowing – it was just like any other expensive perfume she had tried at the airport.

However, to be fair to Vuitton, she knew very well from Maison H training that only two luxury brands had their own 'nose,' a perfume specialist or tailor, to make perfumes that were unique to the brand. She also wondered whether it was her loyalty to Maison H that was to blame for her prejudice towards Vuitton. She could not believe that she even missed the scent of her old company! Maison H had a scent for everybody. She personally loved the Wonderful Scent that had a unique fragrance that she had never come across, which had a subtle aroma of chocolate mixed with orange. She adored its bottle which resembled a crystal snowball which can be placed either upright from both left and right or laid down flat. Ting Ting, her best friend and ex-colleague was a fan of the house's garden series, which were preferred by most Asian clientele for their light and elegant scents which went very well with the Asian climate and humidity. Priscilla, a strong career woman with a Canadian background and gradual French influence from her husband, wore the Ally perfume, which was a combination of strength, confidence, and sexiness in a bottle. And Phoebe could not deny that it was love at first scent when she met Alex, who was wearing the brand's Earth men fragrance. Alex was not a cologne type of guy; he liked only the Earth fragrance for its simplicity, 'down-to-earth' scent, and its lightness for everyday wearing. Phoebe hoped that she would grow to love Vuitton's products as well as to become its number one salesperson of the brand's first-ever perfume.

Chapter Forty-Two

By the end of her first week at Vuitton Beauty, Phoebe was exhausted, both physically and mentally. She couldn't wait to tell Alex everything when they saw each other. They barely chatted more than five minutes on the phone as Alex was also very busy trying to set up an office in Shanghai. Phoebe got home late every night as she tried to stay in the office to catch up with different systems so she could focus on learning her areas, going to meetings, and making phone calls to her clients to set up meetings during the day.

"This guy is crazy!"

Phoebe was complaining to Alex about her colleague, Bryan Chan, who was her counterpart for the local market in Asia-Pacific and had his office next to hers, about his ridiculous behaviours and Feng Shui set up.

"After rescheduling our induction meeting three times because the lunar calendar did not agree with our Chinese zodiac signs, he cancelled our meeting again because I was wearing purple-blue today. He said it was a funeral colour and would bring on bad luck to him."

"What's wrong with that? Hong Kong has a strong Feng Shui culture, and it seems to work for the city. Even I heard the local government has a budget reserved for making changes according to Feng Shui needs. Sometimes selling is half confidence, half lucky." Alex referred to the infamous bank buildings in Central that had been constructed in a way so to offset the competition from each other.

"Yes, that. He requested me to have my blind halfway down to block away some pointy skyscrapers on the other side of the harbour, which would be bad Feng Shui to business. As our walls are translucent, he claimed that what's going on in my office would affect him. I mean, my office has a sea view for God's sake. Now I can only see the street view that leads to the harbour."

"To make you feel better, I don't have an office myself."

"You can't really compare like your package with mine. You are paid well - we are not. I see the sea view office as part of my remuneration package. Bryan also told me I was not complimentary to his career development, so we should try to avoid business encounters as much as possible. Lucky for me for not being his lucky charm, I don't need to have a male colleague to comment on the colour choice of my outfit."

"Hmm, in that sense, I also don't hire anyone who is unlucky."

"How can you tell if someone is a lucky person? Don't tell me you do the Chinese Feng Shui thing and have a Chinese astrologic background check on every candidate."

"No, my way is very simple. I divide the stack of applications into half. Discard one half and just focus on the other 'lucky" half.'

"Gosh, I hope I never have to beg you for a job…"

Two months into their distant relationship, Phoebe and Alex had fallen into a blissful pattern of communicating and meeting up with each other. They set up a routine to FaceTime each other a couple of times a week and took turns to fly to Shanghai or Hong Kong at least every other week. They also made plans on a couple of short vacations within the next six months, so both had something nice to look forward to. Phoebe no longer felt guilty of her frequent travel and Alex about his long hours in the office. For the first time in a very long time, Phoebe felt contented. She was at the right place for her career and had met the right man to pursue a healthy and happy relationship. She had great friends like Ting Ting, while her parents were not on the other side of the world from her. All these were her own doings and not from the connections of her father.

When Phoebe was with Maison H, she looked after a dozen travel retail boutiques across the Asia-Pacific region. Now with Vuitton Beauty, the reduced in size of the beauty counters were compensated by the increase in quantity. The minimum requirement from the management was to be able to get a spot in the over fifty points of sale that the other beauty brands in the group already existed in. With the Vuitton name, Phoebe's mission was to win a prime location and major promotion areas during the peak seasons.

Instead of the fancy show windows every season, with Vuitton Beauty Phoebe had to coordinate with production companies to alternate the visuals in the display light-boxes and to replace the make-up grids with the new ones that represented the latest make-up trend or colour of the brand, for all the point of sales. The tasks were overwhelming. Phoebe was grateful for her two assistants who were highly efficient and helped her completing those tedious tasks in a timely manner, yet, she found herself working on forecasts, orders, expenses, and budgeting on a daily basis even when she was traveling, which involved lots of preparation on product presentation and negotiating terms with each operator.

When Phoebe visited the airport with her boss, Sebastian, she thought they had walked into a battlefield. When she was at Maison H, she saw the boutiques, both the brand and its competitors. Now every beauty duty-free shop, every light-box, every pillar and corner for promotions, stretching from the main departure area shop to satellite shops near the gates, was seen a territory to compete with other brands. Phoebe could hardly keep up and tried her best to take notes when Sebastian pointed here and there, reminding her to negotiate a better and bigger space. Each promotion corner was valuable, and the major promotion sites would be a holy grail if booked during holiday seasons. Since Maison H communicated mainly through its spectacular show windows, the advertising light-boxes were rarely the brand's concern. Now, however, every single one mattered, especially those at terminals where the richer customer profile would frequent. Koreans, Chinese, Arabs, and Russians were the most popular nationalities to travel retail as they were known as the high spenders. Long after they had left the airport, Phoebe could still hear 'location,' 'visibility,' 'there is no harm to ask if we can have it,' ringing in her head, like some bad tune that would never go away.

At Maison H, as long as guidelines were respected, detailed rules could be adapted within reasons. Besides the endless data input to the dozens of systems under the Vuitton group, Phoebe found some of the rules silly but was still asked to blindly follow, as it would be too hard to tailor-make everything for each brand in the group.

One thing that Phoebe noticed about Sebastian was, he never cared to engage into a conversation with the sales representative or the one or two customers who happened to be checking out the products. Phoebe found it unbelievable as it was the best way to get first-hand information that would have a constructive impact on their business, especially since they were not at the shop on a daily basis. Phoebe would always spare time to have a chat with the staff, whether they were representing the staff or generic sales staff for all brands. She saw them as experts and first agents who could tell her something that figures on the spreadsheet could not. Phoebe knew very well that she was the link between the brand and the staff, too, so she would remind herself to ask the front line staff about the support the company could provide them, be it training, fact sheets of products, more testers, gift with purchases, etc. At the same time, Phoebe would introduce herself to the customers who were nearby and if time allowed, propose some best sellers or new arrivals to them. Most of the time, the travellers appreciated the attention, and some even ended up making purchases of her recommendations.

Meanwhile, Phoebe had to admit the training provided by Vuitton group was more advanced and sophisticated than that by Maison H. At Maison H, a great deal of the staff training emphasized on the brand story, the products, luxury and interaction with customers. It explained why the brand was reluctant to let incapable staff go as the brand invested heavily on each staff member to learn about the brand itself, which was the biggest value for the company. While at the Vuitton group, the focus was more on the soft skills, competitiveness, and ability to adapt of the employee, so to help the group to deliver its bottom line as well as make the capable staff more mobile within the group. Soon after Phoebe joined Vuitton Beauty, she was sent to camps to sharpen up her negotiation skills, to manage new projects as well as learning to handle any PR crisis. Phoebe felt very fortunate to be able to work for both companies, where she learnt about luxury at Maison H and all the powerful soft commercial skills at Vuitton Beauty.

Chapter Forty-Three

"Wait for me, pleeeeease! Don't take off without me! Oh, noooooooo… My plane is gone!"

Phoebe was running late, out of breath, and looking for any sign of her plane. The gate area was completely foreign to her, which meant that she wasted twenty minutes walking around the airport looking for it. Being a jet-setter, Phoebe believed she knew the locations of every single airline lounge, duty-free shop, right down to the restrooms with the shorter queue, etc. like the back of her hands. But this time, she'd underestimated how long it would take her to find the gate areas where most planes bound for China departed from. She'd been discussing some development project with Sebastian right up until after the last minute. Now she had to pay for being arrogant that the plane had taken off without her.

"Chillax, our plane hasn't taken off yet, it's not even arrived."

Veronica, looking relaxed after having been to the smoking-room, probably for the second time, laughed and asked Phoebe to take a deep breath and relax. Phoebe was going to take over Veronica's accounts in China. Veronica had been on loan to Vuitton Beauty; she used to work for another cosmetic brand and was in charge of Greater China within the group. Veronica had taken a sabbatical, and while in the transition of going back to work, she had been asked to establish a relationship with each operator for Sebastian and the brand before an area manager came on board. The excitement of launching the cosmetics and fragrance line of Vuitton Beauty soon faded over her disagreements with Sebastian. Veronica was used to working for an Asian boss, with whom she could give her opinions and expected support from her superior.

In the past decade, more luxury brands had engaged French employees to directorate positions. They claimed to aim at putting in more French value into the brand, despite everyone knowing the truth was that France was running out of jobs, and the brands were pressured to take on more French nationals overseas. With a new French boss, most of the time he would listen and entertain her with a few comfort words, but the status quo would remain the same as he had to follow the guidelines from the headquarters, even if those guidelines might not be able to apply to a certain local business environment. As a result, frustrations mounted over time. Veronica was more than pleased to hand over the accounts to Phoebe and hoped to work with a more compatible director next.

Too embarrassed to tell Veronica that she was lost, Phoebe decided to blame it on their talkative boss for being late. As their boss, Sebastian was French, so it wasn't hard to convince Veronica as she often complained herself that her French colleagues all loved listening to themselves talk.

"What?! How can the plane be elsewhere but here? It's 6:30 pm now, the departure time! How long did they say the delay would be for?" Regretting that she made a promise to her parents to stop by their house to say hello before joining Veronica at the hotel.

"What delay? Anywhere within two hours for a China-bounded flight is not counted as a delay. Apparently, Sebastian did not brief you this when he tried to convince you to take over Greater China, huh?" said Veronica, enjoying the naivetés of her successor.

Phoebe was not a newcomer to China - her parents have been living in Beijing for nearly a year. Her father was a career diplomat who had recently been rewarded an important posting in China by Washington. Phoebe had helped her parents with the move, hence with first-hand experience and that of her parents, she was oblivious about the notorious China's traffic in the aviation sector.

"That's because travellers such as Sebastien or your father who are high up on the food chain," Veronica explained, "usually take what we call 'the Chairman Flights.' These are in the early afternoon when the peak morning traffic has passed, while the delay of later flights has no impact on them as they do to the last flights of the day."

"Oh great, that would give me time to pick up a latte and check out the duty-free shops." Trying to maintain her positive attitude, Phoebe turned her heels away from Veronica and hoped that the next time she looked at the big window again, their flight would be there.

Phoebe went on to look at the duty-free beauty shop at this end of the terminal. She looked for fragrances that she had yet to try the scents. She spared time and made a special effort whenever she could during her business trips ever since she accepted the job offer from Vuitton to try each and every fragrance being sold at a duty-free shop. So far, she'd confirmed that she was not biased over the brand she had worked for five years before Vuitton - it was just that their perfumes were the best. Phoebe also discovered some newcomers in the perfume sector that could become her new favourites, such as Elie from Elie Saab, and Soleil Blanc from Tom Ford. She found the 'just about right jasmine notes' from Elie Saab sophisticated while being sensual. And that from Tom Ford reminded her of happy times and the glorious sun out in the sea.

As Phoebe wandered around this part of the terminal, which was more remote from the main hall than the rest of the other gates, she found there were only a small beauty duty-free shop and a couple of shops that sold gadgets or souvenirs. She was grateful that none of the brands that were under Vuitton beauty were stocked in the small and crowded shop. Most of the perfume and cosmetic products were missing testers. The displaying visuals of most brands were out-dated, and the shelves in desperate need of dusting. It was the same operator who ran the beauty duty-free shop at Singapore Changi Airport but because managed by different teams, resulted in a different standard. The beauty shop would be out for tender soon; Phoebe had little doubt that the current operator would not earn another contract to run the operation.

The competition was going to be fierce as Hong Kong Airport was one of the busiest in the region and these days an important gateway to China, which was the country with the most potential for the travel retail business. The existing operator would compete to renew their contract, against strong operators from the region. The high profile operators who will join the competition came from not only locally but globally. Duty-free operators from China, Korea, Japan, and even far from Europe, all wanted to get into the Hong Kong Airport. Besides, the Chinese operators were being rumoured to be one of the strongest competitors, and their Korean counterparts were also competing to enter most of the airports in the region. Not only had they been in the industry for years and had a high standard of running a duty-free store at the airport, the strengthening Korean economy meant more Korean travellers as well as spending on luxury products.

The Moodie Report, the respected and informative travel retail magazine, believed Asia would be the battleground between Chinese and Korean duty-free operators in the decades to come. The battle among the operators would definitely push up the standard of management. Gone were the days when travellers expected airports merely places for taking a flight; it was also a destination of comfort, dining, and shopping experiences. The competition of being the best airport, airline lounge, and duty-free shop was fierce. As people around the world became more mobile, the potential of travel retail business was enormous, and to the industry, it was literally, 'the sky is the limit.'

Chapter Forty-Four

"How long," Veronica threw Phoebe a knowing look and asked.

"Two hours, maximum three," Phoebe answered with certainty when Veronica asked her how long she thought Nadine could last, staring at her sexy high heels.

Phoebe, Veronica, Sebastian, and Nadine were doing a tour to visit all the airports and downtown duty-free shops after Nadine had settled in her Hong Kong office. The purpose was to introduce Nadine to all the operators. They were to visit every single point of sale, which meant covering all terminals and gates when an airport was concerned. Their first stop was Bangkok International Airport. Sebastian thought airports in South East Asia would be good airports to showcase to both Nadine and Phoebe, as they were very well developed travel retail markets in cosmetics and fragrances for Asia. He asked Veronica to come along for her connections with all the operators in the region.

The Suvarnabhumi Airport covered an area of over eight thousand acres which made it one of the biggest in the region. The terminal itself was enormous and made it feel like a half marathon by simply walking from one end to another. As travel retail veterans, both Veronica and Phoebe knew the drill and always carried a pair of ballerinas in their bags. Otherwise, the pain that followed on their feet was intense. It was worse than dancing a whole night in high heels at a night club. One could hardly cover an entire airport the size of the Bangkok Airport without screaming in agony.

Nadine had chosen a pair of nine inch, sexy Christine Louboutin, because she wanted to make an impression the first time she met her clients.

Phoebe had subtly reminded her they were going to walk a lot during their trip but got dismissed by Nadine who claimed she could run in them.

In the end, Veronica won the bet who guessed Nadine was going to last for less than two hours. Nadine refused to walk any further after an hour. She complained that her new pair of heels gave her blisters and the tile flooring of the airport was simply too slippery for her heels. Phoebe gave her some plasters, which Nadine said did not help much. Veronica made a victory sign at Phoebe, and Phoebe took out a one hundred Hong Kong dollar note and quietly slipped it into Veronica's bag. The party rested in a café for twenty minutes before Sebastian urged them to move on or otherwise they would not be able to cover all points of sales before catching the next flight to Singapore to do the same.

"Are you kidding me? Are we going to walk the whole airport again there, mon Cheri?"

Although Nadine flirted openly with Sebastian in and out of the office, the scene was getting so unprofessional that both Veronica and Phoebe felt uncomfortable to stick around and listen to how they were going to resolve the shoe issues. They told Sebastian that they were going to talk to the sales staff for some market research. Sebastian looked embarrassed and was relieved when Veronica and Phoebe walked away.

Could not stand Nadine's pleading, Sebastian promised to find her another pair of shoes before they did the walk again. Since they were not traveling, they couldn't shop at one of the boutiques on the air side. With the operator's help, Sebastian finally got them both through customs and back to the land side, where Nadine could buy a pair of shoes without heels. There weren't many choices in the check-in area, as most of the shops sold generic Thai souvenirs. In the end, Nadine had to compromise on a pair of Thai woven slippers with royal elephant motifs on top. They looked ridiculous when paired with Nadine's power suit. Yet, they felt like paradise to Nadine's feet, and she squealed with joy when she slid into them. She walked the rest of the Bangkok Airport and Singapore Changi Airport, which was the next stop, in her newly purchased flip flops. And that was the very last time she wore heels to an airport again.

Chapter Forty-Five

"Has it been only a month since you left us? It feels like ages. Especially when you are away on weekends, too, to be with your beau." Ting Ting missed Phoebe terribly now they no longer worked in the same building and she couldn't just run upstairs to share her gossip with Phoebe whenever she was in town.

"Sorry babe, I know I haven't been in touch enough. I hardly have any time to catch my breath before I have to catch another plane. I had to do an induction tour to meet all my clients and check out all the point of sales, which by the way, there are over a hundred. Then I had to help Alex to settle down in Shanghai. It wasn't easy for him to handle the administrative tasks since he speaks literally zero Mandarin."

"Lucky for him to be dating a walking Rosetta Stone. But most importantly, are you happy there? Are you enjoying your new job?"

"Well, I love my new title and office…"

"But?"

"I've already told you the hundreds of systems I had to - and still have to master. The company culture is very different from that of Maison H. Most of my colleagues, except those in assistance roles, are very competitive. Sometimes it feels I like I am swimming in open water with sharks circling around me. They are so reluctant to show you how to get around. Now I've learnt not to take everything they say on face value; otherwise I can easily fall into a trap. I can't believe I am saying this - I miss the oldies at Maison H."

"You speak most of their lingos; didn't that help?"

"Speaking of lingo, even in English, there are multiple meanings of a simple term. We are constantly doing forecasts. We have to 'forecast' on every single thing down to the bloody paper for testing perfume. When I thought I was a bloody native English speaker, it turns out the frogs have some other meaning for the word. The 'forecast' is a bloody 'confirmed order.' If you 'forecast' more than you need, you end up having to pay for it all. If you 'forecast' less, you can't ask for more even it means making more sales."

"Jesus, remind me that again when I moan about my job."

"I got into trouble last week with the Area Manager of Japan. I managed to get a last-minute promotional opportunity from one of my clients, which my new boss Sebastian was over the moon with. Yet, he only enjoyed getting the credit but was nowhere to be found when I needed his support. He knew that I was going to need more GWP… that's Gift With Purchase, by the way, but 'forgot' to ask Nadine our Marketing Manager to help to transfer the stock to cover me. Kobayashi san from Japan literally screamed at me on the phone when I accidentally took the quantity forecasted by her. No one even told me I could only order what I had 'forecasted,' even if there was available stock. Turned out the available stock was set for the whole region under Sebastian, and we could only order not more than we have forecasted. Yet, if we order less, we still have pay from our P&L."

"Probably he was just too busy fooling around with his mistress."

"Oh, don't even get me started with that…"

Phoebe then caught up with Ting Ting on all the new gossips, jokes, and stories in the office or shops of her old company. There wasn't much gossip in the office, but the boutiques were the source of many juicy stories in town, especially concerning the rich and famous. Once Ting Ting told her how a sales staff nearly lost her job over the mix-up of addresses of a delivery. The mistress of the famous, wealthy tycoon Mr. Tang visited the shop in Central one afternoon and had a shopping spree when a new sales staff was in the shop to service her. When asked about her home address for delivery, the big spender left the name 'Mrs Tang.' Any experienced staff in the shop knew that she wasn't the real Mrs Tang but the mistress, which the new salesperson had no clue about. Since the payment would go to Mr. Tang's account, the staff didn't question it, and arranged all the purchases to be delivered to address listed under the real Mrs. Tang.

Luckily, Ting Ting had implemented a policy a while ago that all ready-to-wear purchases by VIPs had to go through her before delivery was made. She wanted to make sure no two celebrities or super rich's would end up buying the same piece of clothing that they would find themselves wearing the same time at a public event. Often Ting Ting would advise the clients who had not received the clothes and asked if they would like something else so that she could assure them no one would be wearing the same piece. That also helped the shop to upsell many slow-moving expensive pieces. In the end, Ting Ting managed to stop the shop delivering the purchases by Mr. Tang's mistress to Mrs Tang, which included many beautiful clothes that were three sizes smaller than the authentic Mrs Tang could fit in.

Phoebe found all these stories amusing and entertaining. It was almost like the Chinese drama series she watched on television. She never shared with anyone that her favourite language was Chinese, and she was an addict of Chinese TV drama. She wasn't sure if it was because Mandarin was what she listened to on a daily basis since she was a little girl, because her father hired a Chinese nanny to care for her when he and Claire fulfilled their diplomatic roles.

Phoebe met Aimee during one of her father's tour to the Far East when she was only three years old. They were visiting a high school in the province of Xian, where the famed Terra Cotta Army was buried. Phoebe and Aimee bonded on the spot. After chatting with Aimee, and envisioning that China would be the future, the idea came to Johnathan to ask her if she would like to be Phoebe's nanny or governess; a job that would take a schoolteacher in rural China twenty-five years ago to travel around the world. Aimee said yes without hesitations. It took a while to process her documents, but it all went smoothly, thanks to Johnathan's status and his in-the-know of the immigration process.

So, Phoebe grew up learning the Chinese language as well as the culture. They loved watching Chinese TV dramas together whenever her parents had to entertain in the evening - a habit or addiction Phoebe still had even after she moved away from home.

Phoebe was also a huge fan of Mandarin love songs. She was amazed by how reserved Chinese could be in conversations but so expressive in melodies. Thanks to the Mandarin pop love songs, she had her refuge whenever she found herself heartbroken, instead of turning to a big bucket of Ben & Jerry's. Even after two years of her break-up with Rayan, Phoebe's heart was still not in one piece. She thought she'd found Mr. Right and fell head to toe in love with the man she met at a diplomatic dinner hosted by her father. She rarely enjoyed those dinner parties as most of the time, the guests were at least twenty years older than she was. Then, especially after she started her career in the luxury brands, she found herself being judged that she did not follow in her father's footsteps or work for a certain non-profit, save-the-world organisation. Phoebe just wanted to be a normal girl who followed the path that fate showed her, just like how she met her boss Priscilla in Buenos Aires and joined Maison H.

A few years ago, her mother Claire went through menopause and struggled a great deal. She could no longer fulfil a diplomat wife's role in hosting with ease and grace. So both Johnathan and Claire agreed that she should take a 'sabbatical' from her state duties, and focus on her own well-being instead. During those challenging days, Johnathan tried to push back the entertaining events or Phoebe would step in and be the hostess while telling their guests that Claire had unfortunately caught a bad bug.

Rayan was among one of the guests during a dinner hosted by her father at his last post in Thailand. Phoebe loved Thai food, its people, and its beaches. Its close proximity to Hong Kong and the fact that Maison H just recently opened a new store at the new airport in Bangkok made it very easy for her to tag a visit to her parents along with her business trip there, close to the date that Johnathan needed her. Bangkok held a trade conference to promote trade between Thailand and the Middle East. Johnathan took the occasion and invited the delegates to the American Embassy for a dinner ball. Phoebe had been seated next to Rayan.

Rayan was a dashingly handsome man in his thirties who came from a powerful family, who had a close tie to the Hashemite Court. Rayan was an architect, and his family was in the construction business that had a majority market share in Jordan's infrastructure. Phoebe always thought the men and women in the Middle East were the most beautiful people in the world. Rayan was not only that, he was also worldly, smart, funny, attentive, and charming when he wanted to be. He carried the charisma and manner of a gentleman. Although he was mainly based in Amman to help look after his family business, he still spoke with a strong English accent he'd picked up back during his boarding school years in the UK.

It was love at first sight for both Phoebe and Rayan. They spent the weekend together after the dinner at the embassy. They lived miles apart but vowed to make an effort to fly to different places to meet up.

Since Rayan's businesses were mainly Middle Eastern based, it was Phoebe who flew more to where Rayan was to see him. Luckily, there was a direct flight between Bangkok and Amman, the capital of Jordan. Once a month, Phoebe would arrange her work trip at the end of the week to Bangkok, catch up with her parents, then take a late-night flight on Friday that would fly her to Amman to spend the weekend with Rayan. Whenever there was a long weekend or a longer work break, the couple would travel in the region and Rayan would show Phoebe the most amazing parts of Jordan. Rayan took Phoebe diving in Aqaba, exploring Petra and to a very romantic luxury camping trip in the Wadi Rum. While under the stars in the Valley of Moon, Phoebe felt that she could spend the rest of her life with him.

Phoebe thought things were going well between her and Rayan and didn't mind the exhaustive trips she had to make to spend time with him. Therefore, when she read the news on the Internet that Rayan was going to marry a niece of the Queen of Jordan, Phoebe started the habit to pay extra attention to the news in the Middle East so to educate herself while fantasizing one day she would live there happily ever after with Rayan. For a brief moment, she checked whether it was a prank or Rayan had a twin brother that she didn't know of. However, later that evening she received a call from Rayan, who'd obviously caught wind that the engagement was already all over the media.

"I am so sorry Phoebe, I wanted to tell you in person. I did not expect the story to be out that soon."

"You are worried about how the story leaked out?! How about the actual story behind the story that we had been dating for over a year and you said you loved me, and now that you are going to marry another woman?" After the initial denial of what she had learnt, Phoebe felt outraged by Rayan's betrayal.

"Listen to me, Phoebe, I do love you, very, very much, and I do not love my fiancée. But I have to marry her out of obligation. It does not mean that things have to change between us."

"Are you kidding me? Why are you marrying someone you do not love? I thought you were educated overseas and are all modern and western. And you are suggesting to me to stay in the relationship as your mistress?!"

"Love and obligation are two very different things where I come from. My father's ailing health means I will have to take over the business soon. I am going to be the head of the family as well as its business. The only way I can have the respect from our other family members and that of our business partner, is to have a family myself. My fiancée is from a very connected family and will be good for our business. Not only that, my parents would have never allowed me to marry a foreigner, least of all an American girl."

"Sorry, I don't think I can be anyone's mistress, least of all yours, while knowing that you are married to another woman who will become the mother of your children. Let's stop it now before it becomes even more painful for me, if not for us."

"I am very sorry Phoebe; we have to look at the bigger picture…"

Phoebe could not believe the phone conversation she just had with Rayan. Her boyfriend, who she thought was serious about her turned out to have treated her as a fling before he had to settle down for the 'bigger picture.' All her life, she thought boys were intimidated by who she was, the daughter of a well-known diplomat. She had never in her wildest imagination thought that she would be looked down upon for what she was - that she was not good enough. It only added insults to the heartbreak.

Phoebe took the following week off work to nurse her broken heart. She listened to the Mandarin love songs all day long; her favourite singer Jay Chou's hit songs one after another, and ordered take away.

Ting Ting finally intervened. She went to Phoebe's apartment. First, she ordered her to take a shower and wash her hair, and then she took her out. Since Phoebe did not want to see anyone, they went to karaoke, and in the privacy of the sound-proof room, they sang their hearts out with songs like 'Someone Like You,' 'Goodbye, My Lover,' and ended with singing at the top of their lungs to Katy Perry's 'Roar.' Although Ting Ting felt gutted for Phoebe, she had witnessed enough heartbreaks growing up with her extended family members. Many knots were tied between rich and powerful families for business advantage. The financially intended unions resulted in countless unhappy marriages, or husbands and wives leading different lives and acceptance that their spouses had affairs in return for blind eyes with themselves doing the same.

Chapter Forty-Six

Phoebe could not believe one of her first assignments at Vuitton Beauty was to destroy products. Due to some document mess up by one of the operators, a shipment of the very first Vuitton fragrance could not go through custom. The tax-free area, also called the bonded area, was a very complex and sensitive zone. There were rules to get the products in, and there were even more rules to get the products out or to sell them. There were occasions when nothing could be done to get the products onto shelves, and they were stuck within the bonded area. The brands that did not wish the products fall into the hands of greedy officers, with the products ending up on the street or in a parallel market, would request to destroy the products on site. Although Phoebe had heard of such practices during her five years working for Maison H travel retail, it did not prepare her at all when she had to witness the process and sign the documents that the items had been destroyed. But, it was a difficult choice that the vendors had to make from time to time. The parallel market was rampant, resulting from operators or owners of stock relieving their heavy inventory that they purchased either based on being overconfident with the market and products, or simply from pressure by the vendors, the brands themselves, with a huge discount to cosmetic boutiques on high streets that did not have direct dealings with the brands themselves. Also, recently operators were facing pressure from the authority to control 'Daigou,' shopping tourism from a country that was of a lower retail price or tax and resold to customers who would have paid more to get the same product. The previous high forecasts in sales took a bad hit, which resulted in large inventories with coverage of tens of months.

"Oh God, please forgive my sins." Rarely going to church, at this moment Phoebe found herself praying for forgiveness every time she saw the hammer down to break the perfume bottles by the custom officers. Two long, frightening hours later, after making sure all two hundred and fifty bottles of perfectly fine perfume to be totally and utterly destroyed in front of her eyes as well as her hearing, she was alright and her conscience was still intact, she left the bonded area hoping that it would be the last time she had to witness something as soul-destroying as this.

On her way to board her next flight to meet her operators there, Phoebe met Daisy, who was her counterpart for a brand that was famous for their nail polishes. Phoebe told Daisy what happened just now, to explain the reason why she smelled like she had just bathed in pure perfume – while making a mental note to herself to wear a biochemical full body suit if in any unfortunate event that she had to do something unpleasant like that, again.

"Wait until you have to destroy nail polish! I don't know which idiot had messed up, but I have done it twice in the past eighteen months since I worked for the brand. The pool of different nail colours mixed together, and the pungent chemical smells were enough to put me off mani-pedis for six months. Me! I joined my company because I loved nail art!"

Phoebe knew that even though Daisy complained a lot about her job, she loved the fact that she got to spend a week or two on a luxury yacht few times a year at her clients' expense since she switched jobs. Luxury yachts that travelled around the world fell under travel retail's net as it was a duty free-zone. Daisy's company supplied nail art and spa products. As a qualified beauty therapist herself, she went aboard different cruise lines to train staff at the spa on the new products, and most importantly, on how to link sell to maximize each ticket sale. Guests staying on the cruise had all the time in the world and often wanted to look their best either in their bikinis or dinner dresses. Daisy worked only four hours a day training staff and selling products directly to customers herself. The goal was to show the cruise company the potential of revenue the spa and related retail products could bring them. She usually did an excellent job, which guaranteed her being invited back every now and then.

Phoebe caught up with Daisy, who knew all gossip in the industry. There were the latest tender wars between two major operators at one of the busiest airports in Europe, while another operator had received warnings and was under investigation for keeping their eyes closed and helping Daigou, or shuttle traders in China, to buy more than each individual to bring back to boost their sales… An hour later they parted ways to board their respective flights. Phoebe recalled all the stories that Daisy told her, and thought to herself that although it was a tiring job which involved travelling all the time, there was never a dull moment in travel retail.

It was also full of characters in the business, and Veronica was one of them. Phoebe loved Veronica. They were at the opposite ends of the spectrum from each other While Phoebe was tall and slender, Veronica was petite and round. Phoebe was elegant and soft-spoken, Veronica was wild and loud. Veronica was such a character that Phoebe found her amusing, and enjoyed every moment working alongside with her when Veronica was handling over the Greater China accounts to her for LV Beauty. She once wondered if Veronica was from a mafia family for she talked about the cosmetics business like she was dealing drugs.

'Don't start a turf war unless it matters;' 'Talk to the chief's right-hand lady first, she was the real deal;' 'Don't touch their people. Sometimes it's easier to hire and train from fresh;' 'Pay up or no supply.' Phoebe wondered if anyone who did not know they were with luxury brands would think that they were in some shady business together.

"So, do you know which brand they are going to transfer you to after you finish with Vuitton Beauty?" Phoebe asked Veronica about her next move as she was only on loan to help to get Vuitton Beauty started, and before that she was on sabbatical.

"I'll find out in a couple of weeks, once I'm done with Sebastian. I asked for a non-French brand or at least working for a non-French boss. Can't stand the frogs."

"I am going to miss you." Phoebe couldn't believe she would ever say that, given how intimated she was by Veronica at the beginning. Yet, Phoebe looked up to her and thought she needed some Veronica in herself in order to survive in Vuitton house and the ever-competitive fragrance and cosmetics sector.

"You do know that I am likely to stay in the same building, having the same clients, and for frog's sake, we are going to sell the same products."

"What do you mean selling the same products?" Considering she was going to sell Vuitton Beauty, it would not be possible for Veronica to sell something more prestigious than she was.

"You no longer work for a single brand house. It is a multi-brand luxury conglomerate. The same resource is shared among as many brands as possible to lower cost and make the P&L look better. All the brands share the same factory and fruits of the research. The revolutionary anti-aging cream of the top brand will become the best-seller of middle-league brands, then the 'must-have' of a lower-tier brand in two years' time. Same content in different jars."

Working for years at Maison H, it was a given for Phoebe to be loyal to one and only one brand. Given the standard of quality of Maison H, it was a challenge for her already to grow a fondness for another.

At least I won't have to go bankrupt myself trying to buy everything I like, Phoebe thought to herself after listening to Veronica about how the same products would flow from the more expensive ones to the lower end ones. The biggest contrast was Double C, who was the queen in the beauty industry. All operators would invite the brand with a prominent location and space to join their duty-free shop. Few outsiders knew the brand had a sister-brand which targeted teenagers with products produced from the same factory, often along the same production lines until towards the end with the brands' respective packaging.

All this new information made Phoebe reflect on how naïve she had been while working in the cocoon of Maison H. She started to question the true value of luxury products. Did the customers pay for the quality of the products or the fantasy of owning a piece of the brand that was marked on them?

Chapter Forty-Seven

Every year after the Christmas and New Year break, Vuitton Beauty would hold a seminar at a five-star resort somewhere in France outside Paris for all area managers and regional marketing heads to gather, to meet with the directors and product managers. In other words, everyone that contributed to the bottom line would review the past year result as well as preview the new collections for the coming twelve calendar months. Even the employees were told that was to mark the beginning of a new year; Phoebe believed it was because the management could book the resort at the lowest rate possible, right after New Year. Who would want to be in a freezing cold non-skiing resort in the middle of January? Some of Phoebe's die-hard, brand loving colleagues, would drag along suitcases of clothes the size of her own entire wardrobe, to the resort. For them, they needed to have a different outfit from underwear to coats, for every meeting, meal, workshop, and party during the five days and four nights' seminar.

As each of the product managers gave presentations to a stadium of sales and marketing executives of the brand, they wowed the sales teams with the most irresistible lipsticks, the most sensual fragrance, the miraculous anti-aging cream, etc.

The travel retail exclusive item was the product that both the domestic and travel retail marketing team was looking forward to, and it was usually unveiled on the last day of the seminar. The product was a carte blanche for the product design team. The retail margin was not the priority; the objective was to create a weapon that would land the brand on the front cover of inflight magazines, airport billboards, and named as the annual must-have item for both the operators and travellers.

There had been lots of noises over this year's exclusive travel retail product because it was the year when there would be a change of operators at several major international airports, including the Hong Kong International Airport - Phoebe's main area of responsibility. Hence, the management was determined to wow the operators with this star product, hoping that it would help Vuitton Beauty to get the prime locations, along with other satellite brands in the duty-free shops.

To an outsider, who did not know how real estate at the airport worked, the space and locations of how different brands were allocated could be confusing. They might question how a bigger and more popular brand would have less space, in a less prominent location. The reason was very rarely one agent managed a single brand unless it was a very big brand such as Double C or Maison H. Usually an agent would be managing a star brand along with several satellite brands. The agent could then negotiate a better term, space, and locations for the small players based on the power and line up of that year of the agent's star player. Vuitton Beauty was planning to launch in the third quarter of last year, the long anticipation and the novelty effect which would bring a huge success to the launch. Entering a full calendar year, the expectation for the brand was sky high, and the group management demanded a magic wand from the product design team to come up with a star product that would shine and blind the whole cosmetic world.

On the day of the revelation, instead of returning to the seminar stadium, like all had been doing for the past few days, Phoebe and her colleagues were told to get onto the coaches lining up at the entrance of the resort. After a thirty minutes' drive, they got off in front of a warehouse-like building that looked more like a factory than a museum. Indeed, it was a museum that had been converted from an abandoned factory. Yet, it was no ordinary museum. Once Phoebe stepped inside, she could not see any physical exhibits. Instead, they were surrounded by probably over one hundred screens on which the classic paintings like Van Gogh's Midnight in Paris, Monet's Water Lilies… came alive. At one moment, they were among the evening crowd at a brassiere in Paris, the next they were crossing over the Japanese bridge above the lily ponds. It was a digital museum that transformed classics art into revolutionary exhibits.

Suddenly, it was all over, and the hundred screens and moving masterpieces came to a pause and vanished. A spotlight fell on one stand-alone glass showcase in the middle of the hall, hidden under a piece of royal blue velvet cover. Then came the music, and a presentation projected to screens that led the audience to travel back in time, to where the legendary Vuitton brand story began - back to the time when the brand established itself in the fashion and traveling world, with its renowned monogrammed trunks. Then came the present time when its loyal customers had been dreaming of owning makeup that was marked with its logo.

No one would have guessed Vuitton Beauty, the legendary money-printing fashion brand, could have come up with such a product. It was functional, stunning, and simply irresistible. It ticked all the boxes of what an operator would look for on their shelves, in their shop. This one, without any double, would be a total winner.

On the screen, Phoebe witnessed the legendary monogram travel trunk shrinking in size, from its suitcase shrinking to the size of its most desired handbag, then the spotlight moved to the showcase standing in the middle of the hall. Then, the beautiful product manager, Amandine, in her white gloves, removed the royal blue velvet cover.

The revelation stirred so many reactions, exclamations, and emotions among the crowd. Phoebe had to fight her way among all the heads to try to catch a glimpse of the product. It reminded her of a similar scene at the Louvre in the hall where the infamous Mona Lisa was showed case.

"Exusez Moi." Phoebe stretched and ducked her head trying to get a glimpse of the star of the show, and cursed her colleagues under her breath from the domestic market team, THAT was a travel retail EXCLUSIVE product.

Luckily, within seconds, the projection became live again and on the screen came next year's travel retail exclusive product enlarged by multiple times - a vintage look-a-like monogrammed travel trunk in the size of a palm. The opening and closure of the trunk were in the same manner of its trunk size. Inside, there were two compartments. In the front compartment, was a space big enough to slide in a smartphone. In the other compartment, the make-up pouch was designed and divided in a clever way to efficiently carry all the make-up essentials. In the lining between the two compartments was inserted a mirror, in a case that bore the same monogram as the clutch. An eye pencil and brush were positioned at the top of the compartment, followed by five classic eyeshadow colours fitted side by side on the second row. A semi-moist foundation and classic rose blush lined in the middle row. The bottom part was filled with a lipstick and a mascara miniature, both elegantly printed with the brand monogram.

Despite the guideline from the product team that photos were prohibited, few actually followed. How could you resist the temptation to share first-hand images with your team back home the excitement of the coming new products? How could you refuse the enormous boost of negotiating power it would arm you with, with your operators, which would set you for the success of the whole commercial year? In fact, Sebastian went to Phoebe a few times just to remind her to snap plenty of photos, at all angles possible, of this travel retail exclusive make-up clutch. It was essential for her to offer a preview to her clients and to demand as much space and exposure for the year to come.

Before the seminar ended, Phoebe was called into a meeting, and was handed over two winning cards. Amandine showed her two limited editions: the luxurious evening party clutch version and a personalised embossing service, which would be exclusively offered to Phoebe, as a negotiation tool. Her only mission was to get the most exposure at the airports in her area of responsibility, especially at those where there would be change hands of operators next year.

Chapter Forty-Eight

Upon Phoebe's return to Asia, the road-show to wow her operators with this star launch was beyond smooth - it was phenomenal. She could basically name her terms with the Vuitton travel retail exclusive make-up clutch. Phoebe secured amazing exposures and prime spots opportunities for the eighteen months to come. The icing on her cake of success was landing the cover of the November-December Pacific Airline inflight magazine, who welcomed her proposal of a personalised embossing service for the home delivery programme with open arms. Advertisers JC-Décor also offered her an incredible discount to feature the star product on a massive billboard on the highway to the airport. It would be impossible for visitors in and out of Hong Kong to miss the It make-up clutch.

After the whirlwind roadshow that ended with triumph, Phoebe flew to Beijing to be with her parents. It was the Chinese New Year holiday in which Phoebe enjoyed time off in Hong Kong as well. Her parents invited her to stay in Beijing where it was more festive, as there were still lots of fireworks and firecrackers blowing up around the city during the festival. Alex was going to be off as well and would fly to Beijing to meet up with Phoebe. Phoebe decided to invite Alex to experience the celebrations in Beijing together with her parents.

Johnathan booked a table at one of the family's favourite restaurants, TRB Hutong. It was a French-Chinese fusion restaurant set up in one of the converted houses in Hu Tong, where it was once filled with traditional Chinese houses in which several generations lived together under the same roof. The design of the restaurant preserved lots of characters of the original architecture of the building. Added in the contemporary Chinese sculptures and artworks, the set-up was a fusion of modern and tradition, and at the same time very chic and elegant. Every time the family dined there, Phoebe was blown away by how stunning the design of the restaurant was. With the temperature at -20 degrees Celsius, the courtyard had an added frozen beauty.

Phoebe was a big fan of these Hu Tong courtyard houses; therefore, Alex booked himself a room in a boutique hotel converted from such homes. Although Phoebe's parents were open-minded and welcoming, Alex never assumed an invitation to stay in their house out of respect for Phoebe, which both Claire and Johnathan appreciated.

The dinner was very enjoyable, and before the end of it, Phoebe's parents invited Alex to visit them again during his stay in Beijing, with Claire telling him he was forbidden to stay anywhere except at their house next time he came to Beijing.

"Alex! What a coincidence!"

A tall man in his late thirties stopped by their table, greeting Alex. His hair was of sandy chestnut shade. Phoebe thought he looked very dandy and full of charisma. Despite his size, he was agile and moved with elegance. Alex stood up from the table and embraced him. He introduced the gentleman to everyone as Daniel, a friend from Shanghai. Daniel listened to Alex introducing Phoebe and her parents with interest. He told them it was a real pleasure to meet them, and he had been invited by one of his clients to spend Chinese New Year in Beijing to experience the celebrations in the capital then fly to Harbin afterward to ski. Harbin was famous for its ski resorts in China. Its annual International Ice and Snow Sculpture Festival, according to his clients, was a must-see for everyone.

Soon after their encounter with Daniel, they left the restaurant and went back to Claire and Johnathan's house for a drink. Phoebe helped Claire choose some dresses for her coming events while having girl talks, while Alex bonded with Johnathan over a glass of his favourite whisky.

"Honey, you look very happy with Alex. Both daddy and I are very pleased for you. We like him. Any wedding plans yet?" Claire teased Phoebe while she tried on a cheongsam she'd had a renowned tailor in Beijing to tailor-make for her. The dress hung perfectly on Claire's slender figure. The silk was soft and divine. Purple chrysanthemums were embroidered all over the dark green cheongsam, which was of the same shade as Claire's eyes. Claire decided on the dress for an upcoming important function to go with Johnathan.

"Mum! I like him, too. But we are nowhere near there yet. We have yet to survive the long distance relationship. Your dress is stunning! Looks like you have found the perfect tailor for Beijing." Phoebe admired her mother's dress and wanted to shift the topic away from wedding and baby talks. Since she was their only child, her parents had been worried about her love life after she had turned thirty. As it was the first time she brought a boyfriend home since college, and both she and Johnathan were very fond of Alex, Claire had been holding her breath for some major development between the two love-birds.

"Who is this, Daniel? I have never heard of you mentioning him," Phoebe asked Alex upon their return to his hotel room, after a long evening at the restaurant then her parents' house. Alex told Phoebe that he met Daniel at a fundraising event for his firm. They bonded over being the only two young Englishmen at the event.

"Daniel is three years older than me. He went to Cambridge while I to Oxford. As you can tell from his build, he was in the Rugby Team; apparently, he was very good at it and was the team captain. I was too much into rowing and paid no attention to anything else."

"He sounds like an American, and with his size, I wanted to ask which college team he played football, American football, for."

"He told me he went to Harvard Business School after Cambridge and pretty much stayed in New York to work in Finance ever since. He moved to Shanghai two years ago to help his company set up a China office there. He divides his time between Shanghai and Beijing as most of the important relationships with the government officials have to be built here. Our business can benefit from each other's contacts. And he's cool, I like him, so we hang out a lot when we are both in Shanghai."

"Well, I am glad that you are hanging with him instead of the gorgeous Shanghainese girls."

"How about YOU be my Shanghai girl tonight? I'm going to close my eyes, and you can speak Mandarin to me…" Alex swept Phoebe off the floor, brought her over to their king-size bed and turned the light off.

While in the room of another hotel in the city, Daniel could not believe his luck of running into Alex and getting introduced to his girlfriend Phoebe and her diplomat father. Wheels started to rotate in his head, and he wondered how he could profit from such discovery.

Chapter Forty-Nine

"Look at your smug face, what's going on?" Daniel found Alex grinning to himself when he arrived at the cocktail bar one evening. They were going to discuss some potential deals they could hammer out together for the respective firms they worked for.

Alex wanted to keep it a secret but could hardly suppress his grins all evening. After a few pushes, Alex finally confided to Daniel that he was going to propose to Phoebe next time they saw each other when they celebrated their first anniversary. He'd just put down a deposit for a special engagement ring to be tailor-made for her.

"Congratulations! More to celebrate! We are going to nail this deal, and you are going to have a fiancée before the end of the year."

"Cheers, it may sound too soon to you as we've only been seeing each other for about a year, but I knew she's the one after a few dates. Now we live apart in two cities, I want to put a ring on her to make it official, then we can have some planning for the future."

"To the future!" Daniel cheered to Alex and signalled the bartender for another round of drinks.

Alex had everything planned for a romantic proposal. He could hardly wait for three weeks to pass before they saw each other again. He had to leave for Tanzania in three days, to climb the Kilimanjaro with several of his university friends. One of them was getting married, and they were doing this instead of having a silly, get-drunk stag weekend. It was on his friend's to-do-list before tying the knot. Imagining his wedding day with Phoebe, Alex thought it was perfect timing to do the iconic climb for him, too.

While Daniel, after hearing Alex's plan to propose to Phoebe and learning he was leaving in the next few days for a long trip, made a few calls, and set his plan in motion to give a big surprise for Alex as his engagement present.

Chapter Fifty

Phoebe looked at her watch which said 8:45 am. The traffic was terrible this morning. There must be some accident ahead on the road that made the cars move at the speed of a snail. Phoebe blamed herself for being lazy and choosing the bus over the subway. The bus terminal was right by her building, so it guaranteed her a seat, but the subway guaranteed a traffic-free journey. Phoebe sent a quick message to Sebastian to apologise that she was running late - could be more than thirty minutes as she estimated looking at the traffic condition. It was late even to the French standard. Nearly forty-five minutes later, she was getting off the bus, but had not heard back from Sebastian. It was Friday, so he was probably coming in a bit late himself that he couldn't care less.

Entering the office, Phoebe could feel something was off but couldn't pinpoint what it was. She was surprised to find all her colleagues at their desks already; unusual for a Friday morning when usually everyone would be chatting and sharing his or her weekend plans. Even stranger was that Phoebe found her colleagues avoiding making eye contacts with her. She had not bonded with everyone yet, but at least she believed she was on a friendly term with everyone. Lily, Sebastian's personal assistant, went to her office just as she put her bag by her desk and told her that her boss was expecting her in his office.

As Phoebe entered Sebastian's office, she was immediately attacked by clouds of cigarette smell.

Damn the French, thought Phoebe and wondered how Sebastian managed to disarm the smoke detector in his room.

After adjusting her breath to the cigarette smell, Sebastian gestured her to sit down. Phoebe guessed there must have been some bad results from other areas that stressed him out, as last she checked, her area was doing brilliantly, and he was so thrilled to learn about the performance of her area, that he'd signed off her extended Easter break.

"Phoebe, I need you to hand over your laptop, blackberry, office pass, and clear your desk. You are to be terminated with immediate effect. Lily will oversee your departure; I don't think security is necessary. HR will be in touch for your pay cheque this month."

"Excuse me? Is this a joke? April fools was last week." Phoebe was shocked to hear what Sebastian just said. To be terminated without notice meant only one thing - an employee had committed a crime, or for serious misconduct, which she was quite sure she had not done anything as such.

"Phoebe, we had high hopes for you and were thinking of grooming you to take over my position once my time here was over. What you did was disgraceful and selfish. You let all of us down."

"Sebastian, I have no idea what you are talking about..."

Sebastian then turned his laptop around so that Phoebe could see what was on the screen. At first glance, Phoebe thought she saw a Vuitton exclusive travel retail make-up clutch on a few snapshots, a high street online boutique as well as night markets in China and South-East Asia. On a closer look, it was not the actual Vuitton make-up clutch she saw at the seminar but a look-alike, a very close copy. They were spread across an article headlined *'Copy of Vuitton's Beauty Secret Out Before Launch, Chinese Factory Ahead of Brand to Enjoy the Profit.'* Shocked to see China was already churning out a copy nearly half a year before the launch, a sub-headline further down the article drew her attention. *'Diplomat's Daughter Suspected of Selling Commercial Secret to Greedy Merchants.'*

Phoebe looked around the room, hoping to have someone jump out and tell her it was just a bad joke. Then she saw a photo of the Vuitton travel retail exclusive make-up clutch, edited by her with a heart art sticker, signed with her name and sent to Alex, after she shared with him that she had got a winner for the financial year to come when she was away at the conference. That photo was pinned on the idea board in a meeting room where the 'undercover reporter' managed to take a snap. Then there was another photo showing Johnathan shaking hands with the owners of that factory with Phoebe standing next to him. Phoebe could not believe what she saw. She sat frozen in the seat across Sebastian.

Then everything was a blur: how Lily helped her clear her desk, and asked her gently to hand over the company possessions, namely, her blackberry, office pass, and company credit card. Her laptop was to be left behind on her desk. Carrying a box of her personal belonging, she was escorted out of the office - witnessed by her colleagues and people in the building lobby. Phoebe could sense some flashes which told her there were some nosy people taking shots of her. She was already in auto-mode, so she did not react or object.

Back at her apartment, she dropped her box down by the dining table, let her body fall onto the sofa, closed her eyes, and let her tears flow freely down her face. She was still in shock and had to process what had just happened. During the taxi journey home, she thought back the scenario in Sebastian's office, the images on his screen, and hoped it was just a nightmare. There was only one person who had access to the picture printed in the media - Alex. Phoebe was first in denial, as she would not believe Alex would do something like that to her.

She took out her phone and called Alex. He'd arrived in Tanzania last night. Everything sounded normal when they were last on the phone. He told her he missed her, and he would make up the time of him being away with his friends instead of her when he came back, and that he had a big surprise for her. A big surprise it was.

The scandal did not stop after she was fired. Before the end of the day, she received a call from her father that he had been pressured to resign due to the accusation that he was the one who connected Phoebe with the copycat manufacturer. All luxury brands sent an individual letter to their respective American Ambassador to express their anger. Not only the brands in Europe but those in the US also joined in force to condemn Johnathan's connection to the scandal. They all signed a unified petition to pressure Jonathan to be removed from the diplomatic service. The US government had recently launched a trade war against most nations, so everyone took advantage of the incident to turn it into a scandal and to put pressure onto the administration.

Phoebe felt sick to her stomach after the call with her father. Like her, Johnathan was confused and felt helpless. They had no idea where the accusations came from. The whole incident was apparently staged, yet neither Phoebe nor Johnathan saw it coming at all, so they barely had time to react.

***

After the initial investigations by the Embassy within days after the news decided there had been no link that either Johnathan or Phoebe could have benefited in any way from the trade leak, it issued a statement to clear Johnathan's name. However, to calm things down and not to have a full-on confrontation with China and Europe where most of the luxury brands had their headquarters, Johnathan was advised to opt for early retirement. Vuitton Beauty made no comment on the new development. To them and the industry, the damage was done, and someone had to take the blame - Phoebe's career was over.

Meanwhile, Phoebe failed to get in touch with Alex. She had many questions that she wanted to demand answers from him. Day after day she tried and still no signs of Alex. Phoebe started to entertain the idea that Alex could be behind the set-up, although she could not understand why especially after receiving a message from Daniel that read:

'Hi Phoebe, I am so sorry to read about what happened. I cannot imagine Alex could sell you out, but I'm afraid he might have a part in it. I should have thought something was not right when he called me to bid farewell, saying he finished what he had to do in Asia and that was time for him to move on… Take care of yourself, Daniel.'

Phoebe read Daniel's message several times, then recalled how eager he was, and not entirely his style, when Alex asked her to convince her father to add two business acquaintances to the guest list of the annual Embassy dinner ball that her father hosted a couple of months earlier. It was a request at short notice, and Phoebe insisted to her father, as she sensed that it was important to Alex. As for Johnathan, he was glad that Phoebe would attend the ball with Alex and believed China was a location of low-security risk, hence he waived a few security protocols to add the two guests requested by Phoebe at the last minute. Johnathan assumed the two guests were Phoebe's clients in the Travel Retail Business and were proper.

As it turned out, the two merchants had a dodgy trade history. The breach of protocol was the official reason to call for Johnathan's immediate departure from his post. He was offered to have a clean record if he was willing to take early retirement. Johnathan took the offer as the last thing he wanted was to leave a stain on the impeccable family history in the diplomatic service for his beloved country.

Confusion turned to anger. Phoebe consumed all her resources to try to get in touch with Alex. Then a realisation dawned on her that she did not really know anyone related to Alex apart from Daniel and several of his friends in Hong Kong. All his friends in Hong Kong had not heard from Alex since he left for Kilimanjaro. Alex had invited her to go back to the UK with him the coming Christmas as he wanted to introduce her to his family, but for the time being, Phoebe knew no one who was related to Alex.

Chapter Fifty-One

As soon as Alex bid farewell to his friends and headed to the airport to catch a flight to Hong Kong, Alex turned his phone on to get in touch in Phoebe. His friend Ben who was getting married insisted everyone to hand in their smartphones and blackberries before their stag trip, so they could focus on having a good time and not be disturbed by work calls or girlfriends and wives. Alex cursed Ben for such a tyrannical idea, but he still managed to compose a message to explain that to Phoebe and promised to get in touch as soon as his phone was released. Only now he found that the message did not get sent in time before Ben turned everyone's phone off including his.

"Bloody hell, Ben, I hate you!" shouted Alex to nobody and called Phoebe right away.

"The number you have called is not valid..." Alex kept hearing the same message instead of Phoebe's voice answering his calls. He checked the number against the many messages he had exchanged with Phoebe and tried to dial as a fresh number, the same number but nothing. He tried again and again until he boarded his plane and settled in his seat. Alex was without doubt that Phoebe must be fuming with him because he'd been out of touch for more than two weeks. He started to panic and scrolled down his contacts. Relived, he found Phoebe's best friend Ting Ting's number. He called Ting Ting, who picked up the phone after two rings and screamed into his ears.

"Alex, you are in big trouble!"

"I know Ting Ting, I can explain, it was all Ben's fault. I need to talk to Phoebe right away."

"Please turn off your phone, the plane is going to take off."

Alex told Ting Ting he had to hang up and that he was flying to Hong Kong and needed to see Phoebe as soon as he arrived.

"Sorry Alex, Phoebe has left Hong Kong, and I am not allowed to tell you where she is."

"Please turn off the phone; otherwise, we will have to ask you to get off the plane."

Alex had no choice but to comply. He did not understand what was going on. It was his bad not to be in touch for more than two weeks - but to leave town and her job behind? What had happened in the sixteen days when he was conquering the highest mountain in Africa? He was planning to take Phoebe to the Maldives and to propose to her when they went sailing at sunset. Now the plan sounded more like a fantasy when he didn't even know where his fiancée-to-be was.

Chapter Fifty-Two

Heartbroken, humiliated, and drowning with guilt for her father's scandalous and forced early retirement, Phoebe packed her bags and sublet her apartment. The subletting tenant did not have her own furniture and appliances, so Phoebe did not have to store them or sell them. The tenant also agreed to let her store her belongings in a spare cupboard until she figured out her long-term plan or the lease of the apartment was due. Phoebe logged into her Pacific Loyal Club account and redeemed a business class one-way ticket to Bali with the mileages she had accumulated from her frequent business travels. Bali was labelled as the island of healing – it sounded like the perfect place for her current physical and emotional states. She then called a couple of retreats she had come across during her business trips to the island and asked for availability of a room.

Upon arrival in Bali, Phoebe checked herself into the yoga retreat where there was still one room available. She planned to practice yoga, read, and lead a raw food diet to restore her physical fitness, and meditate to restore her sanity. She rose with the sun every morning and meditated for an hour together with other guests. Then she would sign up for several yoga classes during the day while allowing herself to be pampered a couple times a week with a massage by the in-house masseuse.

Phoebe witnessed groups of guests coming and going, including those who arrived with baggage and dark clouds surrounding them but leaving with a lightened heart and spirit. One day, one of the gurus at the retreat invited her to enrol in the yoga teacher training certificate course. She signed up without hesitation. At the end of the three weeks training, Phoebe was certified to teach yoga. She became friends with her masseuse Madya, which meant middle child in Balinese, who asked Phoebe one day if she was interested in learning the healing business. Phoebe then followed Madya to her Ayurvedic spa school every afternoon, after a vigorous morning of yoga practice, to learn different massage techniques, aromatherapy, and Ayurveda therapies, the wisdom of attaining balance in dosha.

Phoebe promised Ting Ting to touch base with her once a week to let her know that she was still alive and possibly when she was coming back. From Ting Ting, it sounded like there had not been much change to the outside world, but the glamourous luxury corporate world seemed light years ago to Phoebe. Every week she felt she was transforming into a new person and was evolving into someone who knew what she wanted. Phoebe still had not yet figured out her purpose in life, although she was sure that was not the life she wanted to return to.

One of Phoebe's mentors at the retreat came from a very interesting background. He had the name and look of a porn star, but in fact, he was a self-made business mogul, a philanthropist, a yogi, and a tree hugger. Richard Sampson had met Phoebe's father before, and after learning what happened to her in the past few months, he encouraged Phoebe to take up a temporary teaching position at the Bali Eco-School which he founded, while she figured out what she wanted to do and where she wanted to go next.

Chapter Fifty-Three

Ting Ting could hardly hold back her tears when she dropped Phoebe at the airport when she left for Bali. Phoebe made Ting Ting swear that she was not going to tell a soul where she was heading to; only Ting Ting and her parents knew she was leaving Hong Kong for Bali. Phoebe told Ting Ting she had to be alone and would find her way back when she was ready - if she was ever ready. Ting Ting couldn't really blame her for wanting to run away, her career was totally ruined. Her father's life long and spotless diplomatic career was also forced to cease as collateral damage, and not to speak of, she was betrayed by the love of her life.

Ting Ting rang up Aunty Diane and asked her for the contact of her private investigator. All taitai's in every big, prominent family of Hong Kong had a handful of private investigators on their payrolls. Each private investigator had an expertise in certain areas, such as finding out if a husband was cheating on his wife and at times helping end the extramarital affairs discreetly. If they ended up having divorces, there would be private investigators specialised in digging out the husbands' hidden wealth around the world. Other areas that were not as incriminating but equally important was to investigate which designer a certain socialite was going to use in a coming ball or charity event, so to avoid clashing in ball gowns with anyone, which would be gossiped over for years to come at high-tea tables.

The private investigator Aunty Diane referred to Ting Ting was Frank, because of his connections in China, after she shared with her Phoebe's very unfortunate story. Two weeks later, Frank came back to

Ting Ting with some initial findings. Frank dug into Alex's personal background, career history, personal life, parents' profile, etc. and stumbled into something when he was looking into Alex's academic history. Both Alex and Daniel were from the elite school league in the U.K. While Alex graduated from Oxford University, Daniel graduated from its adversary Cambridge University, with three years apart as Alex was a few years younger than Daniel. Interestingly, both were in their respective school rowing teams. Both universities were famous for their rowing teams and how fierce the competition between the two universities to be the rowing champion. Frank checked in with Ting Ting to confirm if a guy named Matthew Scott rang any bell to her or Phoebe.

"Well, Phoebe is out of touch, as you know, and I do not want to call Alex until I find out more to decide if he is guilty in the whole scandal. So tell me what you've got."

"This Matthew Scott could be the link connecting all the dots to the question mark here. As he is the only brother of Daniel Scott, Alex's supposed best buddy in China."

"I remember this Daniel, I met him once when both he and Alex came back to Hong Kong for some business dinner. Keep going."

"Hmm, the question mark here is why they were buddies, given the history they had back in the UK."

"What are you talking about? What have you found out?"

It turned out Matthew was in the same year at Cambridge to Alex in Oxford. They both rowed for their colleges. That year, the competition was fierce, and the results were very close. So close, that all technologies and arguments were brought in to determine the winner. In the end, it was decided that Oxford was the winning team. That evening, both teams ended up coincidently at the same pub in the competing town, one for celebrations, while the other team to be numbed by alcohol after losing the race by such a small margin. It all started with only verbal insults and accusations, then one guy pushed another which soon turned out to a full-on fight. The young rowers were all big and pumped up after a long day of racing, while their anger was fuelled by alcohol after a few pints. It was nearly impossible to separate the boys and stop the fight; also, the spectators were enjoying a hell of a show. No one was seriously hurt except for some cuts and bruises. However, Matthew, very unfortunately, stopped a glass bottle which ended up having a big piece cut through its arm. The injury was nothing life-threatening, but it altered his life completely. The injury touched some important nerve, which was irreversible. Matthew was a medical student and was studying to become a surgeon. He was in his last year and was about to start his internship at a hospital in Scotland, which was famous for its orthopaedics surgeries. Not only could Matthew never perform any surgery which he'd studied very hard for, his arm would never be strong enough to row again. Although he was drunk at that time, Matthew was convinced that it was Alex, the leading member of the winning team, who threw the bottle at him. Alex got into legal trouble for a while because of the accusation. However, due to lack of concrete evidence and only with hear-say by some heavily intoxicated young hotheads, the case was finally overturned by Alex's very successful lawyer father.

"So you are telling me that Daniel spent months cosying up with Alex to pay him back a big-time revenge? And my best friend Phoebe, who was unlucky enough to fall for Alex, became the ultimate victim as collateral damage?"

Ting Ting never liked Daniel, even just from one or two evenings hanging out with him when he visited. She thought he had this cunning aura seeping out all around him. What he did to Phoebe was unfair and unforgivable, and poor Alex, who probably was still clueless about what had happened. Ting Ting was glad that she had commissioned Frank to find out why.

"Hurt who you love most, the worst, and most powerful kind of revenge," said Frank, who sounded like he had passed on some wisdom to some of the taitai's whose husband went for a younger woman. There, no wonder all those taitai's hired their own private investigator. Every penny well spent.

Chapter Fifty-Four

Ting Ting was saved by the attendant who threatened to kick Alex off the plane if he did not hang up. Alex asked Ting Ting to meet him at the airport and tell him everything as soon as he got off the plane. Not trusting herself that she would not tell Alex where Phoebe was, Ting Ting turned her phone off afterward to avoid his calls. Instead, she emailed Alex all the articles of the events over the whole saga which were fairly self-explanatory. Ting Ting trusted her own instincts that Alex had nothing to do with Phoebe and her father getting fired. What Frank found out proved her instinct was right, although she had no idea how Alex would be able to get Phoebe back and she regretted that she promised Phoebe not to tell a soul her whereabouts.

Twenty hours later, Alex finally checked himself into the hotel. It was a last-minute booking he did during the brief transit. He saw Ting Ting's email in his Inbox. There were many attachments which at first glance, he didn't understand why they had anything to do with Phoebe running away. Despite desperately needing a shower, Alex fired his laptop up, opened the attached articles from Ting Ting, and read them one by one.

Realisation finally dawned on Alex. Phoebe had been terminated with disgrace by Vuitton Beauty being accused of selling a commercial secret to greedy merchants in China, and it was also implied that Phoebe and the merchants had been introduced by her father who was Consulate General at the American Embassy. Her father was pressured to resign a week later amid the heated scandal. Anger gradually built up within Alex. He hit the desk with his fists numerous times after reading several work-related emails. The few big deals referred to him by Daniel fell apart at the same time, and his firm had lost a significant amount of the set-up cost as results. The counterparts claimed the reason for withdrawing was due to Alex's integrity being in question. His firm had been trying to get in touch with him and asked him to report back to the Hong Kong office. They were sending his replacement to Shanghai the following week, and he was asked to do the handover over in the next few days. Alex immediately called Daniel to try to find out what happened. The number had been disconnected.

Going back to the articles that Ting Ting sent him, all the pictures showed the events all happened after Daniel ran into him having dinner with Phoebe and her parents. He did not understand how it was related, but the first impression told him that Daniel was behind all this. The greedy merchants mentioned on the news were guests requested by Daniel to add onto the guest list at a dinner hosted by Phoebe's father where Alex was also invited. Daniel insisted it was quite important if he wanted to close one of the deals they were working on together.

To give face to their business partner by taking them to a dinner hosted at the American Embassy, Alex recalled how Daniel pushed him to ask Phoebe for the favour. The picture of the 'commercial secret,' the Vuitton travel retail exclusive make-up clutch, was sent to Alex by Phoebe signed with her name and a kiss emoji No wonder, Phoebe disappeared. On the surface, he was the prime suspect of the set-up. From Phoebe's point of view, it could even be Alex who sold the commercial secret and used Phoebe as the scapegoat, with her father as collateral. Only Alex knew that he was innocent. Now the prime suspect had been shifted to Daniel, as he was the only one who could have accessed his phone when they were hanging out. He recalled the final days before he left for Africa that they often ran into 'deal prospects,' who led Alex out of the bar for a chat. He often left his phone on the table after messaging Phoebe. There was a window of several minutes before the phone locked itself.

"Ting Ting, thanks for sending me the articles. It was NOT me. It was my friend Daniel, although I don't understand why he set me up like this." Alex sent a quick email to Ting Ting.

"Hi Alex, I have hired my aunt's private investigator to find out. I will explain to you in person."

While waiting for his meet up with Ting Ting to hear what her aunt's private investigator had found out, Alex wondered how on earth he could win his fiancée-to-be back.

Chapter Fifty-Five

Alex thanked Ting Ting on the phone after she promised to tell him everything she had learnt from Frank. He quickly arranged his flight to Hong Kong. He had been in Singapore the past few weeks working on a financial project for a previous client of his. It was his way to gradually put his career back on track and to stay within a short flight away from Hong Kong, for him to get back to as soon as Ting Ting could dig out something for him.

Alex met Ting Ting at Aunty Diane's house on the Peak. Aunty Diane only agreed to loan Frank to Ting Ting on the condition that she had to share with her all the juicy details of the investigation. There was nothing that Aunty Diane enjoyed more than a dramatic love story that involved betrayal, revenge, and romance. Her aunt also wanted to be involved in the part that would lead to a happy ending. Aunty Diane insisted Ting Ting meet Alex at her house, and she would host teatime - since Aunty Diane offered to pay Frank's bill, which ended up being quite a big number as he had to fly all the way to the UK on business class, and 5-star hotels, to dig out the truth about the root of the revenge.

Upon greeting Alex at the foyer, Ting Ting quickly explained the situation and apologised half-heartedly to Alex about Aunty Diane's nosy involvement. Although, Ting Ting had to admit it was both amusing and entertaining to watch how Aunty Diane's mouth watered when she saw Alex. If Aunty Diane was not so keen to team up with Ting Ting and play cupid to get the two love birds back together, she might have tried to go all over Alex herself.

Alex thanked Ting Ting for what she had done. He greeted Aunty Diane like a gentleman and thanked her profusely for offering her help with the investigation.

"Karma, karma," Aunty Diane sighed dramatically, referring to how Alex's recklessness in his youth had cost him the love of his life.

"After Ting Ting sent me the report, I spoke to my father and a few mates back at uni about the fight in the pub after we won the rowing championship. Daddy did not play dirty to get me out of trouble. A witness later came forward to say that Daniel's brother Matthew was actually injured by a random drunk-head. They first started pushing each other, then it escalated to a fight. Most of us were either drunk or at least not sober, so everyone made up a story. Luckily, the witness was a pregnant woman who was having an after-work drink with her husband before heading home. Since she was not drinking, her statement stood. As soon as Matthew got hit and everything let loose, her husband got her out of the pub and to safety at home. It was only later police found her as a witness during the investigation of Matthew's accusation of me injuring him, that my case was dismissed even before it went to court. Unfortunately, they couldn't find the drunk person who attacked Matthew. The police believed he wasn't a local and could be from anywhere. No one had ever seen him before. Back in the police station, the file was still marked as an unsolved assault. I cannot believe Matthew's families still thought it was me who attacked him, and Daniel decided to play judge and decided his sentence for me."

Ting Ting could tell Aunty Diane was enjoying too much of the story. She insisted both of them to stay for dinner, and lay out a plan in detail, on winning Phoebe's heart back for Alex. She even offered to exhaust her resources to help.

"Sorry Alex, if you want her unlimited resources to help you find Phoebe and win her back, you will have to offer to supply unlimited fantasies and stories for Aunty Diane to tell when she goes to the spa with her friends." Ting Ting patted Alex's shoulders and told him he would have to endure Diane's affection if he wanted to get Phoebe back.

Chapter Fifty-Six

Growing up, Phoebe was very privileged to be able to take up interesting interning positions trying out different innovative projects thanks to who her father was. Yet, teaching at the Eco School was the most eye-opening and inspiring experience to date for her. The school was funded by a billionaire and a visionary, Richard Sampson. He also took part in the design as well as the construction of the school building.

The Eco School was constructed with both nature and the future in mind. There were no walls in this school. It was an open space where students, teachers, even parents gathered together to learn to build a sustainable world and future together. Solar panels lined above the roof to collect the sunlight which was converted into electricity for general power usage on the campus. It was perfect for an island that was blessed with plentiful sunny days.

Instead of using traditional wood, the campus was constructed with bamboo. Bamboo, with its tensile stronger than steel and compression better than concrete, would withstand earthquakes better, which was a risk for the Balinese geography. As its tube was hollow and grew at a much faster rate compared to other trees, bamboo was a much more environmentally friendly material, being more sustainable and easier to transport. It wasn't hard to imagine that paper used at such a school would be made of recycled paper. Yet here, the effort went beyond that. All paper consumed at the Eco School was fabricated on site, by students and teachers, from discarded writing paper and packaging mainly from resorts. The surplus was then resold to their paper waste suppliers.

Richard also invested in building on site a small scale water treatment plant to treat the water before relieving it back to nature. The building had been constructed in such a way that water was not usually used only once. For example, water flowing out of basins would be gently treated then recycled for flushing toilets. All cleansing detergents were naturally prepared on site as well such that the water released at the end of the chain would not be contaminated.

Students who attended the school were mostly children of expatriates who had been attracted by the Balinese lifestyles and relocated there, mixed-raced children between foreigners and locals, and also local students who had received scholarships from Richard to attend to the school. Disregarding nationalities and cultures, they were taught entrepreneurial skills as well as the sciences that would equip them to achieve that. One very practical example was that students, teachers, and supporting staff on campus gathered waste oil from restaurants and hotels – which was abundant in Bali - and learnt how to turn it into biofuel that fuelled school coaches to bring students to school and back home every day. In the near future, they would have more than enough and could sell to hotels and resorts to fuel their commuting vehicles on sites.

The Home Economics and Cookery classes happened in the school cafeteria kitchen. Students in the senior year were in charge of meal planning, cooking, and sourcing the ingredients. The school hired certified nutritionists to guide the students to prepare their meal planning, such that the menu each day could meet the nutritional requirements of school kids. Richard, with his vast connections, invited celebrity chefs to be guest lecturers and create occasional excitement among the students. The source of ingredients would be from the farm surrounding the campus. The school offered local farmers free use of land to grow produce, in return for teaching the school students how to grow their own food, organically. After ensuring enough supply to the school cafeteria, the local farmers got to keep the rest of the produce, either for their own consumption or for sale. For the students who were involved in the catering work, their meal fee would be exempted, so they earned their meals through hard work and learnt how to appreciate food.

There were thousands of yoga teachers on Bali island, and the competition to get a teaching position at the prestigious Bali Eco School founded by a businessman who was rich and famous worldwide, was fierce. Phoebe's yoga teaching experience was zero. However, Richard liked the fact that Phoebe had years of training in Krav Maga. Richard asked Phoebe to teach his students, especially the girls, defence skills, balance the practice, and calm their minds with yoga.

Phoebe immensely enjoyed teaching at the eco school. Not only was the campus itself eye-opening. It was simple, yet at the same time ahead of its time. Technologies were implemented in such a way that human activities could be blended with nature in harmony.

On the other hand, Phoebe was in awe by how educated, informed, innovative, respectful, and at the same time entrepreneurial, students were there. In the brief time she taught world history and yoga there, she learnt a great deal from these students. They respected and learned from each other's cultures. Their openness to new ideas and enthusiasm never failed to impress her. The school was grooming citizens of the world and leaders of the future. Time and time again, the line between teacher and students was fused.

Phoebe started to reflect on her decade of work in the luxury world. The amount of unnecessary materials used and then wasted. She recalled the heated discussions she had with Priscilla regarding how the luxury brands handled the out of seasons ready-to-wear items.

"Burn what? I beg your pardon? Burn those beautiful leather jackets that are so smooth as silk and those stunning cashmere pieces?!"

Phoebe could not believe what she had heard. She repeated her question to Priscilla three times, hoping she was going to correct her when Priscila told her those fashion items that could not sell during the season and post-season sale would be incinerated.

"How about selling to the staff? I am sure all of us would like to pay a bit of money to own a piece of a Maison H garment. A little money is better than no money, right? What about the craftsmanship they keep talking about? Isn't being eco-friendly is one of the most important trends?"

"Allor, mademoiselle, you are wrong. To our Finance Controller, selling at a fraction of the price to staff would dramatically drag down the margin." Priscilla explained to Phoebe the rationale behind such wasteful and unforgivable behaviour of burning perfectly fine, retailed at more than 2,000 Euro a piece haute-couture, artisanal creations, for the sake of P&L. Now living and working among a community who cared about the environment, who believed in reuse, reduce waste, and recycle, led her to reflect on the business practice of the industry she was in, as well as her daily consumption behaviour as a customer.

Chapter Fifty-Seven

When Phoebe was not teaching at the Eco School, she continued to learn holistic treatments from Madya. One day, Madya invited Phoebe to spend a weekend in her village with her families. She wanted to show Phoebe their medicinal garden where they grew all the herbs she brought over to the spa school where Phoebe learnt different kinds of therapies.

Phoebe shared a room with Madya's teenager niece, Gede. She was intrigued by foreigners and requested to be her chaperone during her stay in the village. Phoebe brought her a makeup sample gift set she'd saved from her previous cosmetics years. Gede was overwhelmed and danced with joy when she unwrapped the gift - she had never owned anything like that. Phoebe thought she must be joking and asked her where she found the colour to put make-up on her face. Gede then opened the drawer of her dresser and showed Phoebe what she used to colour her face; she did own make-up products, but nothing like what Phoebe had and used daily. All beautifying items that Gede, or any woman in the village owned, were picked up from their farms. Their eyeliner, lipsticks, and blush were extracted from plants in their garden that gave the colours naturally. Gede told her they prepared batches each time, then again when they ran out.

Phoebe was also equally intrigued by the elegant boxes that carried Gede's makeup. Each girl in the village would be gifted a set of beautifully handcrafted bamboo makeup boxes when she reached puberty, to mark the beginning of womanhood. She was moved by such a sweet gesture, and an idea began to blossom in her head.

The idea began to develop throughout her stay with Madya. Every personal care item was produced from their farms or garden organically.

Fruits and plants were dissected for multiple purposes while what little was left would be composted to become organic fertilisers for the soil. Even the peels of an orange or lemon would be zested to be added into the soap or bath salts handmade in the village. Phoebe couldn't find any plastic bottles in the bathroom of her guest room. There was a shampoo soap bar, a bar for washing her body and another one for cleansing her face, with which she was pleasantly surprised by how clean and moisturised her face felt afterward. There was a little jar with some salt mixed with citrus zest and essential oil - the aroma was divine, and her skin was beyond soft after she used it for a body scrub. No wonder everyone smelled so lovely around her. Out of curiosity, Phoebe asked Gede if they even made perfume for themselves, half-jokingly. To her amusement, Gede took Phoebe to meet with her mother the next day, who showed her the art of perfume making.

The perfume there looked very different from what Phoebe used to sell, and the way they were applied were not exactly the same as what she had been taught at work. Gede's mother explained the different pulse points on the body to apply the fragrance for various purposes. Phoebe wondered where else she could apply perfume beyond her wrists and neck. Who would have thought you could apply fragrance on your hair? Gede's mother demonstrated to Phoebe how she sprayed her hairbrush with fragrant oil before she combed her hair. She explained that way her hair would be moisturised at the same time. The fragrance trapped within the hair fibres also ensured the fragrance would stay in for a prolonged period of time; and she claimed that her silky, shiny, and fragrant hair put a spell on Gede's father the first time they met! In the evening after her bath, she would apply it on the pulse points or where the body emits heat to let herself feel more sensual. She giggled while telling Phoebe the best place to apply perfume before going to bed with her boyfriend. That made Phoebe feel sad for a moment, but she quickly pushed away thoughts of Alex, and focused on finding out more on the fragrance-making business.

Since there was no alcohol among the ingredients, except during process to extract the essence, the perfume did not give a burning sensation against the skin, which Phoebe suffered from at the beginning trying to test out all perfumes she had to come across. Gede's mother told her that the base oil was coconut oil or jojoba oil, cold pressed locally. Then different essential oils or essences would be added.

Each lady in the village experimented with different recipes to find the right fragrance for herself, for a number of occasions, including seducing their husbands! The source of fragrances was abundant thanks to the wide variety of botanical life on the island. Frangipani, the iconic flower of Bali, was apparently one of the most popular for its seductive scent!

The abundance of plants allowed the community to extract or distil them into essential oils in their specialised kitchens, which supplied their produce to spas all over the island of Bali. In fact, their essential oils also served as a little clinic for the villages for minor ailments such as minor cuts or stomach upsets. Since over 80% of the Balinese population practised Hinduism, most of them believed in Ayurvedic holistic ideals for general health, in which the principle was to strengthen the body's immunity against disease and illness - the approach was rather restorative than invasive. To them, there was a high medicinal value in their farms and gardens. Phoebe was very intrigued by all those naturally made personal caring products and asked humbly if she could take part in the production and learn more about Ayurveda during her stay with them.

What she learnt from Madya and her community, and from her teaching post at the Eco School Bali, led Phoebe to reflect that she did not have to give up looking good in order to be a tree hugger. On the other hand, she believed cosmetics was gradually destroying the planet in the name of beauty. She also noticed that the beauty approach from her new school of training was to enhance one's natural beauty and promote a healthy glow from within a person, instead of hiding faults as what the mainstream was in the beauty industry. Her new teachers believed one could be beautiful while protecting the environment, as well as being gentle to the skin and faithful to the body.

She remembered how shocked she was when Veronica brought along skincare products that were over four years old to gift to clients. She questioned whether the products would have been expired but was assured by Veronica that there was enough paraben among the ingredients which could give the product another four years of shelf-life.

She went back to Madya's village several times more to learn the natural way to make cosmetics. She also challenged them on the issue of shelf-life and enduring being transported to far destinations. To Phoebe's surprise, Madya and her friends came up with very good suggestions that convinced Phoebe, with some effort and creativity, those challenges could be overcome.

Phoebe brought a wide range of samples as well as a set of make-up boxes to the school. She wanted to discuss with Richard and his team of 'scientists' there to see how they could scale it up, overcoming the shelf-life and transport issues, and eventually turn it into an eco-business. While the scientists were hard at work, Phoebe typed up spreadsheet after spreadsheet, and finally, a business plan that she was pleased with was drummed up. She also prepared a 'look book' that carried at least thirty looks that could be created by the products she had in mind. Although the colours would be from the farm, the looks could not remind the consumers as such. Phoebe took reference of her experience with Vuitton Beauty as well as all the elegant figures she had met in her life to produce looks that were modern, elegant, timeless, youthful, sensual, casual, evening; that would cover a wide range of occasions and impressions, and most importantly, to promote a healthy glow of a woman's face. Finally, thinking she was ready, Phoebe gathered up her courage and showed it to Richard, her mentor. Phoebe very much wanted to hear what he had to say and whether he thought it was a feasible business.

A set of make-up boxes was gifted to Phoebe by the women in the village during her third visit, who'd started to make them after her first stay with them. A butterfly flying around a bush of blossoms was engraved on each of the boxes. They said Phoebe would be that butterfly, ready to take off when the flowers bloomed next time. She was floored by their kindness and believed when her idea was ready to bloom, she would have found her future destiny and be ready to go home.

Phoebe did not hear back from Richard for two weeks. In fact, he was nowhere to be seen. Was her business plan so bad that he could not bring himself to tell her to her face and was avoiding her? As days passed by, Phoebe was filled with bigger and bigger embarrassment, until she finally made peace with it. What was she thinking to pitch her business idea to a legendary entrepreneur? Phoebe told herself that she had still learnt about making cosmetics naturally for the rest of her life, and accepted that nothing would come out of her business plan, nonetheless.

"Phoebe! I've been looking around for you." Richard appeared out of nowhere one day at the campus. It turned out he'd had some emergency to deal with back in the States and had just returned to Bali the evening before.

"I hope you haven't pitched to other people about your natural, zero waste cosmetics business idea yet, because I am in."

"I beg your pardon? You like my business idea?"

"I love it! And I am going to invest in it. You will have my full support - spiritually and financially."

Phoebe could not believe what she heard. She did not expect Richard to put a dollar into it. In her business plan, she was going to launch a campaign on one of the crowdfunding platforms.

"Do that, too. It will help you create noises and get feedback on your project, and if you manage to raise more funds, even better." Richard encouraged Phoebe to go with what she had in her business plan, too.

"It is a very solid business plan, accompanied by a very revolutionary product. They trained you well at the luxury houses."

"I could not have had such an idea if I had never come here. You opened my eyes and a world of opportunities for me, Richard. Whether the idea succeeds or not, I am forever grateful." And Phoebe was glad that she'd decided to go back to Bali - where she was finally healed, both physically and emotionally.

Chapter Fifty-Eight

Richard owned an airline and offered to sponsor Phoebe freight allowance on commercial flights to deliver her products all over the world, as part of its corporate social responsibility programme to support eco-ethical businesses to reduce additional carbon footprints. He also invited Phoebe to partner with the Eco School to produce the packaging materials. Phoebe's eco-business was aimed at reducing waste from packaging, but some were still essential - especially for worldwide delivery. The Eco School had the perfect know-how to be the right supplier that could meet the requirement. They were going to use the recycled paper produced at school for packaging. The branding design and marketing plan became the real life project in their business management classes. The school also organised a competition in their computer engineering class to design websites for the brand, and create a seamless program to process the orders, logistics, reporting, as well as analyses. Phoebe was more than grateful and knew that she could not have a better dream team than the students from the Eco School. She had to admit that they were way better than her when it came to digital marketing. Those young people were incredibly savvy with social media and handy with the computer. As the school infused entrepreneurial teaching in their courses, Phoebe knew that she would not have difficulty explaining the business flow to them - a challenge she had while working at both Maison H and Vuitton Beauty. There she'd found her colleagues at the IT departments had little knowledge or interests in their business practice, which was not very helpful when the brands these days were getting more digitalised in recent years.

Phoebe shared her business idea with her friends and sent them the product samples to get their thoughts. She was overwhelmed by their support and positive feedbacks. Ting Ting was glad that she did not have to pretend she liked the products because they were best friends.

"LOVE! LOVE! LOVE!" was the first message she sent Phoebe upon trying out the samples. She swore she was going to be Phoebe's first paying customer and made all her aunts buy the make-up sets. She even offered her 'bible,' the black-book that contained all her media contacts, when Phoebe was ready to launch. Kannis, who found out she was pregnant with twins several months ago and had become more eco-conscious than ever that she was going to become a mother, asked to be a silent partner; Phoebe was floored and touched by the request. To show his support to both Kannis and Phoebe, Charlie offered space for their pop-up stores at all the commercial sites that were under the Kwan's real estate empire. This generous offer would doubtlessly help Phoebe to have her products reach out to customers at the beginning as she planned to run the business mainly out of the internet as online sales. She wanted to keep the retail price reasonable and affordable while implementing a fair trade policy towards Madya's community; so, keeping the operational cost as low as possible was key.

Valerie in Paris put herself forward as the spokesperson and volunteered to sample her products on her Instagram and Facebook page, where she had a big following. Kenji, Phoebe's best friend during her teenage years in Japan, was a renowned make-up artist who was sought after by Hollywood big names such as Beyoncé and Lady Gaga. Phoebe had made a short trip to Tokyo to take a crash makeup course with him before she'd started with Vuitton Beauty. Kenji promised Phoebe to do a demo at her debut press conference and make a marketing video for her makeup products. Recently converted to veganism and more eco-conscious himself, Kenji vowed to use Eco Beauty as the primary makeup line for his celebrity clients and endorse the products on his social media where he had over a million followers worldwide.

Both Ting Ting and Kannis reminded Phoebe not to forget what she had learnt at Maison H about how to entice its customers with the brand story and how the artisans skilfully crafted each product to its perfection. They urged Phoebe to make some footage of Madya's village, the farms, and gardens, as well as the 'kitchens' where everything was prepared.

They told her they could not wait to go visit and meet with Madya and her community. Coming from Maison H, they had the utmost respect for the artisans who were behind the beauty products. Phoebe sent them the design proposals on the brand logo, the idea board for the colour theme, and materials. Both Ting Ting and Kannis were amazed by the quality of the works produced by the students at the Eco School and told Phoebe the students should go work for them when they graduated, and they each took over their family businesses.

In the end, they narrowed it down to three themes. Phoebe wanted to seek the opinions from her parents, the most important mentors and cheerleaders in her life, on both the branding and the business idea, to make the final decision.

Chapter Fifty-Nine

"Honey, it's so great to have you back. We missed you so much. Look at you, you've lost so much weight."

Phoebe's mother did not waste a moment to fuss over her after her return to the States. She and her father had settled down in her family home after his forced early retirement. After three generations of diplomats, her family home was more like a retirement home. Yet, Phoebe had very fond memories from this charming little town on Long Island. Centerport was family friendly with its residents physically very active. It was hard not to be when there was a beautiful port for boats and beaches at your doorstep. For years they had been moving from one country to another, and her family home was let out to several families, so by the time her parents moved back in, the house still had the set-up for a young family instead of for a retired couple.

Although Phoebe's father was still upset with the early retirement, Claire was secretly glad that they were finally 'back home.' She was tired of moving from one country after another. As glamourous as it got for a diplomat's spouse, she'd had enough of the state parties or to entertain yet another ambassador's wife.

"Don't tell your father I say this, but I suspect he doesn't hate this retired lifestyle at all. Beijing was so landlocked and getting more polluted; here we can walk along the beach without worrying about the air we breathe in. Not to mention, he could get back into his favourite sailing."

Every man in Phoebe's family loved sailing and was trained to sail from a very young age. As the only child, her father raised her and introduced her to the sailing world the same as she was a boy. Phoebe loved going out to the sea with him, most of the time, just the two of them when Claire would be having tea or spa time. It was the perfect father-daughter bonding activity.

"Where's daddy?"

"Where do you think he is?" Claire said, glancing at a terrace that led to a small dock telling her that Johnathan had gone out sailing. "Sorry darling, we didn't expect you to be early, but he can be back any moment."

"Not at all, mom. I'll go out and wait for him."

In a few minutes, Phoebe saw her father's sailboat rising over the horizon. Despite in his late fifties, Johnathan Downlington was dashingly handsome. Johnathan and Claire had Phoebe when they were very young. They were high school sweethearts, married right after college, and had Phoebe soon after.

Johnathan quickly secured the boat to the dock and nearly jumped off the boat, ran towards Phoebe, and gave her a bear hug - just what a girl needed from her daddy. She would always be her daddy's little girl.

"Darling, you're back!"

"I missed you, too, daddy. How was your sail?"

"Marvellous! But not as marvellous as having you back home. Tell us everything about your adventure in Bali."

Phoebe told Claire and Johnathan about her encounters with all the wonderful people and the inspiring places she had been in Bali. She shared with them her business idea on the eco-friendly make-up line and received an enthusiastic response.

"That sounds wonderful darling! We were worried that you were going to hide in Bali forever, but you did not let those people bury you. This business idea of yours is going to take off and succeed. We are proud of you."

The next morning, Claire and Johnathan told Phoebe that they would like to invest in her business and be a silent partner. Being a diplomat all his life, Johnathan was not cash rich, yet he had much faith in his daughter and decided to support her both emotionally as well as financially.

"No daddy, I can't take your money. I have already cost you your job, and reputation. I cannot risk losing your life's savings."

Not wanting to argue with Phoebe, Claire and Johnathan promised to be her first customers. They planned to get everyone they knew Phoebe's products as gifts from now on for years to come.

Claire couldn't sleep the previous night, overwhelmed with joy that Phoebe was back to her normal self, and eager to help, she'd stayed up the night and did some research. She then made a few calls first things in the morning and managed to secure a booth in the coming family market before Thanksgiving, which was the biggest event in town. By then Phoebe's make-up line would be ready for a test-run, and Claire volunteered to run the booth and promote the products.

"Thank you for the support. You should be very mad at me for what happened."

"Darling, Ting Ting has already told us what happened. It wasn't your fault, or Alex's. It was just bad luck and timing that Daniel used us to hurt him, which in a way is evidence that Alex was serious with you. The idea only came to Daniel to target you when Alex shared his plan to propose to you. We think you should give this poor lad a chance. We like Alex very much and wouldn't mind to have him as our son-in-law."

"No, daddy, bad luck or not, I just want to be alone and focus on launching Eco Beauty for now."

"Of course, darling. We only want to remind you that true love does not come along often, it's all we have to say to you. Do not let Mr. Right slip away because of some evil deed."

On that note, Phoebe thought back the investigation report that was sent to her by Ting Ting as soon as she received it from her private investigator. It was very clear that Alex also fell victim to Daniel's evil plan. The last time she'd asked Ting Ting about any news of Alex, he'd been forced to take a sabbatical from his firm. She had not heard from him, ever since she'd ignored his hundredth call and message. Now, after all these months had passed, she didn't know where or how to pick things back up.

Phoebe stayed with her parents the following weeks to discuss her business plan, set up the legal documents and arrangements with the bank such that the investment from her parents and Kannis could go to a proper company. The operation of Eco Beauty was launched officially.

Chapter Sixty

Phoebe commuted between her parents' home and New York to interview designers for Eco Beauty, while Madya in Bali worked hard together with her team at production. Before Phoebe left Bali, she worked with Richard and his team of architects to set up Atelier 21 - a workshop where the artisans on the farm could produce as well as experiment with different products for the Eco Beauty collection. Phoebe named it after the renowned workshop Atelier 17, to pay respect to the artists she met through Madya who possessed much knowledge and love for nature, while giving her a fresh start in life.

On the other hand, Claire wanted to roll her sleeves up and help as much as she could. She had retired from being a diplomat's wife and wasn't used to having so much time on her hands. She put her diplomatic skills into good use for Eco Beauty; she used her network to create a buzz for Eco Beauty as well as drafting communication statements for the brand story and mission. She even managed to secure a booth at the Sunday Market at Centrepoint which usually had to be booked months in advance. Phoebe and Claire thought it would be useful to do a test run in their hometown to see the customers' feedback first-hand, and make necessary changes when it was still early days into production. The family crowd at home would be perfect, as well as the brand's target audience who were health and eco-conscious consumers.

Claire told Phoebe that their handyman and carpenter volunteered to build her booth for the Sunday market as a gesture of support. Phoebe was touched and grateful for the offer since the venue only provided a cover and a long table with a few chairs if requested. Although she felt bad about not being able to meet with Claire's builder in advance to brief him on the concept, she couldn't help it as their schedules often clashed. During the day she would be running around to deal with the logistic company to have all products and testers flown over on time, or she would be with the printer to go over every printable item from leaflets to signage displays. In the evenings, she was on hour-long video calls with her team in Asia due to the time difference. In any case, Claire told her that the builder was a private person and he built most of the items at his own workshop quite a long way from where they were. Claire assured Phoebe that she would check on him as she could use the excuse to visit a couple of girlfriends who lived out there, too. Phoebe trusted her mother, who was now a shareholder of Eco Beauty, to relay the concept to the builder while she occupied herself with preparing the other hundreds of details for the Sunday Market.

On the day of the Sunday Market, Phoebe expected to catch the builder in the morning to express her gratitude in person to him, after he pulled an all-nighter to bring all the pieces from his workshop and put them together at the assigned booth for Eco Beauty. Annoyingly, the moving company who would help her transport everything to the venue was late, shamelessly blaming the Sunday traffic, giving Phoebe less than an hour to set up the products and testers before the market began. Already filled with nerves and anxiety of the day, Phoebe was overwhelmed with worries on the journey to the Sunday Market that she would never have enough time to clean up the venue before she could bring her precious products out. Experience in the past had taught her that builders often left layers of dust for her and the sales team to clean before any product could be laid out.

All these worrying thoughts did not prepare Phoebe for what she was going to see in front of her. Her booth stood like a gem shining among other shabby booths of the Sunday Market. The booth was built entirely with bamboo with other complimentary natural materials such as stones and teak wood. The whole set up reminded her of the simple, elegant, and luxurious spa she had been in Bali, while integrated lots of plants and herbs that Phoebe knew the builder must have acquired from some of the vendors at the market. It was beyond her expectations and totally conveyed the message of the brand concepts: from farm to face, nature to nail art, plant to perfume. When Phoebe could spare a moment later during the day, she noticed that the pieces had been cleverly crafted and assembled in a way that they could be easily dismantled, stored, and transported for future events. She made a mental note to thank her mother and her builder profusely.

With the social connections of Claire and Johnathan, a much bigger than usual crowd was drawn to the Sunday Market, which other vendors were also grateful for. Several socialite friends of Claire made special visits to the booth along with a few lifestyle media, bloggers, and vloggers. Eco Beauty was a massive hit, and the day was a huge success. Phoebe barely had a moment to herself, running between customers and the media to be interviewed on Eco Beauty, it's brand story, concepts, and products. At the end of the day, all products Phoebe had brought with her were sold out, along with many orders to fulfil and more coming from the brand's website, after the media gave a raving review on everything of Eco Beauty from the products to its packaging and brand values.

Phoebe asked her mother to thanks the builder and said would like to thanks him in person. She was thinking of giving him a big tip to say 'thank you,' and probably some of her products for him to gift his loved ones. Regrettably, Claire told her that the builder had to take some time off for some family affairs, and wouldn't be back before Phoebe had to depart for New York. Phoebe then passed the gift on to Claire with a handwritten 'thank you' note for her fairy helper - who she never quite managed to meet.

Chapter Sixty-One

After the successful test run at home and hearing many constructive feedbacks, it boosted Phoebe's confidence with the official launch of Eco Beauty the following month in New York.

As an American, Phoebe knew she was more Asian on the inside than the outside. She admitted to her parents she barely knew nor understood the US market but her friend Kenji, who, on the other hand, was more American than the Asian he was, advised her that she must launch her collection in the US first to get the most noise. Then, when she went back to Asia, it would have been packaged as an American-founded brand, which would be more appreciated by the Asian clientele. Kenji also had the contact of all the media that mattered to the Beauty business. A handful of lifestyle editors owed him a favour when on more than one occasion he'd played magic to finish several divas' make-up with time to spare for an exclusive interview or preview with them. The glimpse of the diva's appearance just before getting on stage guarantee the Instagram or Tweet go viral within minutes.

On the day of Eco Beauty's official launch, Phoebe was a nervous wreck. Kannis, who was now the official silent partner, flew all the way to New York to support her. Pregnant with twins, Kannis could not physically help much, but she brought Caroline, who'd been in charge of the successful launch of Charlie's night club, with her to help. Caroline was half-French half-American, and she'd founded her PR company in the US and had an office in Paris. Her expertise gave a powerful launch to a brand that would bring the most media attention so that it would be the most talked about business within the first month of the launch when it most mattered. She had a strong influence in Europe as well, so many luxury brands hired her as their PR for both the American and European markets.

Caroline had proposed to the Eco Beauty team to have the launch party at a hip and chic organic juice cocktail bar that had opened recently. Caroline did their launch party and managed to get glorious praises from media across the city. She also convinced the bar owner let Phoebe to have the launch party there for free; that Eco Beauty echoed with their ethics and the launch party would keep the momentum of their recent launch going and continue to draw attention and crowds to the bar. It would be a win-win situation.

Special cocktails were created for the event, and named after the collection and the places in Bali where the make-up line was inspired. One was particularly named after Madya, as if it wasn't her opening the door to another world, Phoebe could still be somewhere dark and grim, licking her wound. The cocktails were such a success that the bar decided to keep more than half of them on their regular menu.

On the other hand, a couple of senior students from Pratt Institute were hired to use spices to create artworks on canvas, to showcase how natural plants could also give vibrant colours.

Several of Phoebe's students at the Balinese Eco School created the music played at the launch party. One of Richard's initiatives was to teach students of the Eco School music. Not only the students could learn different kinds of both traditional and modern music instruments, Richard also invited famous musical engineers from all over the world to take temporary residence on the school campus and teach his students to make music in the music lab he designed and built himself. Albums were displayed and sold during the launch. The proceeds went to a trust fund that offered scholarships to impoverished students in Indonesia who showed potential to go to the Eco School to develop their musical talent.

As both F&B and Beauty media had been invited to the event, the bar was totally packed and spread out into the neighbourhood. The owner of the bar was more than pleased with the outcome and offered Phoebe to advertise and showcase her products for free at his location for the next twelve months.

Chapter Sixty-Two

Kenji's appearance might have scored high on media coverage for Eco Beauty. Yet, the team knew that to sell the products, they had to keep the momentum going on after the launch. Caroline caught wind of a vendor giving up a pop-up store at Time Square due to the delay of a shipment. Kannis quickly snapped it up by offering 10% more of rental payment. That allowed Eco Beauty the best three weeks of the year before Thanksgiving that people were looking for special gifts for their loved ones. Phoebe flew two of Madya's uncles over to New York to do personalised engravings of the make-up case on the spot. Both Madya's uncles were over the moon as they had never been anywhere out of Indonesia in their lives, not to mention going to the Big Apple.

Everything seemed to be perfect except Kenji was no longer available to do demonstrations after the debut. He was all booked up to his neck without a break until the New Year. He was not only booked by shows, Kenji was also in high demand among the rich and famous for doing make up for them during the festive seasons when there were endless balls and parties to attend. Phoebe knew very well from experience with both Maison H and Vuitton Beauty that, the easiest way to sell the products was to show the customers the ease of using it. Valerie could sell dozens of scarves in a single hour by demonstrating different ways to wear the scarves. Kenji assured her that he would send one of his trusted apprentices to support her pop-up event. Still, Phoebe had never met this apprentice so she wasn't sure if he or she would be any good. She had met some make-up artists with very arrogant attitudes that in the end, pushed customers away rather than drawing them in.

The first day of the pop-up store came, and Phoebe was running late because of New York's notorious traffic. She wanted to take the subway, but with two rolling suitcases and two hand carry bags, she had no choice but to called an Uber. The pop-up space had limited storage and nearly no security. It meant that Phoebe had to carry the extra stock back and forth every day, while her assistants helped to carry the other tools, and Madya's uncles their own tools for engraving. She hoped that her luggage would reduce day by day and be emptied out by the end of the pop-up event.

Catching her breath at the corner where the pop-up booth was, Phoebe tried to perceive the scene in front of her. She couldn't see any make-up artist but instead Alex, sitting on a high stool, giving a make-up demonstration to a customer using Eco Beauty.

As soon as the customer left with a full bag of purchases, Phoebe went to Alex to confront him.

"What do you think you are doing here? Trying to ruin my second career?" Despite Phoebe having read all the investigative reports from Ting Ting and receiving dozens of apologising emails and voice messages from Alex, Phoebe could not help scolding Alex, out of the frustrations and heartbreaks, for all the time they were apart.

"Phoebe, I am very, very sorry for what happened. You and your father became the collateral damage when Daniel pulled his revenge on me. I cannot apologise enough and turn things around. But I am hoping I could make things easier for you from now on."

"Exactly WHAT are you doing here?"

"I AM Kenji's apprentice. I have been learning to do make-up from him for the past few months as soon as I heard about your new business."

Just as with the typhoon when she first met him, Alex had come to her rescue in her time of need. Phoebe was very touched to find that Alex followed Kenji around the world for two months to learn to do make-up and look the part. However, for the ordeal she and her father went through because of him, she decided not to soften up that easily.

"As far as I understand, Daniel had mistaken you as the guy who wounded his brother and took revenge on you; my father and I were collateral damages. In my book that is bad luck, YOU are bad luck. I am not sure if I want to work with someone who is unlucky." *A taste of his own medicine*, thought Phoebe.

"Considering I just sold the full Eco Beauty collection to three different customers before you arrived, I would say my luck has turned around for the better."

"You what?" Phoebe wanted to pump her fist in the air but suppressed the urge. "Alright, I will give you a day to day probation. You get to come back the following day if you perform. You'd better pray for your good luck to stay."

"I'll take things one day at a time." Alex was thrilled to have the chance to work alongside Phoebe, to help her out with her new career and most importantly, to win her heart back.

Kenji had not only taught Alex make-up skills, convinced that Alex was perfect for Phoebe and she deserved all the happiness in the world after what Daniel had done to her, he had also taught Alex the trick to link sell. Kenji believed in Phoebe's products, and he wanted her to succeed in both her business and relationship with Alex.

During the three weeks of the pop-up event, Alex proved himself to be the most valuable staff Phoebe could wish for. He'd learnt all Kenji's signature touches with make-up, which even impressed Phoebe. By now Phoebe was convinced that Kenji had taught Alex how to talk to the customers, especially the desperate housewives. They just couldn't get enough from Alex, and were more than happy to part with their money. It was rare that Alex could not sell everything available on the table to whoever was willing to stop and watch him do a make-up demonstration.

Every morning and evening, Alex helped Phoebe to do all the heavy duty to set up and close the booth, and carry everything back and forth between her hotel and the pop-up store. There were days that Phoebe's team took turns to fall sick, and Alex would step in. He worked every day non-stop from start to finish, with only a few minutes break here and there to grab a bite or go for a sip of water. On top of all this, he was an absolute gentleman; he did not try to take advantage of the moments Phoebe was tired or weak. He gave Phoebe space and time. He wanted to earn Phoebe's trust and love back through hard work and commitment.

On the second day of the pop-up event, some teenagers were fooling around and did some damage to the booth set up. Phoebe panicked as she knew the design was clever, while at the same time complicated. She had no idea where she could find a handyman to fix what the talented builder of her mother had created. When she walked back to the booth, feeling defeated after talking to the mall's contractor whether they could help, she peaked. Alex was working hard at the back of the booth, quickly putting the pieces back together with precision and ease, like he was the one who had built it. Just at that moment, realisation dawned on her. No wonder she was never able to meet the builder; Alex was the builder. Phoebe then remembered he actually had a double-degree - while one was in Finance, the other one was Architecture. That was why he was in infrastructure finance. Despite feeling immensely touched, Phoebe kept quiet and did not make a big deal out of it. She thanked Alex for fixing the damage and carried on with the event.

The pop-up at Times Square was a huge success for a new beauty brand that was not selling a mainstream product nor had the backup of a conglomerate. The series of PR events laid out by Caroline had generated much buzz across the media. Gwyneth Paltrow, who was an icon in chic health lifestyle these years, tried the products and gave her endorsement to Eco Beauty. Caroline was going to negotiate a deal with Paltrow's agent to become the brand spokesperson.

Not only the marketing feedbacks were beyond Phoebe's expectation, but she also underestimated the sales volume. Thanks to working with production directly, for the first time in her professional life, she didn't panic when her forecast of sales had been totally off. Madya, who had become Eco Beauty's Production Manager, had been checking with Phoebe daily, regarding the sales. She had the ladies in her village, who were now employed by Eco Beauty under a fair trade agreement, started on preparing more ingredients, ready to go at any time when the replenishment order arrived. The constant two months' supply was already halfway sold through one week after the launch. Madya diligently went to work and managed to expedite a big shipment to New York to support the pop-up store, as well as fulfilling the online sales, which was increasing on a daily basis when more media talked about the latest eco beauty line.

As part of the curriculum at Eco School in Bali was to develop entrepreneurial skills, Richard and Phoebe struck up a deal to hire students in their last year at school. They were to run the online business - including order fulfilment, online shop management, marketing, and social media - under the guidance of the Sales and Marketing Manager hired by Phoebe, who was more than happy to be based in Bali. The students would receive both training and commission during their internship with Eco Beauty, and a recommendation upon graduation.

Chapter Sixty-Three

Daniel looked out of the window while his plane was taking off down the runway. Four years ago, when he came to Shanghai, he was very ambitious to develop the ever-growing China market and make his career. He did not expect to meet Alex and imagine he could finally get revenge for what Alex did to his baby brother. Matt could have become a brilliant surgeon as he always aspired to be since he was five - he loved taking things apart and putting them back together. When he had set his goal of becoming one, he liked playing the game of picking up beans and grapes with both hands, both for fun and for preparing his hands for his future role on the operation table. Only it was tragically ruined by the stupid fight over the rowing championship with Alex. The cruellest revenge was to hurt someone with what he or she loved the most. The plan started to come together after the evening when he ran into Alex with his girlfriend Phoebe and her diplomat parents. Daniel thought Alex had himself to blame for his girlfriend's suffering since he could not shut up about her. Alex often messaged with Phoebe when they couldn't see each other during the week, and shared the jokes and news with Daniel while they were hanging out together. Daniel saw his opportunity when Alex showed him the picture of the Vuitton's secret exclusive make-up clutch that was going to be launch into the market a year later. He made a few calls to some shady people he knew, tricked Alex to leave his phone for a few minutes to steal the photo Phoebe had sent him, created some encounter occasions between the major characters in his plot of revenge in the new few months, and the rest was history.

Yet, after causing the damage done to Alex, Phoebe, her parents, and eventually leading to their breakup, sadly, the sweet triumph did not bring joy nor satisfaction to him. For the past several months he was so lost in setting Alex up, he realised he'd spent every spare minute with him or thinking of him. Now with no more revenge, he seemed to have lost his purpose. Without wanting to admit it, he had grown very fond of Alex and came to enjoy hanging out with him very much. He believed if Alex had not had the unfortunate history with his brother, it could have been a genuine friendship worth cherishing. Phoebe was one of the most beautiful, talented, and kindest girls he knew. His only regret was he did not meet her before Alex did. Last he heard was that Phoebe had left Hong Kong permanently soon after the scandal broke out, soon after that message, the final nail in Alex's coffin - that he'd sent Phoebe. Daniel knew that Alex would be out of touch when the news broke. He had made sure of that by convincing the groom to be, who turned out to be an ex-colleague of his that he was still in touch with, to confiscate everyone's cell phone during his stag to ensure a good time among mates that there would be no disturbing calls from wives and girlfriends. Without a job, heartbroken, and surrounded by unpleasant media attention because of the scandal, Daniel was certain that Phoebe would leave Hong Kong as soon as possible. By the time Alex got his phone back or flew back to China, Phoebe would have long gone. The two love birds would have missed the opportunity to find out the truth, and hopefully, sadly apart ever after.

Six months on, Daniel started to feel depressed over the whole ordeal. He flew back to the U.K. to see his brother and shared the success of his revenge to Alex. Surprisingly, Matt did not seem to be grateful for what he did. Matt told him Alex actually did him a favour in disguise. He met his wife Beatrice at his practice with whom he now had two beautiful daughters. Matt wished Daniel had shared his plan with him earlier, and he would have tried to convince him to abort. Looking back, Matt wasn't even sure if the guy who caused his injury was a student. He was so drunk at that time, and there were so many people in the pub. It could have been a random person as he was so angry from the loss that he was trying to pick a fight with everyone.

That led to further depression for Daniel. Upon his return to Shanghai, he asked his boss to transfer him to South America to set up a branch and to develop the emerging markets there. He wanted to put all of it behind him and start afresh. Daniel never reported to his superiors about the deals he had brought to Alex - as they did not actually exist. Although he had not achieved a lot in the China market, especially in the past six months, his fundraising record was flawless, and within a week, he got the green light and budget from the big boss to relocate to the other continent. Now, looking at the diminishing city, he realised he had not achieved anything he could be proud of in the city, which had been his home for the past four years.

Before Daniel left Shanghai, he sent out a few anonymous emails to several popular newspapers and magazines. Attached with the emails were written and audio evidence that could help clear both Phoebe's and Johnathan's names over the scandal he'd orchestrated himself. News of Phoebe's business of an eco-makeup line had travelled to Daniel's ears earlier, so he felt that was the least he could do to make up for what he did to ruin both hers and her father's career. On the other hand, Daniel respected and admired Phoebe more than ever that she could climb up from the bottom and build something totally inspirational. He cursed that time and fate had not been kind to him. If it was him who met Phoebe instead of Alex, he wondered whether he would have had a chance with that gorgeous, kind, and talented girl. Yes, Phoebe might not be with Alex anymore, but Daniel knew very well that Phoebe would never forgive him after knowing what he had done; she deserved someone better.

Chapter Sixty-Four

Towards the end of her second trimester, Kannis started to feel the fatigue from the first trimester coming back, accompanied by a belly that was growing bigger by the day. Worried that her doctor would no longer sign her off getting onto a plane while carrying twins, Kannis decided to take indefinite maternity leave from Maison H and relocated back to Hong Kong temporarily. There she would have the care of the Peak Hospital, which usually served the city's most affluent, and an army of help to look after both the babies and Kannis herself.

Growing up as a very independent girl who was fearless and never shied away from anything, Kannis was now filled with worrying thoughts, and grew more and more protective of the little ones growing inside her belly. The recent terrorist attack in Paris and other parts of France reminded her that Europe was not as safe as it used to be when she was there as a student. She finally understood how her father felt when she was far away from home and bad news travelled to his ears concerning her safety. Besides, with the size of her belly bigger than a watermelon, she no longer felt comfortable with commuting daily to work, even with the luxury provided by either a taxi or an uber.

There were days she found herself browsing on the Internet for hours to shop for baby clothes or reading parenting websites and forums. The analyses and new developments of the brand became less and less interesting nor important to her.

Charlie was more than pleased about his only daughter's return. He was getting more worried with Kannis, especially after learning about her pregnancy. He wanted to send a team of security to look after her but every time faced strong objection by Kannis and Jeremy who found the suggestion ridiculous and not Parisian at all. With the return of Kannis, he could start planning to hand over part of his empire to her one day, with the other part to her brother. Charlie was certain that Kannis would stay in Hong Kong as his grandchildren grew, for more accessible childcare, a safer environment, and as well as more aunt and uncle times for them especially now she was getting closer to Ting Ting more than ever.

Kannis and Ting Ting were as close as any sisters could be, only these days they did not have to meet in secret. Not only they could be friends in public, they could also be sisters who loved and supported each other. Edith visited Kannis at her residence apartment at the Four Seasons hotel often and brought her nourishing Chinese soups and dishes. Although growing up and educated most of her life in Europe, Kannis embraced the Chinese wisdom in how to nourish a woman's body. She believed in the 'chi' and 'meridian' in Chinese medicine. She even took a Chinese medicine class at university as an elective to learn more about it. Growing up without a mother, she did not have the pass-me-down wisdom from the women in the family, but the youthful faces of the female family friends of hers and Charlie never failed to amaze and inspire her to turn to her own roots when it came to looking after herself against the hands of time.

Charlie gifted one of his many houses to Kannis. The house was close to his and of a good size for a young family. He hired an interior designer who flew to Paris to meet with Kannis and Jeremy a couple of months earlier to hear their brief on their preference. Since then, the designer flew back and forth a few times more too get their feedback and make changes to the design. The house was now finally under renovation according to their requirements.

On the other hand, there were still many whisperings and gossips wherever Edith went, which she paid little to none attention to any of them - she was grateful for having both of her precious girls back. The doctor finally gave Ting Ting a clearance after several months of close monitoring post-transplantation. That was an enormous relief for her.

She and Kannis took their time to get to know each other. Edith accepted that she and Kannis would never be as close as she was with Ting Ting, and Kannis might never totally forgive nor forget that she gave her up, even though it was under lots of stress. Still, Edith was comforted by the fact that Ting Ting and Kannis were now bonded forever by Kannis's selfless act to donate one kidney to Ting Ting.

Edith finally made peace with Charlie, too. She would never forgive his cowardice and not standing up to his mother for her. Yet, Charlie took full responsibility for breaking up Edith with Kannis and sang her praises to Kannis whenever the subject came up ever since his daughter learnt the secret. Edith was grateful for the gesture. Charlie would even extend invitations to Edith and Simon for family celebrations during festive seasons so Kannis and Ting Ting would not be put into difficult situations and torn between both sides of the family.

This change shifted the sentiments between the two families in a positive direction. Gradually, there were fewer rivalries and more collaborations. This had lightened the stress and pressure not only at social occasions but also made Ting Ting's work a lot easier. While she still missed terribly, both Phoebe and Kannis working at the same company, her work had become more enjoyable. Due to the success of the grand opening of the flagship store, Maison H had promoted her to take over the Marketing and PR Department. Her previous superior had been relocated to look after the communications and events in Macau, where there were many new developments of the brand line, and her project management experience could be made the best use of. With that, Phoebe teased Ting Ting to accept defeat her own theory about career advancement in French companies.

Chapter Sixty-Five

The taxi stopped in front of a handsome house full of grandeur on the Peak, and the driver paused the meter. Phoebe checked that she had both her presents for a baby girl and a baby boy were in the shopping bag. Kannis was still more than two months from her due date, but she was carrying twins and wanted to be over with the baby shower before she grew even bigger that she could hardly leave her room. She sent out a last-minute invitation for her twin's baby shower.

Phoebe was running late as she was doing a final touch up to Eco Beauty's presentation. She was so absorbed in writing the story for the brand that by the time she glanced at the clock again, she realised she had to be at the shower within twenty minutes. She quickly changed into a wrap dress - one of the many she'd gathered during her travel retail years, for they did not need pressing, and could be easily rolled up for packing into a suitcase. She found it strange that Kannis would choose to do an evening baby shower as most mums-to-be would do it during lunchtime to get the best daylight for photos. Nevertheless, she dismissed her question as she had never expected any baby. Moreover, Kannis was expecting twins, a boy and a girl. She might want to have a little bit of fun and partying before the chaos began.

Phoebe got out of the taxi and stood staring at the house that belonged to Ting Ting's aunt, Diane. From the look of it, it could be bigger than the walk-up building she used to live in, while in Happy Valley, and she bet to herself Aunty Diane's bathroom alone would be bigger than the apartment she used to call home in Hong Kong. Her sublet tenant had finally taken over the lease, and she was just staying at a studio she found from Airbnb for the time being. Kannis's house had just finished being renovated, and under Edith's advice, Kannis should give it a month or two to air out all the chemicals from the renovation and let the dust to settle before moving in for the sake of both mummy's and baby's health. Kannis told Phoebe that Aunty Diane insisted on hosting her baby shower when she called her to invite Phoebe to her baby shower a few days ago. She said it was a last-minute decision as her twins were in a position that her OBY/GYN advised to have a caesarean in two weeks' time.

When Phoebe got to the doorstep, she saw the door was slightly open, and there was no noise coming from inside the house. Phoebe paid no attention to that as she knew very well the mansion of these rich people were massive. There could be a hundred people gathered in the house, but they could be in one of the many giant halls, so that no one would hear a thing by just standing outside the house.

It was Phoebe's first time to visit Aunty Diane's house, and she hoped she wasn't going to get lost. Phoebe walked towards the courtyard, hoping she would run into one of the amahs who could point her in the right direction. The sun was setting, and she could feel the cool autumn breeze flowing to the back of her neck.

As Phoebe passed the carp pond and round the corner into the courtyard, her jaw dropped, and she was in awe of the scene in front of her. Candles lighted along the four sides of the courtyard with red and white roses lying up behind them. There must have been about a thousand roses. The courtyard opened up to an open view of the city landscape. The sunset brought a mix of romantic colours to the sky - orange and purple - and with the hundreds of roses lining up, it was like a scene in a movie.

Then from out of a corner, she saw Alex holding a bouquet of the same roses walking towards her. Phoebe froze and could not move. When Alex reached the table, he first gave Phoebe the bouquet and a peck on her cheek, then he went down on one knee and took a small velvet box out of his trousers' pocket.

"Phoebe Downlington , ever since I met you, my life has never been dull again. Typhoon, revenge, getting fired, stepping out of my comfort zone and trying new things… we went through ups and downs, and there is no one I would like to make more adventures with for the rest of my life than you. I love you so much. Will you marry me?"

Phoebe's sight was blurred, and her eyes filled with tears. Looking at the ring, it fit the descriptions of her dream ring to a 'T,' that she casually mentioned while watching Meghan Markle marrying Prince Harry on television. It was a three-carat emerald princess cut halo ring with stunning diamonds all around it. Turning to the left looking down to the city's skyscrapers and the harbour, Phoebe saw why Alex proposed to her there; she'd once mentioned to Alex that the Peak in Hong Kong should be among the top ten places of where to make a proposal around the world. Alex had chosen Aunty Diane's house so they would be away from all the tourists visiting the Peak day and night.

Waking up from her brief loss in thoughts, Phoebe realised Alex was still on his knee.

"Yes, there is no one else I would like to share my adventures with, although I wouldn't mind to have things easier from now on."

Alex let out a breath of relief. He slipped the ring onto her ring finger, which was a perfect fit. Alex reminded himself he had to thanks Priscilla who'd told him Phoebe's ring size. Priscilla knew all Phoebe sizes from head to toe as they used to try different clothes and accessories on during buying seasons. Alex could not stop kissing Phoebe until she made him stop.

"Listen, there's music in one of the rooms ahead… oh, the baby shower! Or is there a baby shower?"

"Well, let's go find out." Alex then led Phoebe to the room where the light and music came from.

When Alex pushed open the door, Alex raised Phoebe's hand where everyone could see the ring was on. In front of them stood everyone that Phoebe cared for in her life: Ting Ting, Kannis, Priscilla, Aunty Diane, her team at Eco Beauty, and her parents!

Upon seeing the ring on Phoebe's finger, everyone clapped and cheered. Claire had tears in her eyes and couldn't believe her little girl would soon become Alex's wife.

"Mummy, Daddy, how come you're here?"

"Before you came back from Bali, Alex flew all the way to Centreport to see us. He explained the whole story to us and asked for our forgiveness. He was the one who helped us to convert our house back to the way we liked. He was also behind the setup of your beautiful booth in the Sunday Market.

"Before he left, Alex asked me for the permission of your hand. Of course, we had no hesitation to give you away to this fine young man."

"So, the man who had been helping my parents and living in the coach house was you…" Phoebe turned to Alex and playfully hit his arm at the moment of realisation.

Everyone came to congratulate the newly engaged couple. Kannis was relieved that she didn't have to do a last-minute baby shower at Aunty Diane's place, as she'd insisted should Phoebe turned Alex down, Kannis's baby shower would have to take place in her house to make it a happy place again.

Chapter Sixty-Six

Edith went to see Kannis for the last time before she would stay in and rest until she had to go to the hospital for her scheduled caesarean. Kannis had been very insistent on having a natural birth but was advised by her doctor after finding one of the twins was not in a favourable position. She was disappointed but accepted it for the safe arrival of her babies. Charles had kissed Kannis goodbye and wished her luck with her birth the morning before he left town for business. He promised to fly straight to Hong Kong as soon as his grandchildren had arrived. Kannis had scheduled a caesarean at thirty-seven weeks. Ting Ting was already back from Paris for the mid-season buy. The two sisters had made plans to spend as much time together and party as much as Kannis's heavily pregnant body allowed before she became a mother of two.

"Please take good care of yourself and my two first grandchildren. Put your feet up as much as you can and send your man to get what you want. I'll come see you as soon as you say you're ready. Call me or send me a message - anything you want me to bring over from here." Edith gave Kannis another last kiss and hug before very reluctantly getting into her car. She was sad to have to separate from Kannis now their bond had finally started building. She could not wait to get to meet her first grandchildren.

Kannis felt exhausted. She had been running around these past couple of days to get things sorted for the new house and nursery for the twins. Charles had assigned a staff member to assist Kannis to set up their home before her scheduled C-section. Kannis worked and shopped with the assistant to make sure she got all things right and the way she wanted. She had been feeling cramps all day but blamed her overactive timetable and Braxton Hicks.

She kept piling up baby-related purchases in their temporary home. Luckily, Jeremy's work was computer-based, and he could work anywhere he wanted as long as he had an internet connection. While he wasn't working, he would be reading a manual or watching YouTube tutorials about how to set up certain baby gear.

So Kannis gave him a night off to go out party with his friends in Hong Kong. They both knew it would be months or even years before they could do careless partying again. While Kannis was beyond her physical capacity to be pushed around and wiggling her hips with the other party-goers, she encouraged Jeremy to party on her behalf. Only now, in between contractions, she regretted letting Jeremy go out for the evening. Jeremy was not answering his phone, either - most likely, the ring tone was drowned by the noise at the bar.

The first serious pain hit Kannis when she and Edith were about to say their last goodbye. It was entirely different from the usual period-like pain she'd been feeling. She bent down and could hardly stand up. At the same time, she felt a little bit of liquid running down her thigh. Kannis realised that her waters might have broken and she had gone to labour.

"Oh no, please, I don't want to have my babies now. I can't do it, mum, I can't do it."

Kannis felt her contractions getting closer and closer to one another. She squeezed Edith's hand strongly and urged her not to leave her. Edith urged her driver to call for help right away. Within minutes, an ambulance arrived, and several officers rushed to help Kannis into it.

Upon arrival at the hospital, they wheeled Kannis quickly inside. Edith timed Kannis's contractions on the way, and by the time they got to the hospital, they were less than two minutes apart. Kannis was immediately pushed to the maternity ward, and upon checking, the midwife confirmed she was already 8cm dilated. Luckily, the midwife and doctor managed to set her up quickly for an epidural. Kannis thought that she was going to die from the pain until the epidural started to take effect.

Soon Kannis was fully dilated, and the midwife adjusted the epidural to minimal so that she could feel the sensation to push. Kannis screamed again from extreme pain. The midwife asked if Kannis's husband was going to come and accompany her to the labour room.

"Mum, please don't leave me, I can't do it alone." Kannis squeezed Edith's hand even harder and looked into her eyes begging her to go in with her.

"I am her mother; I'll go in with her," Edith announced to the midwife after Kannis was in too much pain to call Jeremy again.

Once the epidural was reduced to a nearly non-existent level, the sensation came back at full force, and Kannis let out a big scream. Then she felt the urge to push, and the midwife guided her to do the labour breathing. Kannis had not attended any birthing class as she was planning to have a caesarean. She panicked again at the thoughts of having to push not only one but two babies out by herself.

"Mum, tell them to cut me open and pull the babies out already, I can't do it," Kannis begged Edith to intervene and squeezed her hand even harder.

"My darling, it's too late to have a caesarean now, your babies want to come out now. You can do it. I'm here with you; squeeze my hand and breath with me." Edith then made the dramatic breathe-in, breathe-out as directed by the midwife. Suddenly it felt like yesterday when Edith was pushing Kannis out herself. As Kannis was her firstborn, the labour was hard, and it had taken her over twenty hours to give birth to Kannis. She was glad that it wasn't going to take that long for Kannis - she was only two hours into labour, and it looked like her first grandchild was about to crown.

Kannis let out another powerful scream, and the first twin was pushed out.

"The first one is a boy! Keep pushing mama; you are doing great." The doctor announced the arrival of the first twin and encouraged Kannis to push once more. Encouraged by the cries of her baby boy, Kannis felt another urge to push. This time it came easier, and with three pushes, the baby sister was born.

"Congratulations, you have one healthy boy and a beautiful girl." The doctor let Kannis have skin to skin contact with her twins for a few minutes before putting them into incubators as they had been born before reaching thirty-four weeks.

Jeremy finally arrived at the hospital nearly an hour after the twins were born, intoxicated by both alcohol and the joy of being a father for the first time.

The twins did very well, and within a few days, the doctor signed a release form and allowed them to leave the hospital, provided that Charles's medical team had set up everything the twins needed in his house on the Peak. Kannis had been very ambitious during her pregnancy and had planned to look after the twins the first three months by herself and Jeremy, to enjoy the precious moments together as a family. However, once the twins left the hospital and the care of the capable midwives and nurses, Kannis realised the task was impossible.

The first-time parents were clueless about what to do with new-borns. They seemed so fragile and hungry all the time. Sometimes she forgot who she had fed, which ended up with a double fed for one of her twins while the other one went hungry. Kannis was furious with herself as the twins were not identical - they also had very physical differences as one being a boy and the other a girl. She blamed it on her lack of sleep which she barely got any these days as the babies had to be fed every other hour, burped, then changed nappies. When she thought she was finally done with the nappies, one of the twins would cry for milk again.

Kannis was more than grateful for Edith to stick around 24/7 to help, ever since she went into labour. Edith told Kannis little things about the twins that reminded her of Kannis and Ting Ting when they were babies. It was a real bonding time between mother and daughter. Edith enjoyed every moment of it and like Charles, was very smitten with her grandchildren. By the time the twins reached one month, Edith was totally exhausted but was never happier.

Kannis couldn't believe she gave birth to the twins naturally. She felt very helpless when she was in labour without Jeremy around, so she was grateful for Edith's presence. With the twins born and she'd now become a mother, she could not imagine what it was like if someone wanted to take them away from her. Although she still thought Edith should have fought Charles to get shared custody of her, she was no longer angry with Edith; she accepted that it was a different time that was beyond her comprehension, and that Edith was doing everything she could now to make up for the past. Besides, she couldn't ask for a better 'Popo,' a maternal grandmother, for their twins.

Amusingly, the twin boy looked like a mix a Kannis and Jeremy, while his twin baby sister looked a Eurasian version of Ting Ting.

Ting Ting couldn't get enough of her niece and nephew. She would rush to Charles's house every day after work to help with the babies. Kannis joked that the twins barely touched their cribs as they constantly went through a carousel of grandparents, Ting Ting, and all the aunties and uncles from both families.

Chapter Sixty-Seven

Phoebe visited Kannis and the twins when the calendar reached a full moon after the birth. She'd just come back from the U.S. after celebrating Thanksgiving with her parents. Alex went with her; it was their first Thanksgiving together after their engagement. They agreed that after getting married, they would spend Thanksgiving with her parents and Christmas with his as Thanksgiving didn't mean much to his English parents. Seeing Christmas decorations were already up all around the city in Hong Kong, Phoebe felt jolly in the festive atmosphere as well as for all the good things had happened - like the twins' birth, and her engagement to Alex.

There had been lots of discussions on where to have their big day; whether they should have it in Phoebe's hometown, or Japan where they met, or Hong Kong where they had started dating. In the end, they both agreed that they were going to have it in Bali. Phoebe and Alex had a romantic memory there. It was also a place that helped Phoebe heal and pull her up to her feet again from her lowest. They could not think of another place, which was more perfect than Bali to start their life as a married couple.

Alex volunteered to work with their wedding planner to organize all the details for their wedding. Phoebe confessed with him very earlier on that she would not enjoy planning her own wedding like most girls did. Growing up, she spent at least half a day every weekend, planning a dinner party with her mother. Her parents entertained all the time, both out of obligation or for their own social networks, and Phoebe would only do that as it meant spending more time with her mother who had a very busy social calendar as the diplomat's wife. She was tired of seating plans, deciding on menus, arranging guests for speeches. She had first-hand experience on all the stresses during the event instead of enjoying it. She decided that she wanted to enjoy the party of her life, hence having her hands off her own wedding.

Phoebe welcomed Alex's suggestion as she was overwhelmed with the set-up of the Eco Beauty office in Singapore. Phoebe had decided to set up Eco Beauty's headquarter there for its vicinity to Bali, the production base, and its logistic advantage as both a regional and international hub. The bio-technological friendly environment, and incentives provided by the government, would also help Eco Beauty to do research and make further development. After a few brainstorm sessions with Richard, Alex, Ting Ting, and Kannis, Phoebe came up with the idea to develop eco-skincare capsules, which would eliminate the need for conventional plastic packaging. Each application would be simply stored in an algae-based capsule that was biodegradable and harmless to the environment once discarded. Phoebe was confident that such products would also change the Travel Retail Skincare industry forever, since as the frequent traveller she once used to be, she never enjoyed having to carry different jars of products for her beauty routine.

The brand story had attracted Pacific Air, one of the largest airlines in Asia, to publish a full two-page article about the brand and an interview with Phoebe. The airline was keen to carry Eco Beauty as one of their inflight offers. Phoebe was taken by surprise and very flattered, remembering how hard it was to get a product on board for the luxury brands in her previous professional life. However, knowing that the steep margin she would have the pay the airline, and the quantity to fill in the cart of every plane on all routes would be beyond the capacity of her team in Bali, Phoebe explained the situation in truth to the airline. Luckily, the airline was confident that Eco Beauty would bring a positive image to the airline in the field of environmental protection, so the buying team countered-offered Phoebe a much friendlier margin rate and suggested Eco Beauty be a home delivery item. Passengers could order on board and have it delivered to their home address.

Phoebe was relieved and signed up to the program in the end, which would be an invaluable marketing gain for her start-up business. Since Ting Ting and her silent partner Kannis were in Hong Kong, and Phoebe had a network of friends as well as business contacts there, they agreed they should set up a liaison office to coordinate sales and promotions. Thanks to Charlie's support, Eco Beauty enjoyed constant exposure and sales, with pop-up shops at different shopping malls in busy districts of the city every month.

Kannis also generously offered a wing in her newly renovated mansion to be used as Eco Beauty's base in Hong Kong. There were three spacious rooms that would be used as an office, meeting room, and for storage of stock. Both Ting Ting and Phoebe were thrilled with the arrangement and grateful for Kannis and her father's generosity.

Ting Ting volunteered to model for the brand who Phoebe thought had the perfect skin to be the spokeswoman for Eco Beauty. Ting Ting was more than happy to further her modelling gig beyond hair, and it meant that the best friends would see each other regularly, for both business and leisure. Ting Ting could hardly suppress her excitement to soon be on the cover of the inflight magazine for two whole months!

The wedding planner informed Phoebe and Alex that the Bvlgari Resort, their first and only choice of wedding venue in Bali, was fully booked for the next eighteen months. They should consider another equally nice resort which she worked with for many weddings. Phoebe was disappointed but agreed to have it at the alternative resort recommended by the wedding planner. Since then, Phoebe was glad to have deligated the planning out as part of the excitement was gone; the only appeal left was the marriage itself.

Alex had kept the contact of the Event Manager at Bvlgari Resort when they'd pretended to be engaged to sneak a private tour and decided to go meet her in person after hearing the bad news from their wedding planner. The Event Manager was very surprised to hear from Alex and to learn that they were still not married. Alex told her a simplified version of the story - that the engagement had gone through a rough patch, but in the end, they decided each other to be the person they would like to be with for the rest of their lives. The Manager loved the drama and the turn of events, and she promised to study the calendar which apparently was full for two years to come and revert.

Alex did not tell Phoebe his secret quest to book the Bvlgari Resort as the wedding venue as he did not want to let her down in case the Manager could not make any magic. Yet, he couldn't think of a better place to give Phoebe her dream wedding. Alex remembered every single detail Phoebe made up during the fake tour at the resort nearly two years ago. Alex believed she was speaking from her heart and made it his own mission to realise Phoebe's dream.

Chapter Sixty-Eight

Phoebe, her parents, and bridesmaids which included Ting Ting, Kannis, and Priscilla arrived at the resort suggested by the wedding planner as a replacement of the Bvlgari resort, three days before the wedding day. Trusting that Alex and their wedding planner were on top of everything, Phoebe just focused on spending time at the spa with her mother and bridesmaids to get beauty treatments from head to toe. Phoebe saw Alex at the rehearsal and family dinner in the evening. Other than that, they followed the tradition not to see each other before the wedding day.

Meanwhile, Alex was busy at the Bvlgari Resort, the actual location where the wedding was going to be held, to check with the staff there on the last details for the big day.

The wedding day of Phoebe and Alex finally came.

Claire helped Phoebe to put her wedding gown on. She couldn't help tears of joy flowing down her cheek when Phoebe turned around, and she stepped back to have a better look of her only child. Claire thought she had never seen a more stunning bride.

Phoebe's wedding gown was designed by Vera Wang exclusively for her, who later included the design in her 'White by Vera Wang Collection,' named after the bride. Phoebe had met the renowned couture designer at an Embassy dinner hosted by Johnathan in the designer's honour when she had visited China to promote Simply Vera and launching her home collection Vera Wang China. Phoebe thought she was one of the most inspiring women she had met in her life. Claire made an effort to invite Vera to design Phoebe's wedding gown, and to her surprise, the designer said yes to the commission. The designer paid tribute to Phoebe's love of the Chinese culture and incorporated elements of the Chinese cheongsam into the wedding gown, while still maintaining the overall Vera Wang's elegant impression. The result was breath-taking and uniquely Phoebe.

Phoebe paired her wedding dress with satin navy blue heels. Her 'something old' was a pair of teardrop earrings gifted to her by Claire that had been passed down from Phoebe's grannie. For 'something borrowed,' Aunty Diane insisted that Phoebe borrow her diamond tiara on her wedding day, and that would complete her role of cupid in bringing her and Alex back together. Phoebe was speechless when Aunty Diane showed her the tiara for the first time in a room bigger than her apartment that was designed specially to store Aunty Diane's jewellery. For the bouquet, Phoebe chose a simple one that was put together with frangipani, the flower of the island that brought back happiness and hope to her life.

When the buggy that carried the bride and bridesmaids reached the chapel of the resort, a limousine was parked at the entrance. The party was then invited to get onto the limousine. Phoebe was taken back and asked what was going on. Her bridesmaids, who were in the know of Alex's scheme, asked Phoebe to relax and just go with the flow. Ten minutes later, the limousine stopped at Bvlgari Resort. Realisation dawned on Phoebe, and she looked at Ting Ting with a question mark.

"Yes, Fair Bear, yes, Alex did it! You are going to have your wedding here at the Bvlgari Resort!"

Another buggy pulled up to the limousine to greet them. Phoebe, Ting Ting, Kannis, and Priscilla jumped into the buggy which was sweetly adorned with white roses, and headed towards the chapel where the groom was waiting. When they drove past, other guests staying at the resort gave them whistles and rounds of applause.

When the buggy stopped outside the chapel, Johnathan was standing at the entrance, handsome and proud. He held his hand out for his darling daughter.

"Besides your mother, I have never seen a lovelier bride in my entire life." Johnathan gave Phoebe a kiss on her cheek and told her that there was nothing that made him more proud in his life than being her father. Phoebe had to be rescued by her bridesmaids to fix her make-up that was messed up again for the second time of the day.

Arm in arm with her father, Phoebe walked down the aisle with Johnathan. She looked around the chapel and gasped. It was the set-up that she imagined how her dream wedding would be, to the dot: the peony inspired floral decoration of the venue, the harp and violin duet playing the progression, then followed by an opera singer singing her favourite arias to welcome the bride into her own wedding. At the other end of the aisle, she saw Alex standing there, tall and outrageously handsome, who the moment when he saw his bride, his chest rose and fell, barely able to contain his emotions and pride.

Her mentor Richard, her colleagues and students who were close to her at the Eco School, Madya, Gede, her mother, and her indispensable partners at the Atelier 21, Kenji, Valerie, Edith, Simon, Aunty Diane, Charlie, and most of all Kannis, Priscilla, and Ting Ting... Everyone important in her life were all there to cheer Phoebe as she walked down the aisle, towards the next chapter of a new beginning.

The ceremony was light-hearted but warm and touching. The vows that were personally written respectively by the bride and groom brought every guest to tears. Ting Ting, despite having no plans to tie a knot with anyone soon, joined in the fight to catch the bride's bouquet outside the chapel after the ceremony. To every contester's disappointment, the bouquet fell into Madya's arms, who was shocked and shyly glanced the way of her boyfriend who was a bright young man helping Phoebe to manage the production at Eco Beauty's very own atelier in Madya's village.

The reception in the evening was an event, with as much grandeur and glory as the super deluxe resort could offer. The ballroom was sparkling with the many chandeliers lighting up the room. In the middle of each table was placed a stunning arrangement of peonies, similar to those in the chapel. The tables were exquisitely dressed up with Maison H crystal glasses and tableware, kindly on loan from Phoebe's beloved ex-employer, miraculously arranged by Ting Ting across the countries. The lavish dishes were prepared by the chef of the Michelin-starred restaurant at the resort. Yet, the highlight of the dinner was the moving speeches by the father of the bride and the groom himself. Phoebe could not believe her luck in having so much love from everyone there, most of all, her newly wedded husband.

After dessert was served, Johnathan led Phoebe to the centre of the dance floor and led her to dance a piece of Waltz that the father and daughter had done many times and by heart at dinners hosted by the ex-diplomat.

Then the masters of ceremony, an unusual team-up of the humorous Kenji and Aunty Diane, announced Alex and Phoebe were going to do their first dance as a married couple. Alex led Phoebe to the middle of the dance floor. Phoebe thought they were going to do a simple Waltz, not ideal, but the Argentinian Tango was too hard for Alex who was a total beginner to pick up in a matter of months and to be able to lead the bride to do a wedding dance. She would not have had time spared to practice with Alex, either, even if he was willing. She accepted that she was going to have a less than perfect wedding while running her own business.

However, what Phoebe didn't know was, all that time while Phoebe was working hard on developing the Eco Beauty skincare line and having conference calls with her agents all over the world for the make-up line promotion, Alex had been taking Argentinian tango lesson every night for several months in secret in order to surprise his wife with their first dance on their wedding day. When the music played, Phoebe was struck by the similarity of the music but at the same time thought the DJ had made a mistake. Then Alex took her hand and gave her a gentle grip on her waist, then led Phoebe dance her favourite Argentinian Tango. Alex led Phoebe to walk, salida, ocho, and allowed her to do embellishments such as caricias, pasada, lustrada, barrida, enganche… From the eyes of a novice, one would think they had spent a long time to choreograph their first dance.

Only those who knew tango could tell the brilliant leading by Alex, and the two had an amazing connection to be so in tune with each other. The beautiful and sensual movements brought whistles and applause from their audience. Towards the second half of the music, Guillaume led Priscilla to the dance floor and join in the milonga. After one more piece of tango music to let the guests enjoy watching the Argentinian Tango dance, the music gradually picked up the pace, and more popular and mainstream salsa music was played by the band.

Guests gradually filled up the dance floor. Thirty minutes later, the band was replaced by another one that played pop music and pushed the crowd to another high. Alex wanted to keep their guests on their feet and awake until midnight when he had another surprise for his bride. Twenty minutes before midnight, the band started to play more mellow and romantic music. Phoebe was back to Alex's arms after they separated temporarily to dance with other guests. Five minutes to midnight, Alex whispered into Phoebe's ears and asked her to follow him. He took her hand and led her to a hidden part of the garden away from the crowd, but where they were still able to hear the music. Alex helped Phoebe to take her high heels off and walk onto the softness of the grass.

"Ooooooooooh, that feels like heaven for my feet!"

Alex put Phoebe's heels down and led her to the middle, then Ed Sheeran's 'Perfect' started playing. Phoebe looked up to the hundreds of stars in the sky, and suddenly it dawned on her what Alex had in mind. She leaned her head onto Alex's chest while the song played.

'I'm dancing in the dark with you between my arms
Barefoot on the grass, listening to our favourite song
When you said you looked a mess, I whispered underneath my breath
But you heard it, darling, you look perfect tonight…'

When the song finished, the clock struck midnight. Alex spun Phoebe around, then embraced her from behind, and they both looked up when they heard the first fireworks as they soared up into the sky. Neither Phoebe nor the guests expected a spectacle of fireworks. The spirit of the party was pushed to the peak. Everyone could not tear their eyes away throughout the fifteen-minute fireworks spectacular. As each of the fireworks went up to the sky, everyone thought of Alex and Phoebe's story, how their love for each other overcame all the hurdles that were thrown at them and led them to the happy ending.

END

Afterword

Luxe is in the Air is the author Orchid Bloom's first novel. Orchid spent her professional life working for luxury brands, most of which within the Travel Retail or Duty Free sector. She lives in Hong Kong with her husband, daughter and son. She loves doing creative works while looking after her family.

The characters and events cited in this book were purely fictional and created with the author's wildest imagination. The brands were made up and if they by any chance sound familiar, it is solely a coincidence and by no means to portray anything negative. Orchid is forever grateful for her experience and learnings at the brands she worked for.

Certain places mentioned in the book are based on actual establishments, yet the events described were entirely fictional. There is indeed a Travel Retail Conference held in Cannes of France every year. There is also a breath-taking Bvlgari Resort located in Uluwatu of the magical island of Bali. Armani Bar, Sevva and Boujis Club are, at time of printing, still one of the finest and hottest dining and entertainment establishments in Hong Kong.

The historical events such as Occupy Central were real, yet the timeline mentioned in the story should not be taken as a reference about the real-time when the movement happened. "Dream Comes True" is a local charity that aims at helping young cancer patients to realise their fantasies and dreams.

WWW.ORCHIDBLOOMBOOKS.COM